A
SOLDIER
AND
A
LIAR

CAITLIN LOCHNER

Swoon READS

NEW YORK

A Swoon Reads Book
An imprint of Feiwel and Friends and Macmillan Publishing Group, LLC
175 Fifth Avenue, New York, NY 10010

Our books may be purchased in bulk for promotional, educational, or business use.
Please contact your local bookseller or the Macmillan Corporate and Premium Sales
Department at (800) 221-7945 ext. 5442 or by email at
MacmillanSpecialMarkets@macmillan.com.

Library of Congress Cataloging-in-Publication Data
Names: Lochner, Caitlin, author.
Title: A soldier and a liar / Caitlin Lochner.
Description: First edition. | New York : Swoon Reads, 2019. | Summary:
Four supernaturally gifted teenagers—a self-conscious perfectionist, an
amnesiac, a fighter looking for revenge, and a secretive telepath—are forced
to work together to save their sector from the threat of a rebel takeover.
Identifiers: LCCN 2018020073 (print) | LCCN 2018035037 (ebook) |
ISBN 9781250168252 (hardcover) | ISBN 9781250168269 (ebook)
Subjects: | CYAC: Ability—Fiction. | Secrets—Fiction. |
Cooperativeness—Fiction. | Science fiction.
Classification: LCC PZ7.1.L6225 (ebook) | LCC PZ7.1.L6225 So 2019
(print) | DDC [Fic]—dc23
LC record available at https://lccn.loc.gov/2018020073

BOOK DESIGN BY KATIE KLIMOWICZ

First edition, 2019
1   3   5   7   9   10   8   6   4   2

swoonreads.com

Dedicated to my sunshine, who raised me to love stories and has always inspired me to be a better person. I love you more, Mom. And this time I win, because it's in print, and therefore I have the final word. So HA.

1
LAI

SOMEHOW, SNEAKING BACK into prison is always harder than sneaking out of it.

The reasonable part of me knows it's because everyone's asleep when I sneak out at night, and that by the time I return in the early morning, the dreary gray building is already starting to wake. But the cynical part of me thinks it has more to do with how the guards would be only too happy to get rid of me and all too reluctant to take me back in.

Past the distant glass cover of the dome that separates the city from the Outside, the sky is already a weak gray, steadily infecting the clouds with shades of orange-pink. It feels like the whole sector is watching as I pick my way through the trees surrounding the single walled-in block of a building that is the prison.

Running a hand through my hair, I tangle the long brown strands into something resembling bedhead as I assess potential entrances. The barred windows are a no-go. I can usually sneak in through the warden's office, but she's probably at her desk by now. Which leaves the main entrance.

I hold back a sigh. Why do I have to do something so troublesome this early in the morning without any sleep?

I again ignore the reasonable part of me that says it's my own fault.

From the shadows of the trees, I scan the wall's perimeter, but no one seems to be around. I can't hear anyone's thoughts, either, which is a good sign.

I run to the wall and pause, back pressed against it, listening again for anyone's thoughts. The secretary is at his desk. On top of that, I'll have to be careful to stay out of sight of the security cameras. I know where all of them are—it's avoiding them that'll be the tricky part. Especially the one right by the entrance.

With the wall's cameras' blind spots in mind, I carefully scale the wall and drop down to the other side. No alarms sound.

Beyond that, there's no cover, so I sprint to the entrance. I have to be fast for the next part, before anyone comes in or out and sees me.

I grip the small infrared laser in my pocket and concentrate on the secretary behind the front desk. His thoughts are scattered, trying to remember all the things he has to do today. **Report yesterday's prisoner checkups to the warden, arrange visiting time with Martin, call the District Committee to set up the monthly review meeting . . .**

This part is a gamble. My gift allows me to hear others' thoughts and pass along my own—usually when I want to communicate in secret—but when I put my thoughts in another person's head, it's obvious they're not his or her own. However, the secretary is preoccupied, and he doesn't know to suspect that anyone might try to break into his mind, so I'm betting I can disguise my message as one of his own thoughts.

Don't forget, need to deliver yesterday's prisoner checkups to the warden before she gets in.

I feel the sudden surge of panic in the man's thoughts as he realizes the warden is already in for the day. I can't see the secretary, but I can easily imagine him shuffling through the papers on his desk, searching for the documents he doesn't actually need to deliver right now. His thoughts recede as he heads for the warden's office, never once pausing to question the made-up deadline I put in his head. If he didn't have so much to do, maybe he would've noticed it wasn't his own thought.

Honestly. Sometimes Etioles don't even think to suspect things that are obviously strange. A Nyte never would've fallen for a trick like that so easily.

When the secretary is safely gone and I can't hear anyone else nearby, I remove the infrared laser from my pocket. I need to be precise and fast before anyone comes.

There's a single security camera hanging over the front desk that's pointed toward the entrance. After all this time, I know the position of it well. I crack the front door—hopefully slightly enough that no one watching the surveillance feed will notice—and carefully aim the laser at the camera lens.

There's no surefire way to know if I hit my mark. If my aim is even slightly off, they'll be able to see my face.

But from around the corner, I hear the thoughts of an approaching guard. I need to go.

I open the door just wide enough to slip through, careful not to make a sound as I shut it behind me.

Keep the laser steady on its mark. Get out of here before the guard comes.

Closer, closer.

I'm almost there.

The guard's almost here.

Hurry.

In the same instant the guard is about to round the corner into the front hall, I leave the camera's range. I shut off the laser and bolt into the next hall as quickly and noiselessly as I can. I don't stop moving—careful to skirt the remaining cameras—until the guard's thoughts are far behind me.

Once I'm far enough away, I stop to catch my breath. No more staying out past dawn again. This is way too much of a hassle.

When my breathing is back to normal, I make for the hall that'll lead to my floor.

My worn shoes pad silently over white-and-black-patterned tiles, passing wards upon wards of other prisoners. Well, I say prisoners, but this place is hardly a top-security facility. Most of the people here have only committed light crimes.

Their thoughts drift toward me, two dozen voices crowding in my head, and it takes more effort than usual to block them out. It's always harder when I'm tired.

I stick to the shadows and corners and focus all my attention on my surroundings, but I don't see anyone else.

Some security. Then again, what normal person is going to break *into* prison?

Then I turn a corner and run straight into one of the guards.

We both stumble back. How did I not hear him coming? Did I accidentally block his thoughts out along with all the others?

I scan the hall for an escape route, but there isn't one. There's nowhere to go, and even if there was, I've already been identified.

"Cathwell," the guard says, eyebrows slanting down over small, too-narrow eyes. I think his name is Jacobs. **What's the demon doing wandering around?** His bald head shines like a light bulb in a hall already oversaturated with what can only be described as interrogation lights. He rubs his pudgy arm where we collided.

The thoughts I had been working so hard to keep out of my head before rush in with my panic. They press against the insides of my skull, blocking out everything else, even my own thoughts, until I fight them down and reach for my usual calm. When I've finally got everything back under control, I blink and find the guard is watching me with a mixture of expectancy and annoyance.

"Sorry, did you say something?"

"I *said*, what are you doing out of your room?" Exasperation coats his words, but this isn't an unusual exchange. Everyone in the prison knows me as being perpetually distracted. They just don't know why.

"Oh. Walking."

"You're not supposed to leave your room without an escort."

"You're here now. Will you be my escort?" The more I speak, the more my initial dread lessens somewhat. I can do this. I've been doing it for two and a half years. This is the same as any other day. If I can just get him to think I was so out of it that I wasn't intentionally breaking the rules, everything will be fine. I am, after all, the resident eccentric.

Jacobs shakes his head. His eyebrows are dangerously close to merging with his eyes. "Listen here, freak. The only reason we allow you any amount of freedom is because you're an ex-soldier. If you want to keep that freedom, you're going to have to follow our rules."

I tilt my head. "Soldier rules? Salute. Fight."

"Not soldier rules. Prison rules."

"Yes."

He clicks his tongue. "Who's your primary guard? I'll need to tell him you went out after I've taken you back."

My mind scrambles. If my guard finds out I was gone, and then the warden, I'll be put under watch. I might not be allowed to leave my room anymore, ex-soldier or not. Sneaking out to the Order will be nearly impossible.

No choice, then.

I put a hand to my chin and squint, pretending to think. "Omar Khan?"

He freezes. "What?"

"My primary guard," I say. "Was that his name?"

I know perfectly well it's not. That my primary guard is a withered old man named Hallows who seems more suited to be a physician than a guard. But after two and a half years of constantly overhearing everyone's thoughts, I'm well aware that Khan is a good friend of this man, and, should push come to shove, he'll protect his buddy. Someone who allowed a prisoner to wander out of her room and alone in the prison is sure to get in serious trouble. Especially when that prisoner is an ex-soldier and a Nyte.

Jacobs searches my face with doubt and barely discernible distress. **If I tell anyone she went out on her own, it's just going to come back on Omar. Punishments for letting an assigned prisoner escape are harsh.** "Are you certain that's your primary guard?" he asks.

"Maybe?" If I say it as a question, it's not technically a lie.

She's never done anything like this before, has she? Isn't her record clean? Maybe if I let her off the hook just this once . . .

He glares at me and thinks and continues to glare at me and think. Finally, he says, "Look, you can't be going out on your own. Since this is the first time and you've got a good track record, I'll let it slide just this once and escort you back to your room. But if I ever catch you sneaking around again, you can say goodbye to all of your privileges."

I have to hold back a sigh of relief. I lower my eyes and try to appear as remorseful as possible when I say, "Yes, sir. Thank you, sir."

We're not far from my room, so the walk is short. And with a guard escorting me, I no longer have to worry about being seen. Only a little farther and I'll be able to relax.

It feels like a miracle when Jacobs drops me off at my room without further incident. He goes on his way, intending to reprimand Khan for letting his ward out, and I slip in a thought that *no, it wasn't really his fault, it was just an accident, it might be better not to mention it.*

I don't know if he buys the thought like the secretary did, but it'd be better if he didn't bring up my little escapade with anyone. Especially since I don't want him finding out Khan isn't really in charge of me.

With the door firmly shut behind me and locked from the

outside, I let the exhaustion I'd been holding back until now sweep over me. Finally made it.

Right. I'll make some quick notes about the intelligence directives I need to send out, maybe review the supplies count from last night's meeting, and then—

Someone knocks on my door. The sound suffocates in the dead air.

My heart jumps up my throat. Did Jacobs come back? Did he tell someone after all? Am I going to be put under watch?

The door opens. It's my actual primary guard, Hallows.

He doesn't *look* angry, but I'm too exhausted from the long night out and the break-in and dealing with Jacobs to be able to concentrate enough on his thoughts to know for sure. I'll need to recharge before I can focus in on individual thoughts again.

"Good morning, Miss Cathwell," Hallows says. "How are you feeling today?"

I guess I should count myself lucky that the guard assigned to look after me actually respects that I was once a soldier. He doesn't treat me like a prisoner, but rather like a patient.

Not that it means I'm going to act any differently toward him. I stare at him blankly.

A long pause later, he shakes his head. "Well, maybe you'll feel better after meeting with your visitor."

My head snaps up. Who would come to see me? I haven't had a visitor since I entered this prison two and a half years ago.

Curious now, I let Hallows lead me back into the hallway. I wish I could focus enough to read his thoughts and find out who came—I'm not exactly fond of surprises.

The hallway is bathed in sunlight and patterned by the sun-dappled shadows from the trees surrounding the prison. Long black lines cast by the bars on the windows form a sharp contrast against the indistinct shades. The smell of mold wanders the corridors.

We walk down a maze of identical hallways and staircases until we reach one of the rooms off the lobby. It's a small, circular space with two couches facing each other across a coffee table. The wall paintings are obnoxiously bright colors, reds and oranges and yellows with shades of neon green.

Sitting on one of the couches is a tan, square-faced man in his early forties. He stands, smiling, as we enter. His black hair has more streaks of gray in it than the last time I saw him, but he still has that same strict, straight-backed stance and upward tilt of his chin. "First Lieutenant Cathwell. It's been some time."

My heart thuds up my throat. I throw a salute while trying to rearrange whatever expression is on my face into something neutral. "General Austin."

"Why don't you have a seat, Miss Cathwell?" my guard says.

I sit down on the couch across from Austin and the general says, "Thank you for escorting her." When the guard remains standing by the table, Austin adds, "I can take it from here."

"But, sir, I need to stay to monitor—"

"That will not be necessary."

The general's tone leaves no room for argument, and after a few tense seconds, the guard leaves.

As soon as the door closes, I straighten my back and try to smooth the wrinkles out of my prison uniform. I even try to fix my hair.

Austin doesn't bother trying to hide his amusement at the shift. His eyes soften. "It's good to see you again, Lai. It really has been too long."

Despite the fact that I'm a Nyte and he's an Etiole, despite all the trouble I've put him through these past many years, his expression is as kind as what I imagine a real father's to be like.

It takes more effort than I would've expected to hide how happy I am. "You're telling me. What are you doing here? And where's Noah?"

"That's it?" Austin asks. "No 'Good to see you, how've you been?' No saying how much you missed me?"

I raise an eyebrow.

"And Noah isn't *always* with me."

"Yeah, okay."

"Fine, fine. He left for Sector Two a few days ago on a mission from the High Council. He likely won't be back for some time."

"Are you sure you'll be able to manage without your second shadow around?"

Austin cracks a small smile. "Well, the office is already looking a bit messier without him to keep things organized."

"A bit. Right." Austin's version of "a bit messier" is pretty much equivalent to a freak tornado running through someone's office. For his own sake, I hope his assistant returns from his mission soon. "So? If you're here after all this time, something must have happened."

His smile remains, but something about his expression changes. It tempers my happiness at seeing him again. "Well, I hadn't planned on cutting straight to business, but if that's what you prefer." His eyes hold mine. "I want you to come back."

Silence stretches between us.

"Come back?" I repeat.

He sighs and leans against the couch as his gaze drifts to the window. "Last week, a group of civilians transporting supplies to another sector was attacked and killed by a group of rebels. It's the first time they've killed nonmilitary personnel. The High Council has decided to act." He waits for me to say something. When I don't, he says, "If we don't destroy the rebel Nytes' organization soon, this may well turn into an open war. Before they get any stronger, we have to stop them." His hands fold together. "As I recall, you're quite the officer."

I shake my head. "You can't be serious."

"I assisted you in leaving the military over two years ago. Don't you think it's time you returned to help?"

"If the military wasn't so hell-bent on keeping Nytes in its service, I wouldn't have needed your help in the first place," I say. The only way for a Nyte to leave military service is by dishonorable discharge or death. The latter didn't really fit in with my plans. "But yeah, thanks for helping convince everyone I committed a crime so I could be put in prison. I really appreciate it."

"Regardless of how or why it happened, the fact of the matter is that Sector Eight is in a precarious situation right now."

I level a solid look at him. "You know why I wanted to leave the military."

He is, as ever, unfazed. "I do. I am aware that the military doesn't treat the gifted as it should. But I also know we both wish to see an end to the rebels who want to kill all ungifted. Wouldn't it be worth putting aside our differences for this? Besides, you must be going crazy being stuck in here, so far removed from everything."

I resist the urge to bite my lip. Austin isn't aware of the fact that I sneak out of this prison all the time, nor does he know about the existence of the Order. I'm not exactly stuck here. But it's true that being on the inside of the military, the very heart of information on the rebels and the sector in general, would be incredibly beneficial. It'd be a big help to the Order in particular. Especially with my gift.

"Why ask me to come back now?" I say to buy time. "The rebels have been around and threatening to kill all the ungifted for over two years."

Now that I've had some time to recharge, I could read his mind to find out, but Austin is one of only two people whom I swore never to use my gift on. Albeit, at the time, I swore to him and Noah out of necessity than out of any respect of privacy. It was one of the conditions for Austin adopting me off the streets.

He hesitates, which makes me worried. "It was the High Council's wish to both create an elite team to deal with the rebels and to make Nytes more accepted within the military by allowing them the chance to prove how capable they are. Therefore, they have decided to make a team consisting entirely of Nytes. If you choose to return, you will join this team."

I can tell from his tone that he thinks about as highly of that plan as I do.

Nytes have the ability to attain high military ranking through an initial entrance test, so long as they're at least thirteen years old and willing to admit what they are. Most Nytes prefer to lie low in normal society if they can, but the military is a good route for those of us who have nowhere else to go. And the higher your rank, the better the benefits. But a side effect is being hated by the ungifted within the military. Well, more than usual. The fact that Nytes are physically stronger than Etioles, faster to heal, gifted with unique powers, and able to survive Outside the domed sectors without safety equipment doesn't help. A team of only Nytes? That will separate us further.

"That idea sounds about as great as being dropped in a pit with a pack of starving Ferals," I say.

Austin sighs. "The rebels don't want compromise. They're Nytes whose only goal is to completely wipe out the ungifted, and so we must fight back with the intention of destroying them. You know as well as I do that the Council needs more firepower in order to do that. Only Nytes can face Nytes head-on and expect to win."

"I'm surprised the Council didn't think of this brilliant idea sooner."

He taps a single finger against the table, which for him is the same as rolling his eyes. "They've only had twenty years of Nytes being around, Lai."

"More likely people are afraid of what would happen if we banded together." I try to say it lightly, but I falter over the truth of it.

Austin keeps his mild smile, succeeding where I failed. He's waiting.

I need more time. "If I *were* to come back," I say slowly, "I wouldn't want to be constantly responsible for a bunch of stuff like before. I want some time to myself."

Austin shrugs. "You'll only be responsible for the gifted team and normal duty shifts. As long as it doesn't get in the way of your work, you're free to do what you please."

Austin's always been like that. So long as you're capable, he'll let you do pretty much whatever else you care to.

He clasps his hands around his knee. "Then your answer?"

"You won't even give me some time to think this over?"

"I'm afraid the rebels won't wait. The military can't afford to, either."

I blow overlong bangs out of my face in response. I haven't cut or brushed my hair in a long time. After all, physical appearance is important to crafting others' perception of you. The disheveled look helps in convincing people I'm a little off, which generally keeps them at a distance, but it gets annoying.

It's one of many things I'm sick of at the prison. The guards are another major one. Plus, the chance to take down the rebels before they do any more serious damage is rather enticing. I could also gather more information from within the military. I've reached the extent of what I can do while in this place.

But at the same time, I don't *want* to go back to the military. I took such careful measures to leave it in the first place, and then even more so to create the routes and routine that allow me to consistently sneak out to the Order. If I go back, I'll have more responsibilities. Sneaking out will be harder. I won't be able to recruit Nytes wrongfully imprisoned here for the Order. I don't know if I'll be able to support the Order like I have been anymore.

Luke would have said yes. If he'd thought it meant bringing Nytes and Etioles closer together, he would have said yes to anything. But I'm not Luke, and he isn't here anymore. I do things my own way.

"No."

"No?"

"No."

Austin's expression adopts a mildly interested quality, which is his equivalent of wiping all thoughts and emotions from his face. I hate it when he does that. "Might I ask why?"

"You might."

"Then consider it asked."

I can't meet his eyes. "I understand your side of the matter. I know it would help in the military's effort to prevent a full-on war if I returned. And believe me, I want to stop the rebels. But I can't work together with people who treat me as less than human. That's why I left in the first place."

"I see," Austin says. "Even though our end goals are the same, you feel you can't fight for that with us or advocate for better treatment from within the military?"

"That's not what I said. And even if it was, our end goals are not the same. Yours ends with putting down the rebels. Mine ends when there's peace between the gifted and ungifted."

"I would think my goal goes hand in hand with yours."

"That doesn't make them the same." I know full well what the military wants. They seek an end to the rebel Nyte threat, but that's where our similarities end. They have no interest in peace between the gifted and ungifted—the entire purpose of the Order.

Austin does not sigh. He does not shake his head. But I get the feeling he wants to. "Lai, you could do so much good from within the military. I admire your ideals, but you can't do anything in this prison. You have the chance to save innocent lives. *That* is the basis of what you want, isn't it?"

I don't answer.

He stands. "I will come back in four days. Please reconsider your answer before then."

"Didn't you say the military couldn't afford to wait? I already gave you my answer."

"I have made the executive decision that the military can afford to wait four days." He walks to the door without looking back. But he pauses with his hand on the doorknob. "Four days, Lai. Within that time, please consider what it is you really want to do."

2
JAY

"YOU WANT *ME* to talk to Lieutenant Cathwell?" I ask. The low thrum of the air-conditioning is suddenly much louder than it was a few heartbeats ago.

General Austin sits across from me at his desk. His chin rests on threaded fingers. I can hardly see him over the disorganized heaps of papers and documents prepared to topple from his desk. The bookshelves lining the walls of his office have long since thrown up their contents onto the floor. I'm not certain how he can bear the mess.

"That is correct."

"Why me?" I have no idea what the general is thinking. I press my glasses farther up my nose nervously. "Why choose me instead of someone the lieutenant knew while she served at Central?" She didn't even answer in the affirmative to Austin. Why would she listen to what a stranger has to say?

Austin's smile merely widens. Even without using my gift to sense his emotions, I can't help but feel that the greater my distress becomes, the more his amusement grows.

"If you're trying to convince her to rejoin the military, I truly don't think I'm the best person to send." Knowing me, I'd likely say the exact opposite of what would convince her to return. What if I ruined everything and merely ended up convincing her it really would be best to remain in prison? No. Everything about this is a horrible idea.

"Don't worry about things like that," Austin says with a vague wave of his hand. He sends a sheet of paper flying with the motion. "Don't think about convincing her to come back and fight. Just talk to her."

Now I'm even more lost. "What's the point in that?"

"Lieutenant Cathwell is stubborn. If you try to talk her into returning, she'll dig in her heels and never leave that place."

"So you want me to just . . . talk to her."

"Exactly."

I wait for him to lay out a detailed, thoughtfully crafted plan. However, he merely looks at me expectantly. When I reach out with my gift, I sense that he's calm, unhurried. He's not worried at all—meanwhile, I'm struggling to decipher what exactly it is he's asking of me.

"That's it?" I ask.

"That's it."

This is absolutely a bad idea. My gut turns at the mental image of me awkwardly trying to convince a girl I've never met that, despite what she wants, it would be in her best interests to return and fight. What if she turns me away before I even have the chance to say anything?

"So?" Austin asks. "Will you go? I was rather relying on you for this, Major Kitahara."

I straighten in my seat. I still think it's an awful idea. However, if it's something Austin is requesting of me, it must be something he thinks I can accomplish successfully. He's relying on me. "Yes, sir. You can count on me."

I set out shortly after my discussion with the general. Various images of me failing to convince the lieutenant reel through my head, and I have to remind myself that thinking of failure merely hurts my chances of success. It will be okay. It's just a talk.

Early afternoon light blankets the streets outside Central Headquarters. I can barely catch faint strains of music playing from somewhere in the distance. A little farther on and it disappears entirely, to be replaced by the living thrum of chatter, of laughter that pulls back and forth, of shouts that ripple through the air. The sounds of the sector pulse and throb like an undercurrent.

This time of day, the sector is as lively as it gets. People stand on their balconies and hail their neighbors. They call to one another, gather in the doorways of cramped apartment buildings and restaurants and on the overhead walkways that connect most of the buildings, many of them with long lines of stalls of their own. Bycs—lithe, sleek hovering machinery with an elliptical base to stand on and a thick T-stem of a handle—zoom past. Some of the riders race each other as passersby jokingly shake their fists at them. They twist and turn through the empty spaces created by the many levels of walkways and the narrow gaps between connected buildings.

How strange it is that even though the military is abuzz with the rebels' recent attack, watching these people, you'd never suspect we're on the edge of a war. When I let my gift spread out around me, taking in everyone's emotions and presences, shades of warm yellows and oranges dance through the three-dimensional grid in my head.

Perhaps it's better this way. Better that people be happy than in a state of fear and panic.

I press my way through the throng of people, trying to keep my head down, but I don't stay a part of the crowd for long. In my decorated military uniform, at the age of eighteen, I stand out like a three-headed Feral. There are very few teenage officers, and to be one means only one thing.

The air, so lively with sound just heartbeats before, chills to near silence as whispers pass through the crowd. *Demon. Monster. Heathen.* The bright colors I'd sensed previously now fade to dulled grays and blues. Suddenly, it feels as though every eye in a mile's radius is trained on me.

Focus. Don't look around. Don't pay them any attention. Just keep moving.

At least I don't have to push my way through anymore. People make way as I pass, and I let quick steps lead me forward.

Something strikes my back—something small with the hardness of a stone—but I continue walking. If I don't go looking for trouble, nothing will start. The last thing I need is for a scene to break out on my way to attempt a task I'm already sure to fail.

No, wait, I went through this already—I'm *not* going to fail. And I'm certainly not about to be stopped here.

The cool attention follows me all the way to the prison where

Lieutenant Cathwell is being held, but it lessens in intensity once I'm farther from the city center. It's almost a blessing when I step through the prison's front doors.

The secretary is shuffling through papers on his desk and doesn't look up right away when I approach. "Hello, good morning—oh wait, it's afternoon now, isn't it? Where does the time go?" He laughs, and at the same time, he looks up at me. The laugh dies, leaving only abrupt silence in its wake. His presence turns from a busily bright orange to a subdued shade of blue. "Welcome. How may I help you?"

Don't react. Don't let it get to you. "I'm Major Jay Kitahara," I say. "I've come to visit Lieutenant Lorelai Cathwell. I believe General Austin sent word ahead of my arrival?" Not with command. Not too softly.

The secretary glances at a note taped to his monitor. "Yes, he did. But when he said a major was coming, I didn't expect . . ." He eyes me once more and doesn't say anything for an extended period of time. He's clearly trying to make me uncomfortable, but I'm not, nor will I be. I've been through this more times than he has. I'm a patient person.

Finally, he presses a button on a small intercom and says, "Ms. Garcia, if you could come escort our visitor to Miss Cathwell's room?"

A crackle. Then a response in the affirmative.

"Visitors typically meet with prisoners in one of the meeting rooms, but they're both currently occupied," the secretary says. "You're going to have to meet in Cathwell's room." Then he turns his back on me and starts sorting papers.

It's an awkward wait until the guard comes, but I've had worse. The real problem is the stillness around me fueling my unease over this visit. Now that I'm not moving or focused on ignoring everyone around me, there's nothing to distract me from the single thought that keeps pounding through my head.

This is a bad idea.

I'm unable to prevent this thought from repeating interminably as the guard eventually arrives and leads me to Lieutenant Cathwell's room. The halls we pass through are dampeningly quiet and overly bright.

The guard halts in front of a door marked LORELAI CATHWELL far too soon. All the way here, between ignoring the crackling atmosphere around me and making sure I'd been going the right way, I'd been deliberating over what to say. Not something to convince her to come back, but something to merely talk about, like Austin said.

I couldn't think of anything. The only things I know about her are the basics that were written in her file—and even those are sparse. She's seventeen, only a year younger than I am. Raised as an apprentice in the military since she was nine, before eventually taking the Nytes' ranking entrance test and becoming an official soldier. Not originally from Sector Eight, but Sector Four farther west. Her gift is so confidential that only General Austin, who knows the gift of every Nyte in the military, is aware of what it is.

Her list of achievements is impressively long, however, especially during the near war we had with Sector Nine a few years back. Unlike me, she's led teams into battle. She has true experience. I can understand why Austin would want her to return.

Yet I highly doubt she'll want to talk about any of that.

As always when I get anxious, I let my gift spread out in full around me. The 3-D map within my head expands as I take in my surroundings. The guard in front of me, whose presence beats an erratic indigo born of nervousness from being around me. The floors of people whose presences take on an assortment of shapes and pound a multitude of colored emotions. The neutral presence on the other side of this door.

The guard knocks. When no answer greets her, she says, "Miss Cathwell?"

Silence.

The guard glances at me prior to frowning and opening the door.

The room is strangely quiet. And there's scarcely anything in it. The only furniture is a bed and dark upright piano, both of which are nailed down. My eyes catch on the piano. It's nothing grand, but given the setting, I'm surprised to see one at all. Sheet music lies scattered around it—on the bench, the floor, everywhere save where the music is actually supposed to be propped up. Yet despite the messiness, a sudden longing ignites in my chest.

The lieutenant is sitting in the middle of the floor. Her legs are crossed as she huddles over a notebook, sheaves of paper spread around her in a half circle. She appears as though she just rolled out of bed. Her long brown hair is a blind bird's nest, her simple white prisoner's uniform beyond wrinkled. She looks almost deathly pale under the too-bright lights.

"Miss Cathwell?" the guard says.

The girl's head snaps up as her scribbling comes to an abrupt halt. She stares.

Then she begins gathering her notes together protectively. She drops several in the process.

"You've got a visitor today, Miss Cathwell," the guard says

politely. Austin told me previously that the guards here are supposed to treat Lieutenant Cathwell with a certain amount of respect. After all, though the details of her crime are known only to those higher up, it's common knowledge that her misconduct was minor and didn't hurt anyone. Compared to that, her nearly six years of distinguished service to the sector hold more weight. I'm glad this guard appears to respect that. "Two people in only two days. Isn't that nice?"

Cathwell's eyes lock on to my uniform and badges. I suddenly wish I had forgone the formal attire after all. It would have saved me a lot of trouble, in many ways.

She holds her notes a little closer. "I don't want to talk to anyone from the military."

The guard tsk-tsks. "Now that's no way to treat a guest who's come all this way to see you. Why don't you greet him properly?"

"The black butterflies get the same treatment when they visit me, and I never get any complaints from them," Cathwell retorts.

I frown. Black butterflies? What is she talking about? I didn't sense her lie, either, which means she believes in whatever she just said.

Cathwell stands, but rather than approaching us, she glides to her bed and unceremoniously drops her armload of papers atop it. She keeps her back to us as she sorts the sheets into messy piles.

She obviously doesn't want to talk to me. Even though I know it's likely only because I'm from the military, I wonder if she's already decided she doesn't like me.

"Lieutenant Cathwell." My voice is steady. "It's an honor to meet you. I'm Major Jay Kitahara."

"Former."

"What?"

"*Former* Lieutenant Cathwell. I'm not in the military anymore." Not once while she speaks does she look at me.

I glance at the scattering of notes she left on the floor, already at a loss as to what I should do. I bend down to gather the few remaining sheets, but when I glance at their contents, all I see is messily written gibberish. Why was she so protective of them? What was she even trying to write to begin with?

I don't linger over it, but cross the short distance to Cathwell to return the papers.

Her eyes are focused elsewhere as she accepts them.

"Miss Cathwell, this is no way to treat a guest," the guard says. The politeness has left her voice. The nervous indigo her presence had emitted earlier melds into an irritated pink.

Cathwell's eyes narrow. Her presence pulses a brief, irritated pink to match the guard's.

She dislikes the guard being here. In the same heartbeat I think it, her dark blue eyes finally meet mine. I'm unable to read her expression.

"Um, excuse me," I say to the guard.

She appears surprised at being addressed, but hides it swiftly. "Yes, sir?"

"Could you give Lieu—Miss Cathwell and me a few moments alone?" I ask. "I'd like to speak with her privately."

"I'm afraid that is not allowed. We keep careful watch over our wards here, Major."

"I didn't mean to suggest otherwise." I make my tone as peaceful as possible. "I merely thought Miss Cathwell might feel more at ease with less people present. I would get you immediately if I thought anything was wrong."

The guard eyes me suspiciously. I think she's going to refuse me. Instead, she says, "You have ten minutes. I'll be right outside this door. As soon as anything seems wrong, you tell me right away or you'll be held liable for whatever happens."

"Of course. Thank you."

The guard watches us so intently she's nearly glaring as she takes her leave.

I return my attention to Cathwell. Her eyes are following something through the air. Or they would be, if anything was there. She's frowning, but she holds out her hand, forefinger extended, to whatever she imagines she sees. After a few heartbeats and with an unfathomable expression, she lowers her hand once more.

I don't want to ask what just happened. I'd heard the lieutenant can be distracted and eccentric, and now doesn't seem the time to inquire about it.

I choose my words with care this time. "I hope I didn't interrupt any of your plans for the day."

"Do you mean the tests or the sleeping or the being ordered around by guards?" She's returned to not looking at me as she speaks. She's already put all her notes in their respective piles, and with no desk in sight, I wonder where she'll store them.

"Um, all of it?"

"Then don't worry. I won't be missing much." Perhaps I'm imagining it, but she sounds bitter. Her neutral-toned presence offers me no clues.

I wonder what it must be like for her, to have been holed up in this place for so long. I nearly ask how long it's been since she last went into town. Last heard the music of skilled street performers. Last tasted the dried fruits or cooked meats from Market. Last spoke with someone other than Austin who wasn't a guard or another prisoner.

That's too personal, however, and I don't want to make her uneasy or dislike me even more than she already does. So instead, I say, "Nice, uh, weather today, isn't it?"

"I wouldn't know. Outside time isn't for another hour." She waves a hand around her windowless walls, apparently having decided to store her stacks of paper under the bed, because she relocates them with her free hand.

"Why in the world would you choose to stay in a place that dictates when you can and can't go *outside*?" I ask before I can think better of it.

Her eyes flick to me. She doesn't look away this time.

I think she's going to snap at me, but she says quite steadily, "Why in the world would you choose to risk your life in the military for a bunch of Etioles who have only ever looked down on you? For people who would rather see you dead than alive?"

My voice is equally level when I answer her. "No one has the right to kill other people. I believe in protecting all lives, gifted or not."

She laughs, but it's a harsh sound. "Do you think if you just work hard enough, fight hard enough, that you can make things right? That all will be well and the gifted and ungifted will learn to live together peacefully? They will never accept you, *Major*."

I flinch. From her tone, from her words.

Suddenly, I'm fourteen again, standing outside my father's door as he speaks to our maid. Random details are frustratingly clear. The low thrum of the washing machine in the next room over. The rough grains of wood in the floorboards, every speck standing out. The smell of apple-scented candles and lavender. The scratchy wall beneath my palms. And then my father's voice, every syllable pulling a taut string in my chest. *It's his fault she's dead.*

"You don't know that," I say.

"But you do. You've known it for a long time."

"You're wrong. You've just given up."

"Me?" She smiles with closed lips. "And why would you say that?"

"Why else would you stay in this prison?" I wouldn't normally speak so harshly, but the memories of my father are still surging beneath my skin and everything in me is screaming to prove her wrong. "You have the chance to live freely, but instead, you'd rather spend your life wasting away in this place, where those Etioles you appear to hate so much decide everything you do. You gave up your free will."

Her hands clench into fists at her sides. Before, even if she was irritated, she put on a calm front. Now she's furious and letting it show. But even so, her voice grows lower and quieter rather than louder. "You don't know anything."

"Really?" I raise my hands, taking in the whole room, my blood still pounding. "I know I would never let someone keep me in a cage. I know I would choose freedom and fighting for what's right over holing up alone in this place. I know I would at least *try*." There's a tiny voice in my head that tells me I need to stop, that I've already gone too far, but I ignore it. "Just what are you doing here? What can you accomplish inside a prison? You're merely afraid to come back, choosing the easy way out by hiding here."

I'm breathing hard by the time I've finished. I feel so frustrated, so—so *unsatisfied*. As though no matter how much I might say, it wouldn't be enough. I would still feel this gnawing emptiness inside my chest. Suffocating.

And yet, even so, I know what I said was wrong. She's a veteran soldier who's likely had her own share of difficulties. She didn't deserve to hear any of that. I was upset and unfairly took it out on her.

Cathwell is breathing hard, too. The cold fury is gone from her expression and her presence, replaced with something else, something I'm unable to identify. "Get out."

"I'm sorry. I shouldn't have—"

"I said *get out*. Now."

Guilt presses down on my chest. How could I have said all those things? I want to try apologizing to her again, but she's already turned her back on me. The lines of her shoulders are straight and stiff. Unyielding. She's not going to say anything more to me.

"I understand," I say quietly. "It was an honor to meet you. I hope you will consider General Austin's request." The words fall lame and awkward to land straight into silence.

My heart pounds with the knowledge that I failed as I open the door and inform the guard that we've finished.

I barely notice where we're going as I trail after her. How could I have said such awful things to someone who has her own past and problems she's likely struggling with? I think of her notes written in nonsense and the way her eyes followed nothing through the air, hand extended to something imagined.

I was arrogant. I didn't even *consider* her position, and yet I spouted all my unasked-for ideals at her. I told someone I know nothing about that she's taking the easy way out.

Austin was wrong. He never should have relied on me.

3
LAI

EVEN AFTER MAJOR Kitahara has left, his insistent words remain. *Just what are you doing here?*

What *am* I doing? I originally came here to escape the things I didn't want to face, and to be better able to help the Order. In the military, I was under constant scrutiny as a Nyte and a highly ranked officer. There were too many eyes, too many responsibilities. Here, I can focus solely on the Order. No one even thinks to suspect me of anything.

But as my guard escorts me outside to stretch my legs and see the sun, I think how nice it would be to step out into the daylight anytime I liked without someone keeping watch over me. As I write coded notes for the Order back in my room, detailing what supplies are drastically needed and hints of rebel movements that were reported at the last meeting, I think of how much more information I could get from inside the military. Not only on the rebels, but on what the military and Council are up to as well. The Council has been anti-Nyte for as long as Nytes have been around. There's no telling what they'll do.

And considering they're in control of the entire sector, military included, they need watching.

Could I really keep up with both work in the military and with the Order? How often would I be able to sneak out? How much more difficult would it be? This place might be a prison, but it's hardly secure. Central is leagues away in comparison. As a soldier, I could always just walk out the front door, but how long until someone noticed my long and frequent absences and started asking questions?

These thoughts spin through my head all that day and the next as I drag myself through the usual routines. Stuck inside my head with nowhere to go and no one to talk to. Even playing the piano Austin fought to get for me, usually such a source of happiness and peace, can't break me from my indecision.

Entering this prison was never the wrong choice. After I came here, I was able to sneak out and spend my nights helping build the Order up to what it is now. All our members who now have a place to call home, all our established information networks—they're in place because I was able to completely devote my time to the Order. But I'm not necessary for recruiting and information gathering anymore. We have enough members now that others are assigned to those tasks.

What good am I doing here? I could be doing more. I could be doing *better*.

Despite the fact I already told Austin no, and even kicked out the messenger he'd sent, I can't stop thinking about going back to the military. Familiarity. Freedom. Control. But also more responsibility. Bad memories. Expectations.

By the end of the day, I've thought of the same things so many times over that I feel like I've just been walking in circles for the past day and a half. My head hurts, and I'm still no closer to an actual decision.

Come on, Lai, I tell myself. *You're better than this.*

That evening, as I'm practicing my usual strengthening exercises in my room, I catch sight of a dark smudge out of the corner of my eye. A black butterfly. The second in only two days.

My heart rate picks up.

I watch as it flutters purposefully toward me, the edges of its wings hazy and indistinct. Unnatural.

"Can't you just go away already?" I mutter. But verbally and mentally wishing the things away has never worked before, so I hold out my finger for the messenger to land on. As soon as it comes in contact with my skin, it starts to disintegrate like so much dust in a gust of wind. Words as fuzzy as the shadow creature's form sound in the back of my head. *We're moving, Lai. Are you ready?*

The echoes of the words continue ringing in my head even after their deliverer is gone. This is the fourth butterfly in the past week. It's been a long time since I received so many so close together.

Ellis must be trying to get to me. She knows I'll take so many messengers as a bad sign—and with good reason. Ellis isn't the kind of person to make empty threats.

What does that mean? Are the rebels actually about to make good on their promise to start a war with the ungifted? Are they planning to do something huge—soon?

Calm down. What if that's just what Ellis wants me to think? What if she's trying to push me into reckless action?

Uncertainty fills me. Is this a warning or a trap?

And just like that, I'm sick of it all. Sick of my uncertainty, so strange and foreign a thing to me, sick of everyone pulling strings I'm miles away from being able to see.

There's nothing I can accomplish in this prison anymore. The time in which it was useful to be here has come and gone. Complacency, easy routine, a false sense of achievement in being here—all of it an excuse to avoid taking the first huge, risky steps necessary to counter the rebels.

That stupid major was right about me. I'm just hiding here.

If there's anything I hate more than my own weaknesses, it's other people guessing them correctly. And I am not the sort of person to prove others correct about me when it comes to being weak.

I'm going to go back to the military. And I'm going to gain everything I can from that.

I close my eyes. My gift allows me to exchange thoughts with people, but it's harder the farther away the person I'm trying to communicate with is. However, the more trust I have with someone, the farther away I can contact them from.

It's easy to imagine the road I always take to the Order, the bustling main street that eventually goes into the upper-class district before petering out into side alleys that lead to storehouses. *Fiona? Are you there? And is Trist with you?*

Silence. Then, faintly, **We're here. What's wrong?**

Can we meet tonight?

All three of us? You know that's risky.

I know. But it's important.

More silence.

If it was possible to sigh inside one's head, I imagine that's what Fiona just did. **Understood. The usual place?**

See you there.

After sneaking out of the prison some hours later, I pause at the edge of the trees walling the solitary building off from the rest of the city and grab a tattered pack out from the hollow beneath some tree roots. A worn pair of pants, a black shirt, and my green field jacket greet me. I quickly change into them before stuffing my prison uniform inside and stowing the bag back in its place. When the coast is clear, I step out onto the nearest street.

About a fifteen-minute walk later, the streets have gone from deserted to crowded. It takes some effort to mute all the voices shouting in my head to mere background noise. It's easier when I can do something with my hands to anchor my attention outside of me, and harder when there are more people around—and the streets around Central Headquarters are always busy. Yet despite my effort, some stray thoughts still leak through.

Don't forget to pick up bread for the—

Man, this girl is always such a riot—

I bet I can beat him now with my new byc—

Quiet. Quiet. Block it all out.

Red-bricked buildings pile one on top of another, fighting for space. Above them, I can barely see the shine of the dome that caps the sector past all the walkways and added-on floors. There are no trees. The cobblestone roads are haphazard, the only central point being a couple streets down, where Market is set up in a huge open square and vendors man their stalls each day.

I walk in the opposite direction. I pass by several well-trafficked shrines whose thin silver ribbons wave in the wind. The Etioles worship all sorts of gods, none of whose names I know or ever care to learn. Gods for love and loyalty and wrath, gods for air and fire and mountains. When Nytes first began appearing about twenty years ago, the Etioles lost it. First they were ridiculous enough to praise us as being the gods' messengers. Then a plague affecting only children struck right around the same time Nytes were discovered—an incurable sickness that persists even now, though the mortality rate has lowered. So the priests decided that, actually, we went against the gods, that we were demons sent to wreak havoc in the world.

I have never met a Nyte who believed in the gods.

As such, we all have our own theories on how Nytes came to be. Some say leftover radiation from the nuclear war that nearly destroyed humanity hundreds of years ago—the same radiation that created Ferals, the creatures that roam Outside—somehow leaked into the sector. Nytes primarily come from Sector Eight, after all. Much to the other sectors' Councils' frustration. It makes staging and winning a war against our sector to gain resources much harder for them, fortified as our military is with its gifted soldiers. And the Nytes who *were* born in other sectors have a habit of moving to this one, looking for a place to belong. Not that such a place exists here.

Some say the plague was the cause of Nytes. The timing was too much of a coincidence. With the kids it struck, it either killed them or turned them superhuman. Personally, that's what I believe.

Not that it much matters. We're here now, and figuring out the cause isn't going to fix anything.

The atmosphere changes as I move away from Central

Headquarters. The quaint shops and restaurants and cozy homes fitted into their respective high-rise buildings are gradually replaced by blocky concrete skyscrapers and apartments. The first four or five floors are solidly made. Past that, they're hastily constructed, sometimes of brick, sometimes of cement blocks or even wood. The platforms that connect them look precarious at best. But as the population within the sector continues to grow, new residences have to be built quickly to accommodate it.

The "usual place" is a used bookstore located in one of the tall, narrow buildings in the south of Central's fringes. It's where the Order first used to meet, back when it was still just nine of us and the small space could hold us all. The street it's on is nearly deserted, but warm golden light pools out from the windows of the shop.

A small bell rattles when I open the door, and an older man briefly looks at me over the tops of his glasses before returning to his book. "Welcome. They're waiting for you in the back room."

"Thank you, Mr. Clemente."

I have to walk sideways at some points to make it through the mazelike stacks of books, but eventually I'm able to slip through a small door and into a room just big enough to comfortably fit a table and four chairs.

In the past, we used to take out the furniture and sit in a tight circle. Our laughs would reverberate around the room and echo back at us and we'd be so close I could feel the warmth of my friends sitting all around me. The sudden nostalgia of it is like a punch to the chest.

Now, there is no laughter. Fiona and Trist sit in two of the chairs. They had obviously been deep in conversation, but they fall silent when I enter the room.

My spirits pick up at the sight of them—solid, real, *here*. Not everyone is gone. I haven't lost everything yet.

"You're late," Fiona says flatly, killing my small joy. As usual. Her eyes narrow a fraction as she flicks back a loose strand of short, wavy black hair. Her golden-brown hands clasp together in front of her. She's only a year older than I am, but she likes to act so much older and more experienced.

Trist stands, all height and broad shoulders and muscles pulling at taut, midnight-black skin, but his wide smile is disarming as ever. Even though he actually *is* about five years older than me, he doesn't flaunt it. "I am glad to see you well. When Fiona said you called an urgent meeting with us, I worried."

"I'm sorry," I say, ignoring Fiona's earlier remark as I give Trist a quick hug and sit next to him. Just being near his warm, solid presence helps anchor me. "I thought it would be better to talk about this in person."

I tell them about General Austin's offer, omit Kitahara's visit, report on Ellis's increased number of messengers, and finish by saying that I've decided to go back to the military.

"The military wants to use the all-Nyte team as a quick but effective strike against the rebels," I say. "It sounds suspicious to me, but I really think we can use this as a chance to gain more info from within the military—and keep an eye on them at the same time."

After a pause, Trist is the first to speak. "There will be more danger for you, yes? You will be fighting on the front lines."

"I can handle myself," I say. "Who knows, I might even be able to save a few soldiers along the way."

"Your arrogance is showing," Fiona remarks.

"Was it hidden before? My bad."

She throws a scowl at me while Trist hides a smile.

"When are you going to start taking things seriously?" Fiona asks. "The rebels are a serious threat, and you'd do well to start treating them as such."

"When have I ever treated this as anything but serious?" I snap.

"Friends, friends," Trist says. "Focus. There is much to discuss." His hands are raised in peace, both the words and gesture incredibly familiar. Even after five years of knowing each other, Fiona and I can't hold a conversation for ten seconds without getting under each other's skin. Not that either of us really try not to. If it weren't for Trist, we probably would've ripped each other's throats out a long time ago.

"It's true this plan is dangerous, but I think it's well worth the risks," I say with a final, grudging glare at Fiona.

She returns the look in kind. "Well, having an eye on the military certainly wouldn't hurt."

I get the feeling we're both thinking of Luke. I could focus in on her thoughts and confirm it, but it's rare that I ever pry that way with her or Trist anymore. Strange though our friendship may be, we are still friends. I guess.

Trist, with his way of noticing everything, instantly picks up on Fiona's gloom. "If the military starts being suspicious, we will be able to know beforehand," he says. "But let us not worry about that now."

"Trist is right," I say. "Let's focus on the more immediate future." I tap a single finger against the tabletop, thinking. "I'm not going to be able to do as much for the Order after this."

Fiona and Trist share a glance. They communicate silently back and forth, calculating, weighing options. I can read the looks as easily as if I were reading their thoughts. They're ones we've all shared countless times.

Finally, they turn back to me. "We can divide your work among us and the captains," Fiona says. "Save for the things only you can do."

"Of which there happen to be quite a few," I say.

"Are you trying to make this work or aren't you?" Fiona asks.

"All I'm saying is there's a lot I do for the Order."

"It's not just you. That's why we *have* the captains and the rest of us. You think the Order depends on you alone to run? Don't be so conceited."

"Friends," Trist says.

"You think the Order would just continue to run perfectly smooth without me and my gift?" I ask. "How do you think it even got this far to begin with?"

"You act as if the rest of us haven't done anything all this time. You seriously think everything's been down to you?"

"I'm just saying I've done a lot to build—"

"FRIENDS," Trist rumbles. Fiona and I both freeze. Trist never raises his voice unless he thinks things are really getting out of hand. With a last glare at each other, we both reluctantly sit down. I hadn't even realized either of us had stood up.

Trist takes a deep breath before he speaks again. "Plans must be made. Details must be decided. We do not have time for your disagreements. Now. The divisions of jobs?"

Guilt sparks in my chest. Trist is just trying to get things done, and meanwhile, Fiona and I are having a go at each other. Again. How many times has he had to put up with this same thing? His levels of patience are unfathomable.

Fiona and I share a conciliatory glance—a temporary truce, but a truce all the same—and I say, "I'm not going to be able to pull Nytes from my prison anymore, so we're going to be losing potential members there."

One of the reasons I'd requested going to this specific prison was its high number of incarcerated Nytes. Their crimes ranged from insulting an Etiole to being in the wrong place at the wrong time—light things, unproven charges that didn't warrant being thrown in a more severe prison. I'd seek them out, see what kind of person they were, and if I deemed them fit, I'd offer them a place in the Order to go to once they were released.

Although, there haven't been many Nytes coming in recently. Lately they're being put in more high-security facilities even for minor crimes. Tensions with the rebels have been scaring the Etioles into trying to incapacitate Nytes in any way possible—anything to stop us from joining the rebels.

"We will find other ways," Trist says. "Can you still meet with our backers?"

I shake my head. "There's too much I need to prioritize over that. Peter and Paul are good at talking with people. Could they go in my place?"

We go through each of my usual tasks, prioritize assignments, and rationalize what I can feasibly continue to do from within the military. Fiona pulls out a small notebook to write everything down. And we talk, too, about how to minimize putting the Order at risk of discovery. It's been hard work keeping our organization secret over the past few years, and I don't intend to be the one to blow that. The answer we reach is not one I like, but the only rational one.

"You're going to have to choose your visits to the Order carefully from now on," Fiona says. "Only after you've discovered important information that can't be relayed telepathically. That is, unless something big happens."

"Understood," I grumble. Going back to the military really is going to be a pain. "I'll report back to base at Regail Hall after our first mission has been completed, then choose my timing carefully from there on out."

"I have been thinking on this, but could you make a power crystal for the Order to use when you are in absence?" Trist asks. "It could be very useful for the scouts."

It was something I had been considering, too. Power crystals are physical manifestations of a Nyte's gift that can be given to others to use. So long as there is physical contact with the crystal and the user chooses to, the power of the Nyte who made it can be accessed—with limits. Nytes can make any number of power crystals, with any limits or specifications on their gift, but only the specific person they made the crystal for can use it. And the Nyte in question must be alive and currently in control of his or her gift.

People in the Order exchange power crystals as they see fit. When Gabriel, one of the Order's original nine members, left, he gave each of us a power crystal with his ability to cancel out other Nytes' gifts. A power crystal I have found exceedingly useful. I also have Syon's crystal, which creates energy, and Fiona's crystal for illusions—the last of which I use only sparingly. I hate having to rely on Fiona any more than absolutely necessary.

However, my particular gift comes with problems. For one, it's dangerous. There are few people in the Order I'd trust with it, and even then, I'd worry. For another, my gift isn't easily controlled. It wasn't until I was nearly seven or eight that I was finally able to regulate it, to hear only the thoughts of the people I wanted to instead of everyone around me, to shut it off when I chose, to block out the cacophonies that had previously threatened to burst my skull. And even now, I still struggle sometimes.

"No," I say. "I don't think that's within my limits."

Neither Fiona nor Trist ask more. I've told them before of my difficulties with my gift, and even if I hadn't, we don't generally question each other's judgments. Not on something like this.

Fiona gives a small nod to herself and flicks her journal shut with a quick, precise *snap*. "That should be all the major things taken care of. You should head back before it gets too much later."

"Or earlier," I muse.

"Do you always have to——"

"It will be lonely without you in Regail Hall, Lai," Trist says. He hugs me, more tightly than before, and I know he's thinking of the danger of fighting on the front lines against the rebels. He always has been a worrier.

"Don't worry, Trist, I'll be back before you know it," I say as I hug him back. I try not to think of when the next time I'll be able to see him will be. Even just being near him cheers me up. Going back to the military might be a bigger blow than I originally thought.

"Are you sure you're not getting in over your head?" Fiona asks. I'm about to quip another comeback at her when I realize she's being serious. "The work you do is indispensable. The Order needs you. *We* need you."

"I never thought the day would come when I'd hear you say that," I say. "Did the words hurt on the way out?"

"Cathwell."

I hate it when she calls me out. My eyes trail to the table as my feet kick back and forth against the chair legs. "I'm going to be in a position to access information from within the military. Their intel will be the Order's intel. I know it's dangerous to fight the rebels on the front lines, but I have no intention of dying, nor of losing an advantageous chance like this." At her silence, I add, "I'll be careful. I promise. I always am."

She snorts and crosses her arms, which is how I know she's done being serious. "Since when have you *ever* been careful?"

"I'm still alive, aren't I?" I lean forward with my elbows on my knees, a knot inside my stomach that I hadn't even known was there loosening. "Besides, I'm tougher than a four-fanged flying Feral."

"As if I need reminding of that. Just try not to get yourself killed or exposed." She keeps her arms crossed and her gaze focused past my shoulder, but despite how we constantly rub each other the wrong way and pick at each other over everything, I know she's just as worried as Trist. She's a terrible actress.

We might not get along, but we'd die for each other in a heartbeat if we deemed it necessary. And no amount of bickering can get between that or our mutual desire for the Order to succeed.

"Yeah, yeah," I say as I stand up. "Just try not to miss me too much."

As I turn to head for the door, I catch Fiona mutter, "Yeah, *that'll* be hard."

4
JAY

A FEW DAYS after my meeting with Lieutenant Cathwell, I wake up still tormented by guilt. Now, however, the feeling is accompanied by a sense of dread. Today is the day I meet my fellow members of the new all-Nyte team. The team everyone already has a bad impression of.

I'd reported my utter failure with Cathwell as soon as I'd arrived back at Central. I'd thought Austin would reprimand me, but he'd actually *laughed*.

"I forgot to warn you, Lieutenant Cathwell has a way of getting under your skin," he'd said. He'd smiled at me from across his desk. "She always seems to know exactly the thing to say to hurt you the most. I wouldn't worry about it. From what you said, it sounds like you did perfectly."

I could only stare at him. "Perfectly? She wouldn't listen to another word I had to say after that, even when I was trying to apologize."

"Which is how I know you did perfectly. Don't worry, Major Kitahara. Everything is coming together."

Now, as I change into my uniform and prepare for today's briefing on the new team, I wonder what the military decided to do about our fourth member. Were they able to find another Nyte willing to join? I can't imagine we would've gotten the go-ahead with only three soldiers. It's not as though the military doesn't have other Nytes, but not everyone has gifts well-suited to battle.

Out in the halls, it's just early enough to be quiet. Before all the stomping of soldiers' boots create a cacophony. Before doors continuously slam open and closed as a constant stream of people flow through meeting rooms, barracks, and the dining hall. This time of morning is the closest Central gets to feeling peaceful.

I'm the first to arrive to the meeting room. The walls are so thin I can hear the low murmur of conversation from the next room over. The tiled floor hasn't been cleaned in a long time. A table for six centers the room. The walls are a collage of messily overlapping maps— of Sector Eight, of regions of the Outside. They're all covered in markings and notes and tacks. Other than that, the room is empty. I take a seat.

I attempt piecing my thoughts together before everyone else arrives. I review my new teammates' files in my head, but it's difficult to turn numbers and military achievements into personalities. Particularly when I don't know who our fourth member is. I hate missing data.

Sergeant Major Al Johann arrives ten minutes later. He isn't in uniform. His muscular frame slouches into the chair next to mine, black hands rubbing at his eyes. As far as I know, Johann is both the oldest at eighteen as well as the most experienced at nine years of service to two different militaries. When I check his presence on my internal grid, it's a bleary shade of gray. Tired.

"Good morning, Johann," I say. "How have you been?"

"Fine," he says. "Tired. You?"

"Well, thank you. I hope your energy picks up."

"Yeah, well, we'll see," he says around a yawn.

Corporal Erik Mendel, my new roommate, arrives next. Also not in uniform. Also a bleary gray in color.

He sits across from me with a yawn and leans his ruffled blond head in pale, ivory-toned hands. His file was the shortest of everyone's since he joined the military only three months ago. He's the least experienced of our team, as well as the youngest at seventeen. Despite the fact that I've just moved in with him, I've barely seen him around.

"Tired?" I ask.

He nods without looking up.

I wish I could think of something better to say to the both of them—and these are the two whose files I *did* get a chance to read beforehand. We've all spoken a handful of times before, but I've never walked away feeling as though I said anything substantial. Both Johann and Mendel have some sort of wall around them. I get the sense they say as much as they need to, and no more.

And yet Austin said he wants me to lead this team. My first command as a permanent team leader, and it's to a squad that's already the base of rumors within the military, with people I don't know how to talk to.

Then, on top of it all, possibly the last person I expected to see walks in. Lieutenant Cathwell. I'm unable to wipe the shock from my face. When she glances my way, she smiles as though we have some private joke between us.

I can't believe it. After all that, after everything she said—after everything *I* said—she's here. She actually came.

I have to look away from her. The insensitive things I said before are still catapulting through my head.

However, at the continued silence, I look back up. Cathwell is staring at Johann, who in turn is leveling the lieutenant a questioning look. Then Cathwell abruptly bursts into laughter.

"You think there's something funny about me?" Johann asks. His anger comes out through his typically subtle northern accent—he's nearly bristling as he half stands.

Not good. I wait for Cathwell's reply, knowing she'll defuse the situation—she has to—but she merely stares at Johann. And then she wanders away to examine the room.

I nearly have to restrain Johann from going after her. "She just got out of isolation in prison," I say. The words come out calmly, but internally, my heart is racing. This isn't how our first meeting with the whole team was supposed to begin. "She's still adjusting."

For a heartbeat, I think Johann is going to argue with me—but he slumps back into his chair with crossed arms. Mendel never so much as looked up.

Cathwell drifts around the room. She trails her fingertips along the maps. Cocks her head in directions where no sound is coming from, as though attempting to hear the silence better. Stops and starts walking at random.

I'd heard the rumors that she's always been an eccentric, distracted sort of person. I'd hoped the gossip was worse than actuality, but it seems every bit as true as I'd worried. Well, so long as she can do her job properly, I suppose—and according to those same rumors, she was an excellent soldier.

She appears better than the other day, at least. Possibly because she isn't in a prisoner's uniform now. Possibly because her presence on my grid is a less dull color today, more full and bright than when I first met her. She's amused by something. Her long hair still appears as though it hasn't seen a brush in days. Every once in a while, her eyes will become unfocused, as though her attention is elsewhere.

She, too, isn't in military uniform. I'll need to remind them later that soldiers are supposed to be in proper dress when called to a briefing. I hope General Austin isn't disappointed. I should have talked to my new teammates ahead of time after all.

General Austin, equipped with a pile of folders, is the last to join us, but I expected that from him. He's perpetually the last to everything.

It's strange to see him without his copper-skinned, dark-haired assistant, Noah. One of the oldest Nytes alive at the age of twenty, the High Council occasionally sends him to other sectors on secret missions. As is the case now. I'm not certain what his gift is, merely that he's been with Austin since long before I entered the military and that seeing one without the other is an odd rarity.

Austin's presence is a calm, neutral cream. When Cathwell meets his eyes, he smiles, and she ducks her head before taking the chair next to Mendel.

"Thank you all for coming," the general says. He stands behind the chair at the end of the table. His hands rest on the back of it. "The rebels have been getting bolder in their attacks lately, particularly with the recent civilian raiding incident. The Council wants us to eliminate the threat they pose as quickly and efficiently as possible. That is why you are all here."

I don't know how efficiently you can take out a threat when you don't even know where its base is. Due to the fact only Nytes can move freely Outside without protective equipment, our intel on the rebels, particularly their location, is virtually nonexistent. Our technology hasn't been able to pick up anything, either, leaving us at a standstill.

"For the time being, this will be the only all-Nytes team," Austin says. "Think of it as a trial. You four will make up the force of Team One."

Cathwell has started scratching at a hole in the table. *Scritch scritch scritch.*

"So what exactly do we do?" Mendel asks tonelessly. It isn't from being tired—he sounds almost bored. No, not bored, more like this is all just one big hassle.

I frown. Why does he think we're here? If he doesn't care, why is he at this meeting?

"You will fight, just like you've always fought," Austin says. He taps the pile of folders he brought with him. "I've outlined the details of your first mission here. You are to leave two days from now." Our eyes meet. "As the highest ranked, Major Kitahara will be in charge. Lieutenant Cathwell will be second-in-command."

At that, Johann shoots out of his chair so fast it nearly hits me as it clatters to the floor. His presence glares scarlet on my grid, his anger so hot it nearly burns. Even Mendel looks unsettled by the general's statement.

"Sir, you cannot give her a position of command right now," Johann says. His hands are clenched into fists atop the table. "She was only just released from prison. How are we even supposed to trust her?"

Cathwell looks up at Johann, but down once more when the sergeant major glares at her. She resumes scratching the table. *Scritch scritch scritch.*

"She is perfectly capable of taking care of herself and her teammates," Austin says evenly. "If I skipped over the next-highest-ranked officer on the team, wouldn't that undermine both her rank and her confidence?"

My gaze switches between Johann and Austin, who are having a staring match of sorts. Only, in contrast to Johann's vibrant anger, Austin's presence is unchanged in its calm.

I understand where Johann is coming from. He's served more time than all of us, is more experienced than any of us. However, when he came here from Sector Eleven's military to join Sector Eight's two years ago, he essentially had to start over with climbing his way through the ranks. He also likely faced a lot of antagonism at the time from having come from an opposing sector's military. And while his primary strengths appear to lie in battle, his records indicate he's not bad at strategizing, either. Meanwhile, Cathwell has been out of the military and out of practice for the last two and a half years. As a prisoner, no less. Johann's fury is more than reasonable.

But eventually, Johann picks up his chair and sits back down without a word. His jaw is tight, brown eyes trained on the table.

Mendel glances at his watch, discreetly enough that I would've missed it if not for the fact that I was looking in his direction to see how Cathwell would react. What could he possibly have to do that is more important than this?

"Kitahara, are you all right with this?" Austin asks.

I blink. "With what?"

"Taking charge with Cathwell as your right hand."

Oh. "That will be fine." I can't believe I was spacing out. Did Austin notice? I need to stay focused instead of worrying about what everyone else is doing.

Austin finally takes a seat. The chair legs grate across the tiles, scraping against my eardrums. It feels like a private reprimand for not paying close enough attention. "We recently discovered one of the rebels' hideouts. It's a small base, but it needs to be taken out all the same. We're leaving it to you."

Mendel's eyebrows shoot up. "Just the four of us?"

"As I said, it's small," Austin says. "It looks like a storage point for some of the weapons and ammunition they've stolen from us. From what our scouts have reported, there are never more than ten people standing guard. You're all experienced soldiers with strong gifts. You should be fine."

Ten rebels. Four of us. Not exactly favorable odds, especially considering the opponents are other Nytes. We'll have the advantage of surprise, but in a way, so will they. Their unknown gifts will be difficult to deal with.

"And we're not allowed to take anyone else with us?" I ask.

"No. Consider this a test, in order to see how you handle yourselves."

"So if we all die, we've failed?" Mendel asks. Silence follows his words. He asked the question lightly, but the reality of our situation hangs heavy in the still air.

"Well, better make sure you pass, then," Austin says just as lightly. I shouldn't be surprised. He's always been carefree in less-than-favorable situations.

He slides a folder to each of us. "Let's not get to that point. The Council tried very hard to come up with this solution, and there aren't enough Nytes with strong gifts in the military to create another team this well-suited to battle."

Cathwell meets my eyes and I swear she's thinking the same thing I am: The Council doesn't appear to have tried all that hard.

She looks away. *Scritch scritch scritch.*

"Questions?" Austin asks. No one looks at him. "No? Nothing? Then prepare your equipment, read the files I've put together for you, and rest well. You won't be placed on any regular-duty shifts before you head out. It wouldn't be such a bad idea for you to try to get to know each other and train together, either."

Get to know each other? Any of us could be dead in two days' time with this mission. How can we try to become closer with that knowledge hanging over our heads?

We all stand and salute as Austin departs. He leaves an awkward quiet in his wake.

When an extended amount of time has passed and no one has said anything, I realize I'm supposed to take charge here. I exhale slowly. Okay. What can I do to make everyone feel more comfortable? What does everyone need so we can succeed?

"I know this seems like a difficult task, but we can do it," I say. "We just need to work together and create a proper strategy. Why don't we start with everyone talking about their strengths? Whatever you think we should know about your abilities is fine."

I already know everyone's basic information from their files. Gifts, fighting styles, history with the military. Well, mostly. Cathwell's gift isn't in her files, and Mendel hasn't been here long enough to *have* much in his files. But it'd be better for all of us to share these things as a team.

No one says anything. I raise my eyebrows, and when silence continues to reign, I say, "My gift is sensing others' presences, emotions, and whether or not they're lying. I specialize in knives. I prefer long-distance combat, but I can hold my own in a one-on-one."

For a heartbeat, I think still no one will answer and I'm going to have to make plans with soldiers who won't even speak to me.

Then Mendel says, "Telekinetic. I'm best with a sword. I can fight in close-range or long-distance combat given my specialty and gift." He looks at me out of the corners of his eyes. "I prefer long-distance."

Johann snorts. "I'm a pyrokinetic, close-range fighter. I prefer to take on my enemies face-to-face."

"There's nothing wrong with fighting in the most efficient way possible," I say. "At the end of the day, it's the results that matter."

"That's a coward's reasoning."

I'm about to explain why it's perfectly fair reasoning when Mendel says, "What about you, Cathwell?" and once again breaks the uneasy atmosphere. Despite his bored attitude during the meeting, he appears to be a good peacekeeper.

We all look to the lieutenant, who pauses in the midst of her hole-making. She's doubled its original size.

"Lieutenant Cathwell, do you mind telling us about your abilities?" I ask. When she doesn't reply, I add, "We need to know where your skills lie for this mission. Anything you feel comfortable telling us will do."

"Don't go easy on her like that," Johann says. He shoves his chair under the table with a clap as loud as if he'd slammed a door. "If she can't act like an officer, she shouldn't be here. She's barely out of prison, she hasn't fought in years, and she's not exactly trying to cooperate with us. I say we leave her behind. She'll only put us all in danger the way she is now."

"I understand your concerns—I truly do—but the general specifically asked her to come back for this team. He wouldn't have gone out of his way to do so if he'd thought she wasn't up to the task." I look to Mendel for support, but he only shrugs. So much for the peacekeeper.

"Close range is good," Cathwell says.

It's then that I notice the nail on her forefinger is bleeding, the one she was using to scrape away at the table. I resist the urge to sigh.

"When was the last time you fought?" I ask. "Do you think you could hold your own in a battle?" The implications of her being stuck in prison for two and a half years without any training are suddenly very hard to ignore. Her fighting ability has likely fallen significantly.

She shrugs.

This is going to be harder than I anticipated.

"Why don't you two go back?" I say, addressing Mendel and Johann. Perhaps Cathwell would feel less on edge if it was a one-on-one conversation. Johann openly voicing his doubts about her abilities, justified as they might be, likely isn't helping. "Let's reconvene tomorrow to train and talk about strategies. Read the files before then. For now, I'll talk with Cathwell."

Johann opens his mouth, but before he can speak, Mendel says, "Whatever you say, Leader. There's not much else to do here anyway." He directs this last part to Johann, who glares at him before leaving the room without another word.

"Thanks," I say.

"Anytime," Mendel says with a grin. He tips an invisible hat to me and follows Johann out.

I hold back a sigh. Johann's mistrust of Cathwell is going to be problematic in terms of us all working together as a team, but it's Mendel I'm truly concerned about. He stepped in occasionally at the end, but he appeared unconcerned the entire meeting. He can't just be a neutral party when he feels like it and apathetic the rest of the time. But for now, I need to take care of Cathwell.

"I'll walk you back to your room," I say. "We can talk on the way."

She nods and we head out to the hallway. Our boots click on the tiles. A few soldiers stare at us, but say nothing.

Should I attempt asking about her fighting abilities once more? Or perhaps begin with her gift?

No. There's something else I need to say first.

"I'm sorry about the other day." I force myself not to drop my eyes from her as I say it. "I didn't think about your position or the things you've gone through at all. I was insensitive and thoughtless. I'm sorry."

She looks up, clearly surprised. "You're still thinking about that?" She shakes her head. "Don't worry about it. In fact, forget it. It's fine."

I blink. Was I the only one concerned about that awful conversation?

Now I shake my head. If she'd rather I forget about it, then I won't mention it again. *I* certainly don't mind it being forgotten. "Well, we're going to be working together from now on to lead this team. I want to start on the right foot."

"No worries there." She doesn't offer anything more than that, and I'm not entirely sure where to go from there. When she moves to brush her bangs back, I catch sight of the finger she hurt from scratching at the table.

"Is your finger okay? It's, uh, bleeding."

She looks at her hand, then back at me.

I try a different tack, recalling the piano in her room. "I hope it doesn't get in the way of your playing piano."

The pale yellow of her prior amusement turns a more golden tone, into happiness.

Okay. Piano is good. "How long have you been playing?" I ask.

"Since I was five."

"Wow, that's a long time. Do you have a favorite composer?"

"Ashton. Do you know her?"

"She did *Requiem for the Lost*, right?" We turn down a side hall lined with doors. Some stand ajar to reveal glimpses of offices, meeting rooms, or living quarters. When we turn down another corridor, a Watcher—a small, black, spherical machine with video cameras for eyes and a microphone for a mouth—hovers past us. "That's the only piece I truly know by her. I've heard her compositions are rather difficult."

"I had plenty of time to practice until recently."

"You played a lot at the prison, then?"

She looks away. "Less than I could have."

"Will you keep playing now that you're back?"

"Maybe."

After a reasonable amount of silence, I say, "So, what are you good at when it comes to fighting?"

She doesn't answer for so long I worry that I did something wrong. We pass through several more halls.

I should've led up to the question better. The few people I've spoken with about her all said she has a hard time staying focused. Perhaps I threw her off too much.

Just as I'm about to attempt fixing the conversation, she says, "Double-headed spear. Close combat." She stops and looks at me. "Don't worry. I won't let you down."

She dips her head and continues walking. I almost go after her, but I don't know what I could say. In the end, I merely watch her back until she's out of sight.

I open my folder and begin reading the files. This is going to take a lot of work.

5
LAI

THE MORNING AFTER our first meeting as a team, we gather bright
and early in the training hall following a summons from Kitahara.
After yesterday's meeting, I pored over the files we were given, trying to see if there was anything useful that I didn't already know. No
such luck. And the gaping emptiness of my former quarters were
hardly comforting after I finished. All I could see was the bed that
once held my best friend.

I glance around the training hall, but not much has changed since
I left. Most of the place is empty, meant to leave room for sparring,
but doors in the back lead to locker rooms, bathrooms, and the practice weapons. The range is on the left, separated from the main space
by a clear, soundproof wall. A few people are at the weight-lifting section on the right. Some soldiers are sparring in full Outside suits and
gear to prepare for future fights against the rebels.

My new team occupies a relatively empty space near the center.
A few people turn and stare at us. Many of them nudge their buddies
and start whispering. Of course. The infamous Nyte team.

Several of their thoughts bubble up from the sea of voices in my head.

Is getting the demons to team up really such a good idea—
What if they run off and join the rebels—
There's no telling what the demons will do—

Not for the first or last time, I bite back a curse at the stupid Council for creating this sort of team. All they want is to set us apart even further.

A clap of Kitahara's hands brings me back to the present. His glasses are gone today, probably replaced by contacts so they don't get in the way of combat. He wears the same black training fatigues as the rest of us. Despite the early hour, he's straight-backed and alert. He strikes a stark contrast with Mendel, who doesn't bother trying to hide a yawn, and Johann, who watches on with bleary eyes.

"All right, since we're all here, let's get started," Kitahara says. His eyes run over us, surveying but not critical. They stop on me, so I narrow in on his thoughts. **She wouldn't have had the chance to train with anyone since she entered prison. I'll partner with her and we can take it easy today.**

I smile thinly.

"It'll be helpful to be able to watch each other fight, so we'll take turns. Cathwell and I will partner together first and try to get a rough idea of each other's fighting styles. Mendel, Johann, you'll watch us and then do the same." Kitahara thinks a moment, then adds, "For now, no gifts. Let's see what we can each do without them."

"No gifts?" Mendel asks with a single raised eyebrow. **What a pain.** "What's the point in that? It's not like we won't be able to use them on the battlefield."

"What, afraid you can't win without it?" Johann asks, the tiredness from before slowly being replaced by excitement. **Finally something interesting.**

"Just asking." Mendel shrugs with an air of carelessness. **Damn this guy is annoying. How long is this supposed to last, anyway?**

"You never know what might happen in battle," Kitahara says. "Besides, there wouldn't be any point in you two sparring if one of you could just burn your opponent alive while the other flings his partner through the roof." At Mendel and Johann's joint silence, he shakes his head. "This is to help us get to know each other better. A bonding exercise, if you will."

Even without words, I can hear Johann's and Mendel's internal groans.

Well, this is off to a great start.

We all stretch together, and then Johann and Mendel back up to give us some space. Kitahara and I face each other.

Okay, we'll start nice and slow. Ease into it.

If I wasn't mildly amused by Kitahara's misconception about where I am in terms of strength, I might be insulted. It's only because I know he's coming from a logical thought process that I can tolerate him looking down on me. After all, he has no way of knowing I've been training regularly with fellow members of the Order for the past few years.

Still, just because he intends to go easy on me doesn't mean I'm going to do the same for him. He did say no gifts, though, so I flex my hands and tune out all the voices in my head.

"Ready?" Kitahara asks. What a gentleman.

I nod.

He comes at me first. Even though I've stopped listening in on his thoughts, I can tell by the purposeful slowness with which he moves that he's holding back.

He leads with a punch—a hit I easily avoid by skipping sideways—and follows with a swift kick. I catch his ankle and pull him forward off balance. Before he has time to regain it, my leg swings up to land a solid kick of my own to his side. He's not fast enough to block it, and ends up crashing to the floor.

Okay, maybe I should've held back a *little*.

He rubs the side of his head as he sits up. "Nice, um, job."

"Thanks," I say as I loosen my grip over my gift. "You were a little slow."

I noticed. "Yeah. I'll work on my timing." **I didn't expect her to be so fast. Okay, so that was too much holding back. Noted.** He looks to Johann and Mendel. "All right, you're both up."

Cathwell's faster than I expected. The grudging thought belongs to Johann, who glances at me as we trade places. **I wonder if she's actually any good or if it was a fluke.**

Johann puts aside thoughts of me to focus on Mendel. The former is clearly more into this than the latter, who barely looks bothered to hold up his fists.

Mendel isn't going to last like that.

Johann charges forward. Mendel is slow to block the punch that comes his way, and falls back several steps. But he doesn't fall, so the sergeant major keeps throwing punches, keeps pushing him back.

There's nothing extraordinary about the way Mendel fights—or maybe he just can't be bothered to go all out—but Johann's motions are fluid, precise, strong. There are no wasted movements, no reckless shots. That, coupled with a gift over fire, makes for a near-invincible fighting style. I'm glad we're on the same side.

Johann is just about to land what is clearly the finishing strike when Mendel's hands fly up in defense. Despite not actually touching his opponent, Johann gets sent flying several yards back, landing on hands and knees with a fury-filled expression.

"What the hell, Mendel?" Johann snarls. "The rule was no gifts."

Mendel throws up his hands, but it's hard to tell if it's out of self-defense or annoyance. "It was reflex, all right? I just reacted without thinking."

"Is not thinking a habit of yours? Because I can see how that would be hard to shake."

I laugh. Johann and Mendel both turn glares on me.

"What?" I say. "That was funny."

"Everyone, calm down," Kitahara says. His gaze shifts uneasily between Johann and Mendel. "Mendel, you know you weren't supposed to use your gift. It defeats the purpose of this exercise, and puts you at an unfair advantage against Johann, who followed the rules."

Irritation flickers over Mendel's face, but he wipes it off quickly. **Calm down. I don't want to deal with any more annoyances than I have to.** "Look, I'm sorry, okay? I didn't mean to use my gift. It won't happen again."

"See that it doesn't," Johann says. The sergeant major doesn't even glance at Mendel as the both of them stalk back to where Kitahara and I stand.

The major turns to me. His expression is troubled, but he only says, "Let's go again." **Maybe Johann and Mendel can use the time to cool down.**

And so we return to the center and resume our stances. This time Kitahara doesn't ask if I'm ready. He waits for me to come at him.

I'm not usually the first to attack, but I can tell he's still underestimating me, so I lunge forward to feign a punch.

He sees through the attack and ducks both my punch and the follow-up kick to his stomach. He aims a fist near my shoulder, but I drop down and spring up behind him.

He whirls around to catch a punch that would've otherwise connected with the space between his shoulder blades. He tries to drag me forward, but I jerk my hand back, pulling him along with it, and aim another kick at his stomach. He lets go of my wrist and I clip him as he moves back—but not enough to throw him off balance. He responds with a swing intended for my upper arm.

His intention is too obvious, though, which makes the attack easy to dodge and even easier to counterattack. As soon as he swings forward, I kick his ankles straight out from under him. He hits the floor.

"Your movements are good," he says. "Fast, strong, and well-calculated. Very nice." I'm surprised to find no grudgingness in either his voice or his thoughts. He's genuinely pleased I'm a good fighter.

"Thanks. You're not so bad yourself." I offer a hand to pull him up, and he takes it.

Looks like I didn't need to worry about holding back after all. Kitahara looks over to Johann and Mendel, who are silently fuming and bordering an edge between annoyed and bored, respectively. I wonder if either of them even bothered to watch our spar.

They're still mad. Should I split them up? No, whatever

this is, they're going to have to work it out before we head out tomorrow. "All right, you two are up," Kitahara says. He almost adds in a reminder to not use their gifts, thinks that will probably just make them both more irritated, and holds off.

We all switch spots.

Johann, who's realized Mendel isn't taking this seriously at all, is much less into the match this time. Now both their stances are lacking, neither of them looking happy and neither of them about to go into this match with an ounce of care.

This isn't going to end well.

Johann starts again this time, probably because we all know Mendel isn't about to make any moves on his own.

The punches that were before so full of power and purpose now fall with barely suppressed anger. Mendel's blocks are thrown up carelessly, thoughtlessly. It's almost painful to watch.

A crackle ripples through the air before it happens.

A flare of red flames ignites from Johann's fist as it connects with the arm Mendel flung up in half-hearted defense. He shouts and falls to the ground, clutching his arm to his chest with hate in his eyes. He manages to diminish the look to pure anger in seconds.

"Weren't you just harping on me for using my gift?" Mendel demands. "Then two seconds later you turn around and use yours!"

"Sorry," Johann says in a way that is not apologetic at all. "It was reflex."

Mendel looks like he's about to snap Johann's neck. Before he can try, Kitahara rushes to stand between them. Despite the worry in his thoughts, his voice is surprisingly steady. "Look, everyone's tense. We're bound for a difficult mission tomorrow, and with teammates none of us are familiar with. Right now, we need to calm down and learn how to work together."

"Work together?" Johann asks. "I've never needed to work together with anyone in my life. I don't need this team, and I don't need you forcing me to try and accept it. I can take care of myself. The rest of you can figure out how to survive on your own." And with that, the sergeant major stomps out of the room.

Kitahara looks like he might go after Johann, but he hesitates and then it's too late. He turns to Mendel instead. "Are you all right?"

"I'm fine." Mendel examines his arm as he stands, but there are no obvious markings on him, or any signs there was a fire at all. "But I have to say, I agree with Johann." **Much as I hate to say it.** "We're all strong on our own, right? Do we really need to practice together?"

"We're heading out *tomorrow* and we don't know the first thing about each other, let alone how to work together," Kitahara says. The strain in his voice is clear now. I feel a little bad for him, but I don't step in. "Don't you think it would help our chances of survival and success if we could figure all that out before we enter enemy territory?"

Mendel shrugs with what I am quickly recognizing as his signature careless gesture. "I'm not worried about my survival. If you're worried about yours, that's something you should work out for yourself. The other stuff is simple, right? We follow whatever the plan is, we each do our jobs, and then we're done. One less rebel base in existence."

"It doesn't work like that," Kitahara says. "No strategy is ever that simple, and you never know what problems—"

"Then we'll figure it out if and when we need to," Mendel says. He brushes shoulders with Kitahara on his way to the door. "And if we never know what problems might come up, there's no way we can prepare for them, right? Best not to worry about something that might never happen."

Kitahara starts to call after him, but the corporal is already out the door and clearly has no intention of coming back.

The major stares after him, expression lost. The nearby soldiers who had been watching start muttering among themselves, and my unease rises. The last thing we need is fact-based rumors spreading when this team is already doomed to bad made-up ones. But much as I wanted to step in and stop our infighting, I knew I couldn't. Kitahara is our leader. He needs to learn how to lead us and I need to lie low.

Kitahara turns back to me. I wait for his orders—a weird position to be in—but he takes a long time to figure out what he wants to do. Finally, he says, "Let's stop here for today. You should ease back into training after so long, and I need to sort things out with Mendel and Johann. Try to train independently for now so you can get your basic strengths back up, and we'll meet again tomorrow morning to discuss specifics of the plan before we head out."

"Aye, aye, Major," I say.

But as Kitahara walks away, I get the feeling he's not going to have much luck talking with either Johann or Mendel.

6
LAI

THE MORNING OF our mission dawns the same as any other. Our
team meets early to go over the plan—which is to say, Kitahara tells
us the plan and then drills us repeatedly to make sure we've got it. And
then we head out.

The military has its own underground tunnel system for discreet
transportation. So instead of walking through the sector in full combat uniform, where we'd be sure to draw attention, we take the underground passage that leads to the Gate.

The halls are dimly lit and roughly hewn. They twist and turn,
dip and rise, fully intended to lose anyone who doesn't know the way.
One wrong turn, and you could fall into one of the many trap pits the
military's set up.

I have to check my breathing as we make our way. Hold back my
heart rate, avoid focusing on the too-close walls, put one foot in front
of the other. I'm only here temporarily. Everything is fine.

It's quiet, made worse by the strange tension between us. Kitahara
leads the way while I follow a few steps behind. Johann marches with

squared shoulders and lifted jaw. Mendel just trails behind, ignoring us all.

After what feels like ages of navigating the tunnels, we surface in a military outbuilding just off the main street that leads to the Gate. We step outside into the cool air and continue on.

The Gate is one of only two aboveground entrances to the Outside. Almost four stories high, made of two-foot-thick starlight metal—a black, nearly indestructible metal that neutralizes Nytes' gifts—engraved with flowers and several different gods, it is easily the most impressive set of doors in the sector. A small guardhouse squats next to it, pressed up against the diamondlike shell of the dome.

The engineers call the dome "breathing glass," since it's designed to take the polluted air of the Outside and refine it into something everyone can breathe. I don't know much more about it than that, but I've always found the crystalline reflective state of the dome oddly beautiful.

Four guards in blue suits, the standard uniform of the Gatesmen, step forward with hands on weapons as we near them.

Kitahara stops a short distance in front of them. "I am Major Jay Kitahara of Team One. I assume General Austin informed you we would be coming?"

The closest guard eyes us. "May I see your identification?"

"Of course." Kitahara neatly removes his ID card from the pocket inside his jacket and hands it to the Gatesman. The guard turns it over for several seconds, comparing Kitahara's picture to his face—the black hair and straight nose and brown eyes usually covered by glasses but replaced by contacts today—and then inspects the official insignia of the military that serves as proof of its authenticity. He nods and does the same with each of our IDs before he hands them to one of the other Gatesmen, who disappears inside the guardhouse to have them scanned. A moment later, he returns and issues our IDs back to us.

"You're free to pass," the first Gatesman says. He waves his hand and two of the guards disappear into the guardhouse before returning with three hover bycs in tow. "Due to a crash last week, we've only got three bycs right now." He says it unapologetically, and I bet if we were any other team, the military would have made sure we had the right number of bycs. "Keep in mind that the Gate closes at sundown."

"Understood," Kitahara says. He glances at me. **I can't really imagine Johann or Mendel agreeing to share a byc with anyone.** "Cathwell, do you mind riding with me?"

"That's fine."

Two of the Gatesmen place a hand on scanners on either side of the Gate. The thick metal doors slowly slide into the dome until there's enough room for us to pass through single file.

Kitahara takes a byc and resumes the lead. The rest of us follow.

The Gatesmen watch as we pass into the long, tall chamber of breathing glass on the other side of the Gate. At the very end, there's another set of doors, also of starlight metal, also at least two feet thick, also guarded by four Gatesmen. Only, these four are completely encased in the black suits and equipment required for contact with the Outside. The equipment wouldn't be necessary if they were Nytes, but the Etiole-only Council doesn't trust people like us to watch over the sector's Gate.

The Gatesmen say nothing as they let us through. As soon as the second Gate shuts behind us, Kitahara, Mendel, and Johann start up their bycs. The dashboards come to life over the handlebars, three separate transparent screens of stats, graphs, and maps.

It's been a long time since I was last Outside. The monotonous landscape of dried, cracked ground hasn't changed. Nor has the orange-brown murk of the sky, scarred here and there by churning scarlet clouds. Giant rocks and boulders litter the ground. There are no roads, no plants, no signs of life other than the distant howls of Ferals—mindless, mutated creatures that roam the Outside. A sign of life we hopefully won't run into.

"Cathwell, we're going."

The air tastes like ashes on my tongue. I can breathe, but it's like breathing in nonlethal smoke. It smells of iron.

"Cathwell."

Pressure all over my body encases me in a thin veneer of steel.

"*Cathwell*," Kitahara says, and with a jolt, I realize he was saying it out loud and not in his thoughts. I jump up behind him onto the byc, which requires a bit of effort on my part with how high it's hovering off the ground.

I pull a small ball from the equipment belt fastened around my waist and press a button on it. Flaps of lightweight, highly reinforced plastic unfold and enlarge until I'm holding my combat helmet in my hands. The visor slides into place with a satisfying *click*.

Kitahara slides on his own helmet, then adjusts the straps around our feet so we won't be flung off as soon as the byc starts moving.

"Could you hurry it up?" Johann asks from behind us. "We don't have time to mess around." **Wouldn't have had this problem if we'd left the dead weight behind.**

"I am aware, Johann," Kitahara says. **It's not as though there's anything I can do to make Cathwell stay focused.**

A pang of guilt strikes me, but it's short-lived. It's not like I was intentionally ignoring Kitahara before. The Outside has a way of messing with a Nyte's gift if they're not used to it—and it's been a long time since I was last Outside. I remind myself that I need to focus more Out here. At least until I've readjusted.

"Hold on tight, Cathwell," Kitahara says. I wrap my arms around his stomach. He twists the handles and the byc soundlessly kicks forward. Mendel and Johann pull in line behind us.

The wind stings. It pricks at the lower, uncovered half of my face like needles until I bury my face in Kitahara's back. He stiffens but doesn't pull away. **She hasn't been Outside in a while. I hope she's okay.** He's warm.

Even after we've left the sector far behind, the scenery remains unchanged: rocks, spider-webbing fissures in the sand-colored ground, rocks, murky sky, rocks, rocks, and rocks everywhere as far as the eye can see. In the distance, I can barely make out the outline of what I think is a forest.

The initial pressure of the Outside slowly lets up on my body. The air starts to taste semi-normal again.

But my gift is proving trickier to control. It zooms in and out between Kitahara, Johann, and Mendel at random, as though it has a will of its own, and refuses to tune out like I want it to. I twist my fingers around one another repeatedly, trying to create an outside anchor for my attention, but with little luck.

"Where are we going?" Johann's voice sounds directly into my ears from the comm system in our helmets, and I almost mistake it for a thought.

It's a good question. As much as I'd searched for the location of our mission in the files we were given, I couldn't find it. Kitahara must be the only one with the exact coordinates, forcing us to be dependent on him. Austin has always been tricky like that.

"A rebel base," Kitahara says. His voice reverberates in the space Johann's previously occupied.

"No, really?" I can almost feel the eye roll coming from Johann. **Any idiot would know that.** "Where *exactly*?"

"In the west," Kitahara says. "By Nefrin Lake."

Mendel pulls up to join us and throws Kitahara a quick, two-fingered salute. "How long till we arrive?" **Just want to get this over with, need to get back to meet that new information broker and see if she can help me.** "We're open targets out here so long as we're moving through this area."

Now that's interesting. What's this about an information broker?

This time, I deliberately listen in on his thoughts and find that he's replaying a memory.

I stood overlooking a city blanketed in darkness. The night was broken only by lanterns strewn throughout the maze of streets below. Next to me, a girl with deeply tan skin and pale blue eyes leaned against the balcony railing. "The night is approaching," she said.

I didn't look at her when I replied, "It's about time."

"Not much I can do about that," Kitahara says. His voice right in my ears jars me back to the present, and for a moment, I struggle to remember what he's talking about.

The major taps one of the screens in front of him and enlarges a map. Curving lines arc out across the area, red dots skirting the right edge of the screen. Ferals. Judging by the path they're taking and the direction we're headed, we shouldn't run into them. "There's no one around save some distant Ferals. We're okay for now. The emergency system will let us know if anyone comes near enough to attack."

"I still don't like it." Mendel's eyes narrow as he looks around us without moving his head. "Isn't there another route we can take?"

"Not without wasting time for no good reason."

"We could—"

"The sooner the better what with the night approaching," I say. But I'm still half caught in Mendel's head as I try to say we need to get back before night falls. I realize my fumble as soon as the words have left my mouth.

"It's still early morning, Cathwell," Kitahara says. But Mendel's attention has snapped to me and something burns in his eyes. Something that shouldn't have been brought to the surface.

I screwed up. My words were too precise, and too odd, just as he was thinking about that exact memory.

Mendel opens his mouth to say something, but just as quickly shuts it. **I can't bring it up here with the others around. I'll have to wait until later.** It takes some time before he looks away from me again. He falls back in line.

What was that about? I can almost feel Johann's eyes on my back. **Well, whatever. So long as we're not taking some stupid time-consuming detour.**

74

I press my helmeted forehead to Kitahara's back again. This time, he doesn't shift.

We continue on in silence.

I've gotten used to being Outside again, which will be helpful when we have to actually fight the rebels. Even my gift has calmed back down. I hope we get there soon. I'm tired of just holding on to Kitahara and watching the dull landscape pass by.

Finally, after what feels like an eternity, Kitahara slows the byc to a stop. Mendel and Johann follow suit, and they all hide the bycs in a small alcove of boulders.

"Everyone knows the plan?" Kitahara asks. He opens all the pockets of the belt tied around his waist to double-check his equipment. He's the only one.

"You'll take them out from a distance until they notice their numbers are falling," Mendel says, intoning as if from a book. Kitahara beat it into us enough times before we left. "The guards' positions are far enough apart that it should take approximately two minutes before they realize anything's wrong."

"Once they do, I attack from the front and act as decoy." Johann pulls out a thin black metal cylinder about a foot in length. With the press of a button, and several snaps of metal slipping out and locking into place, it extends into a halberd taller than its wielder. The blades on the end curl back toward each other, nearly forming the outline of a circle.

"And I come up from behind for a surprise attack while you continue picking them off," Mendel says. He watches as Johann swings the halberd back and forth. "Adding to the confusion."

"Cathwell?" Kitahara prompts.

"I stay with you." My eyes flick from Johann's halberd to Mendel transforming his compressed weapon into a long black sword to Kitahara. "I guard you."

I can't count how many times it was drilled into me before we left Central that I wasn't to leave Kitahara's side. He seems especially particular about making sure everything goes right, and since he's the only one not going directly into battle, he decided the best place for me—who hasn't been Outside in years, who hasn't seen real battle in ages, who has a tendency to get distracted, who hasn't revealed her gift—was with him. Being his guard is just an excuse.

His confidence in being able to control everything is almost laughable.

"Good." Kitahara nods. He catches Johann's eye, then Mendel's. Glances at the small, three-dimensional digital map projecting from the Military Mobile Assistant attached to his wrist. The MMA is a small device in the shape of a watch that helps us out in the field. It's mostly useful for mapping the area and sending signals to other MMAs.

A red X marks the position of the rebel base. A few squares off, four blue dots huddle together over one spot, marking our position.

Kitahara snaps the map off. "Let's go."

7
LAI

KITAHARA DOESN'T LOOK back as we separate from the others and head out into the open. We duck behind whatever boulders we can. Small dust clouds kick up behind us. After about five minutes of slipping from cover to cover, we finally come up on the base.

It's smaller than I expected, set at the bottom of a crater maybe a quarter mile deep. The slopes are bare and offer no coverage. The walls of the base are built from dark red stone, the same shade as the deeper part of the crater. Rebels patrol atop the outer walls, but the structure itself is small. With the size, camouflage, and terrain, it's easy to see how this place was overlooked before now.

I don't know how we're supposed to sneak closer without so much as a withered shrub to hide ourselves. They might've even found us already, depending on their gifts and technology. Who knows what the rebels managed to steal.

"Which way?" I ask.

"Here is fine." Kitahara glances back the way we came, but I can't see Mendel or Johann. I can hear their thoughts, though, so they must be close by.

Kitahara jerks his wrist down and a thin blade a little longer than his hand appears. The handle has four holes in it for close combat, but he holds it like any normal pocketknife now, only more loosely.

He closes his eyes. Bends his head. Before I can ask what he's doing, his head snaps up and his hand flicks out to send the knife flying. I can't even see the blade as it cuts through the air, it's so fast.

The voices murmuring in my head grow just a tiny bit quieter.

"Down?" I ask.

"Down." Another throwing knife is already in his hand.

We run a short distance, until he can aim at another angle of the base.

Again, he closes his eyes, and again, he deftly sends his blade whistling through the air. This time, I see someone fall off the top of the wall.

"You don't look," I say.

"I don't have to."

We start running again, but a shout goes up from the base. The first part of our plan is up. Time for Johann to step in.

"My ability to sense others' locations is incredibly accurate," Kitahara says. Johann careens down the slope toward the base. "Since I can sense the enemies' positions, I know exactly where to aim to cut them down. It just took practice being able to throw that precisely."

And the strength of a Nyte ensures his blades reach their targets even from a distance like this. That's a pretty inventive use of what sounds like an otherwise battle-weak gift. If my ability to hear thoughts could pinpoint someone's location that precisely, I wonder if I would've thought of that.

Arrows rain down on Johann. The sergeant major doesn't even hesitate before throwing up a wave of fire that crashes ahead toward the base. Flames crackle and roil over each other in a race to reach the enemy's hideout first. Shouts echo throughout the crater, and as the wave of fire smashes into the front gates, flares scream skyward.

Kitahara watches silently, and I think he's waiting for the smoke and flames to clear before he makes his next throw, but then he sends another blade flying. Right. He doesn't need to see to aim.

"How many are left?"

"Five," Kitahara says. "Mendel is coming in on the other side." He winces. "Three. The problem is the flares. We'll have to hope none of their comrades are nearby."

"You'll sense them if they come, right?"

He purses his lips. Lets another knife go. "Yeah."

There's something about the way he says that one word that makes it highly unbelievable. **I can only concentrate on one area at a time and I need to assist Mendel and Johann. I don't know where reinforcements would come from, either. I need to make this quick.**

I turn my back on him to face the area behind us. It is, like most of the terrain we passed through earlier, filled with hundreds of boulders and pillar-like rocks scattered at random. Anyone could be hiding among them.

Glancing back to make sure Kitahara is fully focused on the battle in front of him, I lean into my gift and listen for any new thoughts.

Unlike Kitahara, my range is pretty short unless there's strong, mutual trust between me and the person I'm trying to hear. Which is why I don't notice four people approaching until they're only thirty yards away.

Aim carefully keep the brunette alive kill the other.

I grab the back of Kitahara's collar and practically throw him down the side of the crater. He shouts as he tumbles down the incline, sending rubble and stones clattering after him.

An arrow flies through his former position. I run toward its archer—a rebel dressed all in sand-colored camouflage, crouched behind a boulder, bow still drawn—and decompress my weapon. The cylinder extends into a metal spear a head taller than I am, equipped on both ends with sharpened blades. I thrust one straight through the boy's chest before he can run.

He stares at it. Tries to pull it out.

My heart stutters.

I rip my weapon from him and turn to catch another rebel's sword along the shaft. I tilt my spear and the sword scrapes along the metal, making him lose his hold. Then I kick him in the stomach. He stumbles back, and I run my spear through his throat. I can feel my blood pounding under my skin.

I don't have time to tear it out before another rebel comes down on me. I swing my spear around, still with the rebel impaled on the end, and force the body into a collision with the third rebel. She shrieks as her friend's body hits her, and the force sends them both to the ground.

The smell of blood is overpowering. The growing quiet in my mind—usually such a blessing when I'm finally able to leave a crowd—just makes it worse. I push down my rising nausea. I have to do this. I need to stop these people.

I raise my spear to finish the girl, only to end up using it as a pole vault to avoid a spike of ice as it shoots up from the ground. My boots skid across the dirt, scattering a cloud of dust as I turn to see a tall girl with deeply tan skin, dark brown hair, and pale eyes the color of ice extending her hand in my direction.

Ice Eyes jerks her hand in an arc. I bolt as shards of ice crystallize in the air and cut toward me. I have to duck into a roll to avoid the last few.

My hands and feet shoot out to propel me into the side of a boulder, narrowly driving me out of the way of another spike of ice sprouting from the ground. My right arm takes the brunt of the force as I collide with solid rock.

I push down the pain as I race to avoid her next rain of missiles, only to stumble right into Rebel Three's path. Shit. How did I lose track of her?

She yells as she brings her sword down against my spear. The force shoots through my right arm and I have to bite back a cry. I nearly lose my grip. Blood pounds in my ears as I shuffle back and forth, completely on the defensive as I try to keep her swings at bay.

My mind is still focused on reading everyone's thoughts and intended moves before they make them. Which is why I know exactly when to sidestep Rebel Three's sword and spin around behind her, kicking her into my former position so that she's the one who lands on Ice Eye's crystal spear.

She screams.

I think I'm going to be sick.

Then I bob and weave to avoid getting stabbed by spears of ice myself. My arm screams in protest, but there's nothing I can do except grit my teeth.

It hurts. I don't want to be here. It's been too long since I was last in a real fight. Knowing that I could die with any wrong move. Taking lives that just seconds before had thoughts, dreams, friends, maybe family waiting for them to come back. I hate it. I hate this.

The pattern of falling ice changes. A spear goes straight through my foot, and this time, I can't hold back my scream. I fall to one knee and gasp as I try to hold back the tears of pain.

When I look up, Ice Eyes is standing in front of me. She holds a sword to my neck, but we both know she won't kill me. Ellis doesn't want me dead.

The girl's thoughts burn with barely suppressed fury and grief. For a moment, I can't see her as a rebel bent on killing thousands of innocent ungifted. I can only see a girl about my own age who just lost three of her friends—no, more, counting the rebels we took out at the base.

The tip of her sword presses against my throat. Hot blood trickles down.

"I've got orders to bring you back alive," the girl says very quietly. Her voice is like brittle ice. "But I have half a mind to kill you."

"You wouldn't betray Ellis like that."

She looks like she's about to respond—but then her head snaps around and a wall of ice rises behind her. The sharp, piercing shatter of metal cracking off it rings in my ears.

Kitahara is standing on the edge of the crater, covered in dust and scratches and out of breath from his climb back up, but ultimately unhurt. He's already drawn another knife.

"Don't," I say, but I don't know whether I'm talking to Kitahara or Ice Eyes. He can't take her on. I don't want her to kill him.

Ice Eyes barely looks at me. Her sword doesn't move from my throat. "You killed my friends." She flicks her wrist, and ice spears form in the air above Kitahara. He watches them, trying to decide where they'll fall, but there are too many to avoid. Unlike with me, Ice Eyes is aiming to kill.

"Please," I whisper.

She lets her hand fall. The ice rains down.

And meets a wall of flames.

The rebel pulls up a shield of ice to deflect most of the attack, but the heat blasts past, scorching my skin even through my protective uniform. I close my eyes against the burn. Is Johann trying to kill us both?

Ice Eyes grabs my bad arm, still intent on bringing me back with her. But before she can run, an invisible force rips me back so fast it nearly snaps my neck. When I open my eyes, I'm on the other side of the fire, back on the rim of the crater.

My head is spinning. What just happened?

Mendel is standing in front of me, hands on his knees, focus trained on the wild flames only yards in front of us. Other than a few cuts and scrapes, he seems none the worse for wear.

Then Kitahara is by my side. His hands fly first over my throat with its thin dribble of blood, and then my speared foot. The ice projectile in it disperses in a cloud of steam, letting loose a stream of blood with it.

"You'll be okay," Kitahara says. He says it again as he gets the first-aid kit out of his equipment belt. Again as he gently eases off my boot to better see my injury. Again as he pulls out long strips of bandages and puts pressure on the wound before wrapping it up.

"You're okay," I say. I thought for sure Ice Eyes's attack had gotten him, and if not that, then Johann's flames as they rushed past. I hope he can't sense how relieved I am that he's safe. I really didn't want to be responsible for a teammate's death on my first mission back. Especially not someone so hopelessly sincere.

He doesn't look at me. "Mendel pulled me out of range before the attack hit." Mendel's telekinesis must have been what saved me, too, then. I hadn't expected him to ever be my savior.

"Why did you come back up here?" I ask. "You're a long-range fighter. You should've stayed out of it."

His lips purse as he tightens the bandaging around my foot. I wince. "With the terrain, I couldn't fight from a distance this time. Even if I'd tried, I didn't know the range of the enemy's gift; there's every possibility that rebel could've reached me regardless." He finally meets my eyes. "And I wasn't about to abandon my teammate."

I find I have to look away. My eyes come to rest on Johann, some distance away from us. With an irritable wave of the sergeant major's hand, all the flames disappear. Ice Eyes is gone.

"Is the base cleared out?" Kitahara asks. He finishes fastening the bandages in place on my foot and looks to Mendel.

"Should be," Mendel says, but he glances down the crater like he expects rebels to come swarming out of the smoldering gates any second. "Ten guards, right?"

Kitahara nods. "I don't sense anyone, either. Okay. Let's contact Central and get out of here before any more reinforcements show up. Johann and I will get the bycs. Mendel, Cathwell, wait here for us."

"Yessir," Mendel says.

If I'd thought it was suspicious how fast, and how obediently, the corporal agreed to that command, it was with good reason. As soon as Kitahara and Johann are out of sight, Mendel turns to me.

"Cathwell, why was that rebel trying to take you with her? They tried to kill the rest of us."

I keep my gaze trained on my bandaged foot and half shrug. I'd been hoping no one had noticed.

"Don't play dumb." His carefree act is nowhere to be found now. "You're the one who pushed Kitahara off the cliff, aren't you? Normally you'd want someone there to have your back in a fight. But you didn't. You knew they wouldn't kill you, so you were trying to protect him. Weren't you?"

I'm careful to make sure my expression doesn't change, but inside, I'm fuming. Was Mendel this perceptive before? When did he even have time to notice what Kitahara and I were doing up here when he was in the middle of a battle so far away? Would Kitahara have had time to tell him? "My job was to guard Kitahara," I say. "So I guarded Kitahara."

"Don't parrot that at me." His attention is trained in the direction Johann and Kitahara disappeared. "How is it that someone who's been locked up in prison for the last two and a half years manages to take down three rebels on her own anyway? 'Specially someone who's always so distracted." His eyes narrow. "On our way here, too. You said something about the night approaching even though it was still morning. Why?"

Damn it all. I just *had* to slip up there. "I only meant we needed to get back before night fell. Is that so strange?"

I'm so close to convincing him he was overthinking things. Even his thoughts are split: wanting to believe someone as off-kilter as me really is just that versus his gut instinct telling him something about me is off—and not in the sense of being distracted and fidgety. He knows I'm hiding something. I feel the switch in his thoughts as he realizes it.

"What are you trying to hide?" he asks.

I stare at him, hoping the blank look will work like usual.

It doesn't. The same invisible force from before slams into me, crushing me against the ground with so much weight I can barely breathe. Rocks pierce my skin. My lungs burn. "Answer me, Cathwell."

Then, as fast as it came, the pressure is gone. I'm jerked back upright into a sitting position.

Before I can fully register the sudden change, a clattering of rocks sounds nearby. Kitahara and Johann have returned.

"Any sign of enemy reinforcements?" Kitahara asks.

Mendel cocks a grin. "All clear."

The major nods, then glances down at the base. Smoke from Johann's fire still rises in plumes, but there's no sign of life. "General Austin said to maintain our position until backup arrives to take over. Be on your guard."

"Will do," Mendel says, throwing another of his two-fingered salutes.

I watch him out of the corner of my eye, but he betrays nothing of our exchange.

Fine. If that's the way he wants to play, then I can play just as well. After all, games are my specialty.

8
JAY

THANKFULLY, THE COUNCIL is pleased with the results of Team One's first mission. There were no major casualties and the rebel base was commandeered by military forces soon after it was cleared out.

However, as I walk down the gray stone hallways of Central, I'm feeling much less optimistic about the situation. Johann nearly killed Cathwell in his attempt to stop the rebel near her, and I get the sense Mendel only saved us because it would have been more troublesome if we had died. It's as though neither of them cares.

I'll need to deal with Mendel soon. Of everyone, unexpectedly, he unsettles me the most. I'd thought he was a neutral party, but I've come to realize that isn't necessarily a good thing. It's as though he doesn't care about stopping the rebels. Johann is stubborn and impatient, but easy to understand; he says what he thinks. He does what he wants, but I do think he honestly wants to put an end to the rebel threat. Cathwell is difficult for her own reasons, but at least she's attempting to make this team work. That's more than I can say for either Mendel or Johann.

Three soldiers walk down the hall in my direction. They're joking about something; their voices drift light and nimble in the air—but the words abruptly die when they see me. They keep their eyes down and continue forward in silence as we pass one another. It isn't until they're well past me that their voices bring the hall back to life once more.

I wonder if there will ever be a day when the other soldiers see me as a comrade instead of some "other." If I could ever slip into a conversation with ungifted soldiers without them shying away.

When I enter the infirmary, the hushed whispers of conversation coming from the rear of the room halt. The two nurses who had been speaking watch me. They don't make any move to welcome me in.

Cathwell is sitting up in her bed, staring out the window while her hands pull back and forth at each other. Her presence pulses a low, steady teal.

I'm glad she's calm after everything that happened. I was worried she'd be in shock after such a close mission, especially since she hasn't seen a real battle in so long.

She doesn't look up as I approach.

I sit in the chair next to her. "How are you feeling today, Cathwell?"

"Same as yesterday." She smiles, but it doesn't reach her eyes. Silence descends between us and I don't know what to say. The same thing happened yesterday, the day before, and the day before that, until I eventually excused myself.

I need to figure out how to get her to come around to being more active in the team. Whenever Johann and Mendel go at it with each other, she merely watches. I need her to focus more, too. She needs to be *here*. With us. And yet I can never find the words to convey all this. Part of me feels guilty even trying to bring it up when she's sitting here injured. I just haven't been able to do it.

For the time being, I should get to know her better. Get to a point where we're both comfortable around each other.

"You should be released soon, right?" I say. "That must be a relief."

"Mm. Hey, Major?" Her gaze is still on the window.

"Yes?"

"Why do you keep coming to visit me? We barely know each other."

"You're my teammate," I say. "Isn't that reason enough?"

"You don't personally care about me, then. It's just because we work together?"

"That's not . . ."

I trail off when she finally looks at me. There's something dead in her expression.

The worst part is that it isn't even because she's my teammate that I came to visit her. Starting with Cathwell seems the most effectual way to getting our team to work together. So far, she's shown the most willingness to work with everyone. She tried to protect me when the rebels snuck up on us—though I already told her on a previous visit that it's better to fight together. And if I can figure out a way for her to overcome her distractedness, then Johann shouldn't have a problem with her any longer. Then perhaps Mendel will, I don't know, join in once he sees all of us getting along. It could happen.

"Why are you trying so hard, Major?" Cathwell asks. "Why not let things be?"

Am I that easy to read? "Trying so hard at what, Cathwell?"

"Everything." She runs her fingers down her splinted upper arm. Luckily there were only fractures. Her foot was not so lucky. "You don't have to go so far."

I frown. "If I don't, then what will happen to the sector? Our team is one of the only things potentially capable of holding off the rebels until the High Council comes up with a more definitive plan. If we fail, the rebels may carry out their threat to destroy Sector Eight."

"So what?" She watches me out of the corners of her eyes. "If the rebels win, then don't the Etioles get what they deserve for the way they've treated us? Even when it comes to defending themselves, instead of doing it themselves, they get Nytes to fight for them. And all the while, they continue to treat us like trash."

For a heartbeat, I'm too stunned to speak. How could she even say something like that? And so *calmly*? Her presence hasn't so much as flickered since I first came. Still that same deep, still pool of composure. As if it doesn't concern her at all.

I stand. My hands tremble by my sides as I attempt to keep my emotions in check. "How can you even say that? These are innocent people we're talking about. Even though some of them have abused Nytes, that doesn't mean they deserve to die—and certainly not *all* of them."

"So we'll defend the Etioles despite the fact they continue to treat us as less than human. We'll fight for them, defend them—maybe even die for them—even as they continue to persecute us." Her tone is deadpan throughout. "Even as they continue to kill, and beat, and chase Nytes from their homes."

My fingernails pierce my palms. "Doing the right thing isn't about abandoning thousands of people just because some of them hurt you. It's about defending everyone's right to live. Etioles included."

Cathwell watches me closely—and I abruptly get the feeling she was testing me. Her emotions haven't shifted once during our whole conversation. Not to fear, not to anger, not to any of the usual things people feel when they talk about the discrimination they've faced. But why? What is she even testing me *for*?

"Cathwell, why did you come back to the military?" I ask. "You appear to hate Etioles so much. Why come back to fight for them?"

"I don't hate them," she says quietly. There's no itch behind my eyes that inevitably follows after someone lies. Her fingers twist through the sheets. "What I really want is to change how they view us. To make a world where Etioles and Nytes can live together without discrimination or persecution." Her eyes fall further. "I thought I could better accomplish that from here."

I try to picture it. No graffiti on the sides of buildings saying the only good Nyte is a dead Nyte. No stares, mutters, or thrown stones as I walk through the streets in uniform. No sudden silences or averted gazes when I get near ungifted soldiers in the military—the people who should most be on my side.

Cathwell lets out a deep sigh. "Almost everyone I have ever been close to is dead or gone. And I can't help but think it's because I'm a Nyte. I don't want anyone else to have to go through that anymore."

I truly don't know what to say to that. But her calm wavers on my grid for the first time, and she looks so sad, I reach out and squeeze her hand. She freezes under my touch. "It's okay, Cathwell. I won't leave you."

She closes her eyes; I can't fathom her expression. Her presence on my internal grid has resumed its previous stillness. "Thanks, Major."

"Why do you keep calling me Major and not Kitahara?" I ask in an attempt to lighten the mood.

"Why do you keep calling me Cathwell?" she asks.

"Would you prefer Lieutenant?"

"Lai."

"What?"

"My name. You can call me Lai."

She looks up at me and I notice for the first time just how dark her azure eyes are. They're pretty.

The thought catches me off guard—I withdraw my hand quickly. Too quickly. My face warms.

"I have to meet with the others before my shift on guard duty begins," I say. Gods, that was such an obvious exit. What am I doing?

"Trying to make everyone cooperate with one another?" Cathwell asks. She appears to be thinking something over as she speaks, and that something doesn't *seem* to be my awkwardness. "This isn't going to work much longer if something doesn't change."

"I was thinking the same."

"I can help."

"That's okay." I stand. "You just get plenty of rest so you can come back soon, all right?"

"Going back to the battlefield," she says. Her eyes burn into the back of my neck as I walk away. "How fun."

9
LAI

THE INFIRMARY IS dead boring. At least in prison I had my piano or could work on my tasks with the Order.

It's been less than a week since I physically checked in to the Order's headquarters, but I'm already starting to get anxious. I just want to drop through the nearest window and head there now, but obviously I can't. For one, it's broad daylight. I'd be caught instantly. For another, there are still things I need to do here.

As if on some strange cue, a black butterfly drifts through the wall beside my bed. Luckily the shadow messengers are invisible to everyone except their intended recipient, so I don't have to worry about any of the nurses seeing it and becoming suspicious.

I frown and hold out a finger, but it chooses to circle around me instead of landing. No message, then. Just a reminder. Or a warning.

I need to get going.

One of the head nurses passes by with an armful of freshly cleaned sheets. I wave to him. "Excuse me. I was wondering if I could walk around outside for a bit?"

The nurse watches me with a more guarded expression than I think the situation calls for. "You know patients aren't allowed to leave the infirmary until officially released."

"I wouldn't go far," I say as politely as I can manage. It leaves a bad taste in my mouth. "My injuries are almost healed, and I wouldn't do anything dangerous. I'm just starting to go a little stir-crazy cooped up in here."

The nurse eyes me suspiciously. He's well aware Nytes heal much faster than Etioles, so he knows I'm not lying about my injuries. **She's going to be released in another day or two, so her wounds can't be that bad anymore. But do I really want to be responsible if she does something stupid and reopens them?**

I'm just wondering if I should try a different approach when he says, "All right. But don't take long, and if you do anything to hurt yourself, you better not complain when you get back."

He walks away before I can even say thanks. Rude.

The black butterfly is still here. It circles my head as I swing my feet over the edge of the bed and gingerly place them on the ground. A slight soreness pulsates from my foot that was stabbed, but Nytes are incredibly fast to heal. It's barely more than a scar already.

The soreness fades the more I walk. Out of the infirmary, down the halls, away to the meeting rooms.

For the past several days, I've had nothing to do but sit in my bed and allow myself to listen to any and all thoughts that were within range. Most were mundane, irrelevant, and largely unhelpful in general. Soldiers heading to duty or the mess hall, officers planning missions unrelated to the rebels, like scouting Sector Seven with its recent suspicious behavior to make sure they aren't about to try to launch an attack on us. A lot of people are worried other sectors might try to make a move now that we have the rebels to deal with. A distracted sector is a vulnerable sector.

But yesterday, I finally hit upon something useful. A messenger had been passing by on her way to inform Austin that two High Councilors were coming to visit. They met with the general in his office this morning, a conversation that would have been impossible to eavesdrop on without getting caught. But very shortly, they'll be meeting with a lower-ranked officer to receive a briefing on the rebel situation. *That* meeting I should be able to listen in on—so long as I'm careful.

It's to take place in a meeting room far removed from the usual ones. The only furniture is a table and some chairs and a monitor, which means I won't be able to hide there and listen in directly. So I make for the room next to it. It's similarly furnished, but with the noticeable difference of a many-drawered desk pushed against one of the walls.

I lift the desk and relocate it to the wall this room shares with the one the Councilors will be meeting in. It's not ideal, but it'll have to do.

It'd be a lot easier if I could read the minds of the Councilors. But as befits members of the organization that rules the entire sector, they have a certain amount of protection against Nytes. Their elaborate black robes are woven through with threads of the rare, expensive starlight metal that deflects any and all Nytes' gifts. To protect themselves, to protect the top secret information they possess. I won't be able to hear their thoughts. But the officer they're meeting with won't be so protected. And no one can hide the words they speak.

I climb under the desk and wait. And wait. And wait.

Did I get the day or time wrong? Was the room changed last-minute? Maybe I should use my gift to see if I can find anyone nearby who knows where the Councilors are meeting.

But then I hear footsteps in the hallway and freeze. They're here.

I hold my breath as the footsteps grow nearer, nearer, then stop. A door creaks—the door to the room *I'm* in. The officer leading the Councilors scans my room but doesn't enter. **Not like there's anyone going to listen in on a typical briefing session. And the Councilors' guards are more than enough to take care of anyone who might try attacking them.**

The officer's thoughts are the only ones I can hear, but from the sound of shuffling footsteps out in the corridor, I'd guess there are about six people besides her. Right. The Councilors never go anywhere without their selected guard. They have no reason to suspect I'm here, though, so I shouldn't have to deal with them. I hope.

The officer returns to the others and they move to the meeting room next door. Chair legs scrape against tiles. Formalities are exchanged. I strain my ears as the officer begins speaking.

"The rebel base we spoke of last time has now been requisitioned thanks to Team One's successful strike. As for the stolen technology we were able to reclaim, there are a few things worth noting . . ."

The officer recaps my team's recent mission, but I know all of that already. I lean in on her thoughts instead, but she's fully focused on giving her report without mistakes and thinks of nothing else.

She goes over what the military was able to reclaim from the base—not much, due to Johann's fire—then moves on to discuss a trail frequently used by rebels that the scouts recently discovered, as well as plans to send Team One to investigate after further confirmation. It's interesting, and good to know what our next mission will be ahead of time, but nothing noteworthy. Nothing I couldn't have found out from reading the thoughts of one of the scouts. Nothing worth sitting on this cold, hard floor, hunched up under this desk for.

The officer finishes her report, the Councilors give their thanks, and I think this is it. It's already over. *Great going, Lai.*

But then I hear one of the Councilors say, "Thank you for your time. If you could leave us to discuss some private matters?"

"Of course, sir."

There are footsteps, the sound of a door opening and closing, polite goodbyes as the officer thanks the Councilors' guards outside the door and then proceeds down the hall.

My heart starts racing. What could the Councilors want to talk about privately? Surely it wouldn't just be about the briefing, right?

"Things are progressing as planned," the Councilor who spoke before says. His voice is slightly nasally and gives me the impression of someone self-important. Or maybe that's just my bias. I shove my ear against the wall to hear him better. "We should soon have the demons under our control."

"Indeed," the other Councilor says. Her voice is smoother, silkier than the first. Maybe it's just my general mistrust of the Councilors, but something about that voice turns my stomach. Something that says not to trust her. "The improvements have been advancing smoothly. The newest prototype should be perfected before the month is out. It took a long time, but we're nearly there."

"And it's only a matter of time before the rebel children slip up and we're able to reclaim the fruits of our experiments," Nasal says. "Once they've been put down, Sector Eight will be invincible."

Long-term experiments? There isn't anything like that that I know of going on in the military. But I can't imagine they would bother talking about it if it wasn't important. What did they mean they'd have Nytes under their control? Did they mean the rebels? They did mention them. How are they related? Are the Councilors working on some kind of weapon to defeat them?

Damn it all, if it weren't for their stupid starlight, I could just read their minds and find all this out for myself. I hate mysteries.

"It won't be long before we rein in the demons," Don't-Trust says. Her voice is barely above a murmur. If it weren't for my face crushed against the wall and my Nyte's level of hearing, I would've missed her words altogether. "Then everything will be as it should."

A chill runs down my spine.

"Finally," Nasal mutters.

The door to the hall opens and the Councilors rejoin their guards. I sit very still in my spot under the desk, long after their footsteps have receded down the hall.

What was all that about? Experiments, a goal that involves getting Nytes under the Council's control. Everything about their conversation spoke of ill intent, of *wrongness*, but the information came in only bits and pieces. They spoke too vaguely, too familiar with the topic to explain details. What is happening within the Council? What are they plotting? And how is it related to the rebels?

I can't bring my heart rate down. I can't tell whether it's racing out of fear or excitement. Finally, I've found something useful. If only I knew what it was.

10
LAI

AT LONG, AGONIZING last, the day finally comes that I'm allowed to leave the infirmary. Free again. Sort of.

It took all my willpower not to sneak out to the Order's headquarters the last two nights. I need to tell Fiona and the others what I heard. It's too much to communicate telepathically, especially with that many people, so I forced myself to wait. But tonight's the night. I'm finally going back.

But before that, there's one last thing I need to take care of.

I head straight for the officers' quarters, the rooms of which take up the top three floors of one of the back buildings. Only, this time, I'm not headed for my room.

Team One's first mission was deemed a success, but if anyone else had been there to see our awful teamwork, I doubt our evaluation would have been so kind. It worked out fine enough this time, but what about the next? I need to get everyone on the same page. However unwillingly they might be there.

I stop in front of Johann's door and knock. "Johann, you in?"

For a long time, there's only silence. I can hear thoughts on the other side of the door, distinctly Johann in both content and tone. Pretending to be gone, then.

I continue to knock. And knock. And knock. I don't stop until Johann wrenches the door open from under my still-raised fist. If irritation could be worn, Johann would be killing it in style. "*What?*"

Instead of answering, I slip under Johann's outstretched arm and into the room beyond. If I hadn't already known this was someone's living quarters, I would have thought it a gym. A collection of training equipment is spread out around the space. Johann's cot, dresser, and desk are shoved into a corner to make way for a punching bag and bench press, and without a roommate to occupy the other bed and desk, Johann has clearly been using them as weight holders.

"What do you want?" Johann asks with a scowl.

"Well, I've been thinking," I say. "Kitahara and Mendel room together, and I'm getting lonely in my room, so I thought I should move in with you. Wouldn't things be more fun that way?" Even though I know it'll make sneaking out harder, I also know that I can't stand my old room. Besides, this arrangement has its benefits.

If we were based in one of the smaller command centers, like Eastern or Northern, sharing rooms wouldn't even be a thing. But Central is so crowded, and has seen such an influx of gifted officers, that most of us who are ranked still have to share a room. The only reason I don't right now is because no officer will take the "cursed room." And while I don't believe in Etioles' ridiculous superstitions, recently, it's begun feeling cursed even to me.

When Johann's mouth opens to shut me down, I add, "I already talked to Austin about it. He thought it was a great idea. Good 'team bonding,' he said."

"I don't want you for my roommate," Johann says immediately. **Just because Austin thinks it's a good idea doesn't mean I have to go along with it.**

"He liked the idea sooo much he said he'd make it an official order." I knew Johann wouldn't accept me just like that, so I requested Austin's help when he came to visit me in the infirmary. He'd shaken his head with a smile. And then he'd agreed.

"*What?* Why haven't I heard about it?"

"He said he'd leave it to me to deliver the news. Won't this be fun?"

Johann's thoughts quicken like an adrenaline-rushed heartbeat. **Why would he do this to me? I thought we had an agreement about my living situation.** But there's no refusing an order from the general. Johann's frown deepens. "I've got some pretty strict house rules, you know."

I stretch my arms behind me straight as they can go, fingers laced together, as I start walking around the room. "Mm."

"For one, no weirdos."

"I can handle that."

I almost trip over a pair of weights on the ground. Johann's eyebrows rise. "Two, no getting in the way."

"Yes."

"Three, you leave me alone."

"Okay."

I can feel Johann's eyes on me as I meander around the room. I'm careful not to trip over anything this time.

Maybe I should talk to Austin about getting her put somewhere else. "You know I still don't accept you on the team."

"Yes."

"I'm going to talk Austin out of your assignment until he gives in."

"But I can still stay here?"

Johann sighs. "You seriously want to room with a guy?"

"What do you mean? You're a girl, aren't you?"

Johann stares at me.

And then, in the time it takes me to blink, she's suddenly in front of me, fist bunched in the fabric of my shirt. "Who told you? Was it Austin?" Her thoughts pound by too fast and too furiously for me to keep up with without getting nauseous.

"No one told me," I say. "I noticed it on my own."

I've known from the start Johann's a girl who's been pretending to be a boy ever since she joined her home sector's military nine years ago. The day our team met for the first time, she'd been thinking about how much time had passed since she'd started hiding, and how little ground she'd gained in her search. It was a lucky coincidence that I'd caught it all.

"Have you told anyone?" Johann asks.

I shake my head.

She takes a deep breath. Then another. Her fist is still attached to my shirt, keeping me in place. "This stays between us, understand?"

"Why?"

"Because I don't want anyone else to know."

"Yeah, but why?"

She thinks of her brother, a hazy, indistinct image now with how much time has passed since she last saw his face. She thinks, too, of her fruitless search for him, begun when she entered the military and all but given up now. And she thinks of how she doesn't want to get sent back to Sector Eleven. "It doesn't matter," she says. "Just promise you won't say anything."

"But I can be your roommate?" I ask. "And if you trust me enough to keep your secret, that means you'll accept me on the team and follow the major's orders?"

Johann hesitates. **Did Austin set this up? No, he likes to meddle in others' business, but he wouldn't blackmail, and Kitahara doesn't seem this sneaky. This is all Cathwell.**

A long time passes before Johann finally says, "All right." Her fingers tighten in my shirt before releasing it entirely. I know she wants to throw me against the wall rather than say what she has to. "Yeah. You can room with me, and I'll do like Kitahara says. So don't tell anyone I'm a girl, all right? If you do, I'll kill you in your sleep."

I smile. "Whatever you say, roomie."

11
LAI

I TELL JOHANN I need today to get my things together and that I'll come back tomorrow to move in.

After I've packed my few belongings and gathered all the notes I'll need for tonight, it's still pretty early, so I head for the training hall to get some practice in after my week in the infirmary. Once I return to my room, I check in with a few members of the Order telepathically and go over our tasks for the night.

When the sky has been dark for some time, and I can't hear any thoughts coming from the hall outside my door, I head for the underground tunnels.

The thing about the tunnels is that the military didn't make them. Much like the underground farms and the underground tunnels beneath the Order's home base, they were here long before anyone can remember—a relic of the civilization before, and what they left for us to use. Maps of them are scarce and unreliable. Parts of the tunnels have caved in, rendering them unusable. And some tunnels are hidden.

Luke and Sara and I used to explore the tunnels all the time. It wasn't strictly allowed, but it wasn't strictly forbidden, either, and we enjoyed it. With Luke's gift of invention, he made a machine that allowed us to find and map the hidden tunnels. We would search for ages for the trick to open fake rock walls, the catch that would slide a slab of rock into the ceiling and reveal the dark, twisting path beyond. It was a puzzle, a maze, a game.

Now it's my ticket out of Central. The maps we made then are long burned and gone, too dangerous to keep in existence, but I remember the routes well and go over my memorized version of the maps daily. I can't afford to forget them.

Thanks to my gift, I encounter no one on my way to one of the meeting rooms on the ground floor. The tunnel entrance I'm headed for is unknown to the military, so there are no guards posted. It's the only secret entrance I know of, and what with the room's function, I can only really use it at night—and I'll *have* to return well before morning, before anyone might be there.

The meeting room itself is much like all the others in Central, save for the addition of several monitors lined up on one side of the room. There's a panel of switches that controls them all by the door. I flip the switches on and off, in careful order. Fourth, second, first, fourth, third, first, second, fifth. Then I turn them all off. A hollow *click* resounds through the air. I head for the back corner of the room.

Four tiles are glued together over the trapdoor that unlocked after the combination of switches. Luke, ever the inventor, explained to me and Sara once how the electric currents that operated the room's power also operated the door's lock, but I didn't really get it. I'd nodded and pretended that I did and Sara had nodded and probably actually did.

The memory weighs heavy. I carry it with me as I descend into the tunnel below, careful to shut the trapdoor precisely in place, and then face the pitch-black pathway.

For a moment, panic washes over me. Everything's too close. Too dark. I can't get out. I can't move.

I fumble to pull out the necklace tucked under my shirt and touch the electric-yellow power crystal hanging on it. Light immediately spills into the space, momentarily blinding me as it illuminates even the tiniest of crags in the walls. Syon's gift is going strong as ever.

I give myself a few seconds to calm down. Everything is okay. These walls are sturdy. I can move just fine. There's nothing wrong, so don't dwell on it.

A strange nostalgia for sneaking out of the prison steals over me. It was so much *easier*. Why did I think this was a good idea?

But then I remember what I overheard the Councilors saying. I make my way forward.

With every turn I take and every route I choose, I'm careful. My gift picks up no one else. The rare silence in my head only serves to make me more on edge, though. I double-check my memorized maps, but self-doubt creeps in. If I've misremembered even one path, I could end up stuck in a pit or lost. Two and a half years is a long time in which to forget details.

But eventually—thankfully—I reach the ladder set into the dead end that I was looking for. I climb it and slowly open the trapdoor above, but I don't see or hear anyone around. I push it open the rest of the way.

I'm in the back room of Mr. Clemente's bookstore. The first time Luke and Sara and I discovered this concealed exit, we nearly scared

Trist and his father half to death. That took a lot of explaining. And pleading for them to keep it secret. But funnily enough, that's how the three of us met and eventually befriended Trist. Even through his surprise at a bunch of Nyte soldiers coming up through the floor of his father's bookstore, he was still nothing but kind to us.

Now I greet Mr. Clemente on my way out. He waves without looking up from his book, having already gotten a heads-up from Trist that I'd be coming. And then I'm out in the cool, cool night, sucking in lungfuls of fresh air. Nothing compares to being aboveground.

The route from there is easy enough. Through Market, now closing up, and past the high-end apartments and shops before taking a side street to the warehouse district. Various voices hum in my head along the way, and I tap my fingers against my leg to stay focused.

Normally, I'd head straight to the Order's home base from here. But tonight, I need to help screen potential recruits. And so I keep walking down twisting side streets that grow ever narrower until I reach an alley packed with hole-in-the-wall bars.

Neon lights glow in dirty, dusty windows, raucous laughter echoes off the close walls, people stumble out of one bar and into another. Everything is bright and loud and crowded as I duck through the scattering of people and knock on the door of a bar marked by a sign overhead as THE CROOKED BOOT.

A light voice asks from the other side, "Password?"

"Peace over war," I murmur. The door clicks open.

The inside is as small as you'd expect from seeing the outside. A bar counter takes up most of the space, with room enough for about ten bar stools and the tiniest of raised platforms in the very back. The lights are low, and unlike the alley outside, the space is quiet, subdued. The owner and I exchange smiles as she resumes her place behind the counter and I slip inside. The eight people seated look over at me, and from the raised stage at the back, identical grins split the pale, freckled faces of a pair of lanky, sandy-haired twins about a year younger than me.

"Yo, Lai!" one of them calls with an enthusiastic wave. Peter. "Glad you could make it!"

"It's been a while," his brother, Paul, says. His voice falls much softer than his twin's.

"I know, it's been absolutely ages," I say with a dramatic sigh. "I've missed you both terribly." I give each of them a quick hug. "Have you started yet?"

"We were just about to." Peter waves to indicate the eight people seated at the bar, all of them ranging in age. It looks like we have a mix of gifted and ungifted this time.

"Thanks for coming out to help tonight," Paul whispers so only his brother and I can hear. "We know you're busy, so we really appreciate it."

"It's the least I can do after shoving all my usual responsibilities onto everyone," I say. "Besides, this *is* my job, you know."

Paul's smile widens. "All the same, it's appreciated."

"How's Joan, by the way?" I ask. "I haven't had a chance to ask about her lately."

Paul's whole expression instantly brightens.

"Here we go," Peter sighs.

"She's good," Paul says, ignoring his brother. "We actually met up last night for dinner. She gave me a book she'd just finished reading. She said it reminded her of me and she thought I might like it."

"Aw, that's really sweet," I say. Paul and Joan have been seeing each other for over a year now. I've never met the girl, but from what Paul has said, she sounds bookish and strong-willed. "I'm glad the two of you are still going strong."

Paul ducks his head in embarrassment, but he's smiling. "Thanks, Lai."

"Well, let's get this show on the road, shall we?" Peter asks with an excited clap of his hands. Maybe too excited given how nervous everyone else in the room is. "We do have other things to take care of tonight, after all."

"All right, then I'll leave it to the both of you," I say.

I fall to the back of the room, nearer to the door, as the twins call everyone's attention to them. A few eyes trail me, but soon enough, everyone is watching Paul as he speaks. "Thank you all for coming tonight. We're sorry for the wait. We've already explained in general terms what joining the Order entails, and tonight, as we told you previously, we want to do a simple check of everyone to ensure we're not taking in anyone who might betray the Order."

A few people shift uncomfortably, but when I lean in on their thoughts, it doesn't seem to be for any reason other than the usual anxiety about someone testing you. So far so good.

Here, Peter steps forward. Or as forward as he can on the cramped stage. "And for that, I'll be the one checking everyone. My gift allows me to see parts of a person's past. I'll be using that to see if anyone here has any connections they shouldn't or any reason to betray the Order."

And while he does that, I'll be checking everyone's thoughts to make sure they're not worried about him discovering something he shouldn't. So long as everyone comes up clear, we'll be good to go. To have gotten to this stage, it's a pretty safe bet that everyone here is trustworthy. But risks aren't something the Order takes.

"All right, so who's first?" Peter asks with another clap of his hands.

Do I really have to show my past to join?

Isn't this a little much?

I know they warned us about a screening, but this is . . .

Someone raises their hand. Everyone turns to look at a little girl who can't be much older than eight. She doesn't seem to be with anyone else in the room. "I'll go," she says. Her voice shakes, but she jumps down off her stool and makes her way toward Peter. **Anything is better than going back to the streets.**

My heart twists in sympathy. Peter takes a knee so he's on the same level as the girl, and Paul smiles at her encouragingly. She doesn't seem to know which of them to look at.

"Don't worry, this won't hurt," Peter says with a rare gentleness. He holds out a hand to her. After a second's hesitation, she takes it.

Peter's gift works by question and answer. He thinks of a question—in this case, something like, *Has this person done or experienced anything that would lead them to betray the Order?*—and in return is shown a series of images from the person's past that might answer that question. His gift only works through touch, just like his brother's, which is almost the opposite in that Paul can see random instances of someone's future. But he's firmly refused to use his gift on anyone for years.

Silence falls over the room as Peter and the girl remain very still for a few moments. I scan our group's thoughts, but again, hear nothing suspicious.

Once Peter has finished checking the girl, I send him a thought. *She's coming up clear on my end.*

Peter's hand drops from the girl's and he gives her his trademark grin. "All right, you're all good to go! Welcome to the Order, little miss."

A huge smile spreads over the girl's thin face. "Thank you," she says. I almost think she'll cry. But then she takes her former place at the bar. The owner slips her a glass of chocolate milk, along with a thumbs-up.

And so everyone trickles through, one at a time, all of them nervous but none of them showing any indication of a past connection with the rebels or the Council or anyone else who could potentially give the Order trouble. When the last person has been cleared, the mood in the room shifts noticeably. The anxiety is gone, to be replaced with naked relief. The owner starts serving everyone drinks on the house. A few people even start talking to each other.

I rejoin Peter and Paul. They both look immensely pleased, though Paul keeps his happiness more subdued, as usual. "Nice work tonight, guys," I say. "Looks like we've got a nice batch of newcomers."

"Aw, it was nothing," Peter says with a dismissive wave of his hand. But despite his nonchalance, there were a few people tonight with hard pasts. A not-uncommon trend among our members. I know it takes a toll on Peter to have to sift through all those upsetting memories, but he never lets it show.

Paul squeezes his brother's shoulder before facing me. "We'll let everyone celebrate here for a bit before we take them to Regail Hall. Once we've gotten them settled in, we'll join you and the others for our meeting."

"Yeah, you go on ahead," Peter says. "You don't have time to waste waiting around here, right?"

"Yeah," I say. "Thanks. I'll see you both again soon."

We exchange waves. I give the owner my thanks for her help and for always offering up her bar to us. And then I head back out into the night.

12
LAI

I RETURN TO the warehouse district. After a brief check for thoughts in the area confirms no one's around, I quickly enter an old red-bricked building that looks much like the others. It's dark inside, but I don't switch on the lights. Stacks of crates loom up out of the darkness. I know my way around them, and to the ones I need to move in order to reveal the trapdoor that leads into the tunnels below. I open it and drop through.

Below, lanterns line both walls to bathe the hallway in a honey-coated glow. They make the tunnel familiar. Warm. Not terrifying. I follow them down, down, down through the stone halls until I reach the room I'm looking for. I don't knock before swinging the door open. "Tally ho and all that."

Inside, Fiona and Trist and a young boy, Syon, look up from a long table that fills most of the room. Maps and charts and lists are strewn across the table, some pinned down permanently, others there only temporarily for tonight's discussions. The rest of the room is plain and unadorned. Nothing marks it as our usual meeting place.

"Took you a while," Fiona says. Ever the cheerful one.

"Yeah, well, the twins asked for my help with the new recruits," I say. "It took some time—surprising, I know."

Next to her, Syon signs a greeting to me. He's younger than all the rest of us by a good few years, maybe about twelve now. Even for his age, he's small, and his large blue eyes and round face only make him appear younger. His fluffy blond hair looks like it's been cut recently. Fiona probably decided it was getting too long.

I sign a hello back and look pointedly at Fiona. She ignores me.

"It is good to see you again," Trist says as I sit next to him. "Was there any trouble?"

"Nothing I couldn't handle. But what about things here? How's everything running?"

The Order's leader is a young woman named Walker, but it's Fiona and Trist who all but run the organization. It's true Walker is our head, and she takes care of what she can, but she isn't usually present at our base here in Regail Hall. The managerial work falls to her two seconds-in-command, while Walker herself handles running the organization-wide meetings, doing tasks outside the physical location of Regail Hall, and some overhead organizational jobs. And anything Fiona and Trist can't handle falls to the eight captains and the Helpers. It's a system based on shared responsibilities and trust—the same way the entire Order functions as a society. But without me pulling my usual weight, I can't help but worry.

"Did you think we wouldn't be able to handle things without you?" Fiona asks with a raised eyebrow. By the way she says it, I know there haven't been any major problems. "How cocky. Not that I'm surprised. What you should be concerned with is your current position within the military and making sure you don't get found out or killed."

I flick my fingers at her dismissively. "You worry too much."

She scowls in response. Then again, she's always scowling. "Just see that you don't bring all of our hard work down right around our heads."

"I'll aim for our feet, then."

Fiona opens her mouth, but Trist slips in before she can respond. "Lai, you said you had not much time tonight. Let us talk about our revised self-defense plan before Peter and Paul come."

I give Fiona a look that says *See? He knows what's important here.* She rolls her eyes.

Trist pulls out a folder and lays a few sheets atop the table. He points to them each in turn as he speaks. "Our members' strength has been rising, and the number of volunteers participating in the self-defense program. But with our group growing so much bigger, we need more teachers and organization. We have only so many capable fighters who are free to teach the others."

"And with a possible war with the rebels getting ever closer, we need our members to be able to take care of themselves if it comes to it," Fiona murmurs.

They proceed to describe the system they want to implement, a tournament-style set of sparring matches that would allow members to practice with each other while the teachers tend to the beginners. They go over the finer details of how it would work and show me a chart of shifts and times for the sparring practices to take place. I nod and offer suggestions to some of the organizational points, and when all is said and done, I say, "I think it's a great idea. Good planning, both of you."

"Then we'll begin tomorrow," Fiona says as Trist gathers all the papers, each with a few new notes, back together. "The sooner the better."

Syon signs to me. *Backup energy plan?*

I nod and sign back. *Yes.*

Syon powers the entirety of Regail Hall with his gift over energy. He's one of the rare, unlucky Nytes who has no limits to his gift, which is what makes it possible. Nytes like him are so scarce they're not even common knowledge among the gifted. But every limitless Nyte has a huge drawback. Syon's is that his emotions affect his gift. Even the tiniest amount of feeling, whether it be positive or negative in nature, can send his gift spiraling out of control. It's happened before. It'd be terrifying to witness again.

I want to know why he's thinking about a backup energy plan now. Did something happen? Is he worried he might lose control? I don't know if he'd want to discuss this in front of the others, though, so I put a thought in his head to ask these questions as well as to ask if I can actively listen in on his thoughts. He nods.

If we weren't so close, I would've just done it. But the five other remaining original members of the Order are special. I respect their privacy. Even now, I merely skim over his thoughts, listening only to what he wants to convey to me.

I'm worried about the possible war. What if I can't stay in control? The Order shouldn't have to suffer because of me.

The words pierce my heart like blades. Syon shouldn't have to worry about things like that. A kid as young as him shouldn't have to worry about how his possibly *feeling* something could affect those around him.

But I know showing sympathy or pity doesn't help anything, and it's true that the Order would be in a hard spot if we were to lose Syon's gift.

I withdraw from Syon's thoughts. *Understood*, I sign. *Ideas?*

He signs, but my ability at signing is too poor to understand the details and Fiona has to translate. "He's wondering if it would be possible to ensure every member has a flashlight. That way, if the power is gone, everyone would at least still be able to navigate the tunnels and escape if need be."

I bite my lip. The Order has a thousand members and little funding. Would it actually be possible? And how could we cover the tracks of that many flashlights suddenly being bought around the sector?

I brokenly sign these concerns and Syon's expression falls infinitesimally.

Fiona, ever his protector, immediately jumps in. *Not bad idea. We just need time. Don't worry.*

I try my best to sign as well. He's mute, not deaf, so he'd understand if I just said it aloud, but we all try to communicate with him in the same way he does with us. *Continue thinking ideas. Talk more later.*

He nods.

A knock sounds from the doorway and we all look up to see Peter and Paul standing in the entrance.

"Yo, Lai!" Peter says with an enthusiastic wave. Paul echoes it, albeit more calmly, beside him. "Long time no see, right?"

"Absolutely ages," I say with a laugh. "How are the new recruits liking the base?"

"They were a little nervous about it being underground," Paul says. "But I think they'll take to it. Amal and Jair are with them now, explaining how things work and answering questions."

"Good work," Trist says warmly. "Now please, sit."

Now that all the remaining original, core members of the Order are here, I can finally give my report. The twins take a seat and I quickly fill them all in on Team One's first mission and what I overhead the Councilors talking about. Something about experiments, getting the Nytes under their control, making Sector Eight invincible.

It feels pitifully little once I'm done. I wish I could've learned something more concrete, more useful, something that could've helped us going forward. Given that most of my time back in the military was spent in the infirmary, I didn't really get a chance to do much investigating.

Trist and Fiona and Peter share an unsettled look. Syon keeps his eyes focused on the table, thinking, careful. Paul is quiet.

I leave them to their thoughts a moment before I ask, "What do you think it could mean?"

Fiona shakes her head. "It could mean anything. There's too little context to make an accurate guess. Whatever it is, if it's the Council's doing, it can't be good."

"I don't like how they talked about getting Nytes under their control," Peter says uneasily. "That doesn't sound limited to the rebels."

"The experiments are worrying," Trist says. His head is bent in thought. "That they are almost complete more so."

"I'll try finding out more," I say. Their disquiet is starting to get to me, too. I don't know that I can lighten the mood, either, seeing as how my specialty is getting under people's skin.

"Be careful about it," Fiona says. "Don't take any stupid risks."

Peter rolls his eyes, but only after making sure Fiona isn't looking. He'd never admit it, but she scares him. "You just do what you have to and leave the rest to us," he says. "And don't worry about things here. We've got everything covered."

"I know you do," I say. "Thanks." I glance at my MMA. "I should be getting back. Don't want to risk exposing my only way in and out."

Fiona opens her mouth to speak, but then shakes her head. "Just be careful out there, all right?"

"Aren't I always?" I ask. The same concern as always. The same reply as always.

She rolls her eyes. As always.

"Be safe," Trist says as he gives me a hug. "Do not put yourself at risk for information. We can do without. You, we cannot."

"I got it," I say gently. "Don't worry, I'll be okay."

"Yeah, our invincible Lai isn't gonna go down that easily," Peter says. He kicks his feet up on the table, but immediately removes them when Fiona gives him a withering glare.

"Take care, Lai," Paul says.

Syon adds in his concern as well, and I sign back not to worry. Everything will be okay.

As I take my leave and wave goodbye to everyone, I can't help but wonder when the next time I'll see them will be.

It's very early morning by the time I reach the meeting room with the secret tunnel entrance. I hear no thoughts either in the room or out in the hallway beyond, so I quietly make my way out.

As I walk the halls, I can't get my mind off what I heard the

Councilors talking about the other day. Everyone's unease over the matter only reinforced the feeling that whatever they're plotting, it can't be good. But how can I find out more? Considering how big whatever it is sounded, I doubt just anyone in the military would know. And those who do are probably protected by starlight. What are the odds of the Councilors returning and talking about it again? Maybe I can see if anyone knows of another scheduled visit from them . . .

I'm so caught up in my thoughts that I nearly run straight into someone when I round the next corner.

"Sorry," I say as the other person rubs his shoulder where we knocked into each other. In the dim hall, it takes another moment for me to recognize him. "Mendel? What are you doing up and about this early?"

"Looking for you," Mendel says. His hand drops back down to his side, but something about his expression puts me on edge. "You weren't in your room last night when I came by."

"I was in the training hall for a while," I say slowly.

"Until right before curfew? And just now when I went to check, you still weren't there."

"Why would you be looking for me at this hour?"

"It was more like I was seeing if you were still gone. Where've you been, Cathwell?"

"Around."

"Obviously." He crosses his arms and waits. When my silence continues, he says, "I was on guard duty last night. I watched the security camera feeds, but I couldn't find you anywhere in Central.

Not even just walking down a hallway. Funnily enough, you obviously weren't in your room, either." My heart starts pounding. "And yet, here you are in Central, as if you never left. How'd you leave and get back in?"

"Leave?" I repeat with a mildly blank look. I can hear the blood rushing through my ears, but I force my voice to be devoid of emotion. "There are cameras all over Central. How could someone leave without being recorded?"

"You expect me to buy that?" Mendel asks. His eyes are flat, any semblance of his usual carefree act long abandoned. "You don't fool me, Cathwell. What are you hiding?"

My stomach knots. The usual blank act won't work on him, especially not after our last conversation. I hadn't anticipated running up against him this soon. I need more time to think before I deal with him.

I take too long to answer.

Mendel says, "It's fine if you don't want to talk to me. But I'm sure Kitahara and Johann and, oh, I don't know, all of the higher-ups, would be very interested to hear about all this. That rebel trying to take you with her on our last mission, you sneaking out. It doesn't paint a very nice picture of you, does it?"

My irritation flickers, and I know it shows on my face, because Mendel smiles sharply. It's such an annoying look I jump to wipe it off his face without thinking. "And what about you? Poor little Mendel, missing all your memories from before the military picked you up injured Outside the Gate three and a half months ago." The smile is gone. "What you wouldn't give to know even a hint of your past. But your string of information brokers can't tell you anything except that there was never any Erik Mendel in Sector Eight. You must be desperate by now. I wonder what the others would think of that?"

Unlike Johann, Mendel does not immediately jump for my throat. He sticks instead to shutting down and staring at me with dead eyes. "None of that has anything to do with the team, the rebels, or my loyalty to the military. Even if I can't remember, I'm not the one sneaking around and keeping secrets. That would be you."

Before I can respond, we both freeze as a nearby door opens. We were so wrapped up in our conversation that neither of us were paying attention to our surroundings. The gray, early light of dawn is already seeping into the halls. Footsteps are beginning to echo around us. Central is waking up.

I focus on Mendel again. It's clear he's as reluctant to continue this conversation around others as I am. Despite what he says, he's very cautious about his lack of memories. He sees it as a weakness. One he doesn't want others to know about or be able to use against him.

"Let's continue this later," I say cheerfully. Being too serious will only draw attention, especially from two Nytes. "I'll find you, okay?"

I don't wait for his response before skipping away down the hall, back to my room and away from the reality that someone is onto me. But no matter how much distance I put between us, I know I can't pretend my way out of this one.

13
LAI

I FEEL MENDEL'S eyes on me all day. Now that I've been discharged, Kitahara gathers all of us together for a joint training session. Johann comes because of our recent agreement about her working together with the team. Mendel comes to see me.

Much as Kitahara doesn't want to pair Mendel and Johann together after last time's disastrous outcome, he's worried about either of them going too seriously against me when I was only discharged yesterday. And so, it's once again me against Kitahara and Johann versus Mendel.

Yet even though his sparring partner is Johann of all people, I feel Mendel's gaze on me the whole time. It's obviously distracting him from his practice, but he can't seem to stop himself.

Eventually, Johann snaps at him for his lack of concentration. "What are you even doing? You think you can win against me using only half a brain?"

Annoyance flickers over Mendel's face and he starts fighting her seriously after that. But it only seems to lead to them bickering even more.

I shake my head, understanding for the first time how Trist must feel when Fiona and I go at it with each other.

"You okay?" Kitahara asks. We've had a few matches by now, all of them ending in my win, with the result that Kitahara is finally starting to face me seriously. **I don't know how she's still so strong after this long, but I'm glad. I hope she's not pushing it with her recent injuries, though.**

"Mm." My attention roams over the many soldiers training in the room while I try to keep all their thoughts at a distance. My fingers drum against my leg. "Want to go again?"

But Kitahara's eyes slide to our teammates as Johann's fire flares up yet again. He sighs. **What am I going to do with these people?** "No, that's fine." He claps his hands and raises his voice so Johann and Mendel can hear him. "Let's take a break."

Johann and Mendel trade one last glare before stalking toward the benches. Kitahara and I follow after them.

Mendel reaches out toward his water bottle, clearly intending to use his telekinesis to bring it flying to him, but after remembering where we are and all the ungifted soldiers around us, he chooses to physically pick it up instead. Casually using our gifts outside of battle or training is one thing. Casually using them in plain sight of Etioles is another.

I sit on the floor and try to ignore Mendel's continued staring as Kitahara speaks. He's standing, looking out across the room of training soldiers. There's something distant about his expression. "We're setting out again in a few days. This time, we have to be ready."

"The mission details from the file sounded easy enough," Mendel says lightly. He may have dropped the carefree act around me this morning, but he clearly intends to maintain it around the others.

"It's better not to underestimate your opponent," Kitahara says. After a look around the room at all the people present, he lowers his voice so only we can hear him. "We'll proceed with caution. But the important thing for this mission is to stay hidden and inconspicuous." He stares pointedly at Johann and Mendel, who, despite their personalities, have been very good at hiding certain things up till now. But I know what he means. They're both too . . . much. "This time, we don't want to engage with any rebel forces."

"Roger," Mendel says.

Johann rolls her eyes, but answers affirmatively at Kitahara's look.

"Okay," the major says. "Let's go once more."

Even after the training session has ended, Mendel follows me around like some kind of target-locked Watcher. I make sure to go only where there are other people present while I consider my plan, but by the end of the day, I'm worn out from his constant supervision. Which was probably *his* plan.

I finally duck into the one place I know no one will interrupt us: Mendel and Kitahara's room. Kitahara is in the library drafting the plan for our next mission, and if his perfectionist nature is anything to go by, he'll be there awhile.

The door is locked, so I have to pick it open with a hairpin I carry around specifically for times like this. In a handful of moments, the door springs open under my fingers.

Kitahara and Mendel's room is a strange mix of two different minds. I'd heard Kitahara was transferred over from Eastern Headquarters for this team, but any signs of unpacking are already gone. Books and binders are placed in neat rows along his desk. His bed is perfectly made. Reminders written on varying colors of sticky notes form seamless squares over both his bed and his desk. Nothing is an inch out of place.

The other half of the room is chaos born of creation. Drawings and schematics hang over Mendel's bed, mostly for buildings, quite a few for furniture. Tables and chairs and other woodwork creations clutter his half of the room. They're stacked one on top of another in teetering piles. Cities of model buildings cluster together in the empty spaces between chair and table legs.

The door opens behind me and I ask, "Is the woodshop always where you go when you're off duty?"

"Shut up," Mendel says. "How'd you even get in here?"

"I opened the door."

He decides it's not a topic worth pursuing, which, really, it should be given I just proved I could break into his room. "You said you'd talk, so get to it."

"So impatient." I turn around to face him and hold up a deck of cards. "Let's play a game."

"A card game. Are you serious?" He searches my face for any sign of a joke or trick. When he finds none, he frowns. **What is she up to?** "I wasn't looking for you so we could play games."

"No. You were looking for me so you could get answers."

He eyes me one last time, carefully. "Fine."

Mendel waves his hand and one of the tables scattered around his half of the room rises through the air and comes to rest between us.

He also manages to telekinetically pull two semi-matching chairs out of the mess without sending anything toppling.

Mendel falls back into his seat. I wonder if he's trying to show off his sturdy workmanship. "So. What's the game?"

"Pass." I sit and push the deck across to him.

It's a simple enough game. Each player starts with five cards. The goal is to trade them out to get a chronological sequence of number or face cards. You get other cards for your sequence by asking the other player if they have a card you need. If they don't, you draw, then discard a card. If they do, you trade cards.

"You don't just want to play cards, do you?" Mendel asks. I watch him. He taps the deck. "What's the real point of this?"

A corner of my lips curls up. "Information."

"That's why it's pass, right?"

I nod.

It's about time I met someone interesting. Whatever she's hiding, now's my chance to find out.

Mendel shuffles and deals the cards, then waits for me to start. Waits for me to set up the rules of this game.

The idea is simple: If he has the card I ask for, he has to answer the question I ask. If not, he can ignore it.

But I don't necessarily need him to answer my questions for them to have an impact. I'll show my intentions and get him riled up first, and then ask my real questions.

"What would it take for you to work together with the team?" I ask. "Five."

I take it back. She's as boring and annoying as the rest of them. "Pass."

When I pick up a card from the deck and set another facedown on the table without saying anything more, he realizes how this game is going to work.

"Where were you last night?" he asks. "Jack."

"Pass."

Mendel picks up a card and discards another on top of my facedown one.

"How come you want to find your memories so badly?" I ask. "Three."

His eyes narrow. **There are only a handful of people who know I have amnesia. I might not trust any of them, but I doubt they would say anything without good reason. Which means she really does know something.** He remembers how I mentioned the night approaching on our last mission. Something I accidentally pulled from the one scrap of a memory he does have of his former life.

"Shouldn't that be obvious?" Mendel asks. "I want to know who I was, if there's anyone waiting for me, what I planned on doing with my life. Why I was injured and Outside when they found me." He hands me a three of hearts. "I want to know everything."

I give him a card I don't need.

"What's your gift?" he asks. "Four." It's not a card he needs, but he knows that since I asked for a three and a five, the probability of me having a four is high.

My nose scrunches up and I stare at my cards. He just *had* to start playing to get information instead of playing to win the game. Too late to go back now. "Telepathy."

He stares at me. **Is she joking? She wouldn't lie. Would she? There's nothing to gain from a lie like that.**

"It's against my policy to lie," I say, still examining my cards. "I'm a decent actress, but not a liar. Not through words, at least. Which is why, unlike you, I'm safe around Kitahara."

I flick my four of spades at him, but it floats down to lie on the table, where it remains untouched. He stares at it.

"You should probably fix your line of thinking, too," I say. "Not everyone does or says things just because they can get something out of it. We're not all you." I tilt my head in his direction. "Oh, and I do hope you won't tell anyone what we discuss during this game. That wouldn't be much fun."

He meets my eyes for possibly the first time since we met. It's hard for him to wrap his mind around the fact I can read thoughts—*his* thoughts, specifically. **No wonder she knew about my memory loss. What else does she know? Not just about me, but everyone. Wait. Could she go into someone's head and dig up forgotten memories?**

He opens his mouth to ask the question aloud, but before he can, I say, "I'd like for this team to work out. Which means everyone has to cooperate with one another. Will you help me? Four."

Mendel blinks. He'd forgotten we were playing pass, and it takes him a moment to understand why I tacked a four on the end of my question. He slides the four still sitting between us back to me. Normally players don't ask for a card they just gave up, but it's not strictly a rule that you *can't*. "What about Johann?" he asks.

"The sergeant major seems willing to work with the team now."

Blackmailed. Johann definitely isn't the type to make deals or be persuaded. Whatever Cathwell heard from his thoughts, it must've been important enough to get him to bend.

He squints at the deck as if willing it to give him answers. **What kind of person is this girl? Manipulative, clearly. But she seems smart. If she's asking me for a favor, then she must have something to offer in return. I doubt she'd bother otherwise.**

Disagreeable though Mendel is, he's perceptive.

"If I agree, will you help me get my memories back?" he finally asks. When I just keep looking at him, he adds, somewhat irritably, "Four."

"It's against the rules to ask for the same card as your last turn. An automatic pass." I was expecting more from him. To correctly guess a card from my hand like last time, maybe. Did I overestimate him?

But I can tell he's been thrown off. Mendel said the card we'd traded back and forth instead of guessing a card I might have because he didn't care about the game. He was more concerned with our conversation.

I take up his side for him. "If I said I would try to help you get your memories back, would you work to make the team a success? Which would, of course, include not prying into my affairs or talking about them with anyone. Ace."

"You're not sure it would work." He's careful not to phrase it as a question. That would require asking for a card. Besides, he needs to answer my own question first. "Using your gift to get my memories back, I mean."

"My gift isn't going to be able to help you," I say. "I can only hear what people are thinking in the moment. Dipping into memories is beyond me. But I know someone whose gift *is* to see into a person's past. I can ask him to help us. I don't think he's ever used his gift on someone who has amnesia, but if that doesn't work, I'll help you in other ways."

"And what ways might those be?" he asks. I raise an eyebrow, but he says, "I'm not going to agree to such a flimsy deal. I don't even know this person you're talking about—if he even exists."

"I did say I don't lie."

He scoffs. "Look, I want concrete proof that you'll find a way to make me remember my past, or at least get me closer to it."

"You wouldn't trust me if I said I could absolutely do such a thing." I lean back in my chair until I'm balancing on its two back legs. Mendel's craftsmanship really is solid. "And I wouldn't, either, if I were in your position."

We stare at each other. He knows I'm reading his thoughts. He knows I probably know exactly how to counter any argument he could think up before it even crosses his mind. **Her gift must be so helpful when she wants to manipulate someone into doing what she needs. There's no way I can trust her.**

I don't so much as bat an eye when he comes to this conclusion. Even among Nytes, a gift like mine isn't something that's easy to have or share with others. It happened a few times when I was younger, before I knew better, where I told someone about my gift and was met with revulsion and hate. I didn't understand then. Now I know some things are better left secret.

"You're asking an awful lot of me in return for this one favor."

"The one thing you want is your memories, right?" I ask. "If there was more you wanted, I would offer it to you. But there isn't. You have no leads, no allies, and only three and a half months' worth of memories. I have the means to help you. If you don't accept them, who knows how much longer you'll remain at a standstill. You need help, Mendel. I'm offering it to you."

"At a price."

I shrug. "Everything comes at a price. I help you get what you want, you help me get what I want. If we both benefit, what's the problem?"

His eyes shift to the rounded edge of the table. He thinks about how he didn't sand it well enough. It's almost too small a thing to notice—certainly not anything I would've ever caught on my own—but a part of it is uneven.

What do I really stand to lose? Forced cooperation with the team or whatever, which would be annoying but doesn't actually take anything from me but effort. The possibility of what I could gain in return is huge. It could end my search.

But that thought also makes him hesitate. For as long as he can remember, which, granted, is not very long at all, his only goal has been to find out who he is. **What comes after that? Will the person I am now disappear once I remember? Will I go back to my old home, go after my old goals?**

He shakes his head. **That's exactly why I'm trying to get my memories back. So I can decide where to go from there.**

"Okay," he says. We trade cards. "I'll cooperate to make the team succeed or whatever. In return, you get my memories back or show definite signs that you're making progress on finding out about my past. Those are my conditions."

It's hard to hold back a smile as I lay my hand down on the table. Ace, two, three, four, five. "Deal."

14
JAY

TWO DAYS FOLLOWING our failed group training session, we're sent Out once more. We reviewed the plan early this morning, but that's the limit of our team's recent interactions. I can't help but worry how this mission will go.

Everyone is astonishingly silent as we ride. Though the wind is strong, I can faintly hear the thrum of my byc and the varying beeps from its radar. Blackened trees jut crookedly out of the ground like giant sticks. Brown-gray dust billows out behind our bycs.

We follow Ferals' trails of packed dirt and flattened underbrush. The trails are difficult to traverse; however, if we were to take the single main road that leads through this deadened forest, the rebels would see us coming.

Luckily we encounter only smaller Ferals—strange, mindless creatures that somehow manage to live Outside. They say no two Ferals are the same, but they share a few similar characteristics. They all have the same thick, hardened gray skin pulled so tightly over their bones you can actually see their entire skeleton. They can have anywhere from one head to four, sometimes with ears or noses, sometimes without, always with gaping black holes in place of eyes. Some have wings, some tails, some teeth sharp as knives. They all attack as soon as they smell blood.

As none of us are bleeding, it's easy enough to back away from the Ferals we run into. But we do then have to get off and walk our bycs through the trees until we find a new trail. It's slow going, but for some reason, no one complains.

A branch cracks under my foot as we transfer from one path to another, and Mendel must nearly break his wrist whipping out his weapon. The sound echoes through the still air, up through the tops of trees that tower so high above us the orange sky is barely visible. We pause.

Mendel opens his mouth, appears to consider, then closes it.

"We're almost there," I say. I don't know why everyone is so quiet today, but it's nice. Well, truth be told, it's unsettling. Previously, Mendel and Johann wouldn't listen to a word I had to say about the team. I have no idea why they're being so cooperative today, and their sudden transformation makes me wary. Whatever the reason, I have my doubts about it being out of the goodness of their hearts.

Cathwell is the same, I suppose. Her arms circle around me as we board our byc and shoot forward. The Gatesmen still haven't had the other byc repaired yet, so she's riding with me once more.

I can feel her heat through my back. I'm not used to physical contact with others; even though she's merely using me as an anchor, her presence is strangely comforting. Like the others, she is silent.

The trees blur by. Shriveled leaves and branches pelt my visor. The usual iron scent of the Outside is overpowered by freshly turned dirt.

When we're nearly to the coordinates specified in our mission files, I lift two fingers in the air and point to a grouping of dead bushes ahead. We dismount from our bycs and hide them as best we can in the skeletal underbrush.

I allow my mind to go blank and the three-dimensional grid unfolds in my head. Four spheres, each slightly pulsating different shades of emotion, stand at our location. In the distance, a small amber presence is walking, far enough away that I think we'll be safe from detection.

"Everyone knows the plan?" I compress my helmet back into its ball, stow it in its proper compartment, and commence double-checking the equipment in my belt. I look up when I hear the click of everyone's compartments opening as they do the same. No one else checked their equipment the last time I went through this procedure.

I'm not able to ask about it before Mendel says, "Large amounts of rebel traffic have been seen passing through this forest, specifically at point thirty-eight north twenty. Our scouts suspect they're either setting up a new base or else trading information here, but couldn't risk getting close enough to confirm. We'll split into groups and find out what we can via undetected observation."

"Mendel and I've got west," Johann says. He looks up; however, it's not me he's looking at. It's Cathwell. "The major and lieutenant have east."

Ideally, it would be better to pair Cathwell with Johann or Mendel since they have stronger offensive gifts, but I don't trust either of them enough to watch out for her. Mendel is too whimsical, Johann too impulsive. Plus the fact that the latter nearly burned her alive on our last mission.

"Remember, try not to be seen or engage in a fight." I refasten each of my belt's compartments. "If the rebels become aware we've found their new base or information trading spot, they could potentially abandon it, or else strengthen its defense in preparation for future attacks. It will only make more trouble for us later on if that happens."

"Trouble if it doesn't go well," Cathwell says. She isn't looking at either Mendel or Johann as she says it—her attention is focused somewhere down the Ferals' path we took to get here—but both their presences flicker with irritation. Whatever their change in behavior, it has something to do with the lieutenant. I just can't comprehend how.

"We'll regroup here in three hours, whether we've discovered anything or not," I say. Much as I want to interrogate the three of them about their behavior right now, the mission comes first. There will be time for questions later. "If you find the base, come straight here and send the all-clear. If anything happens and the rebels discover you, send the red alert so we can regroup and help each other out." I tap the small screen of the MMA strapped around my wrist and am rewarded with a roll of the eyes from Johann.

"Understood," Mendel says lazily. Cathwell remains staring into the distance.

Gods help us. "Okay. Let's go."

Surprisingly enough, we are not instantly discovered. Silence is key; we don't want to risk setting off any audio-based technological traps or bugs by being too loud.

Cathwell and I stop a few yards short of an enormous tree located near the coordinates we were given. Bare branches twist around one another as they fight for the small amount of sunlight available.

For the time being, the four of us are the only presences in the area. Mendel and Johann are heading toward the other side as Cathwell and I hunker down under a cracked, fallen tree trunk overcome by clinging ivy and red-black moss. Now we wait.

Cathwell taps me on the shoulder. Using standard military sign language, she asks, *Orders?*

Hold, I sign back. *Quiet.*

She struggles for a heartbeat with the hand signal she wants. *The scouts found something.*

I think she's asking if my gift would pick up any incoming rebels prior to us seeing them. At least, it was the question I had been anticipating, and it matches closely enough.

Someone with a gift that circumnavigates mine could appear. There could be enemy Watchers patrolling—my gift doesn't pick up technology. We could have unknowingly already set off some kind of trap that would alert them we're here; they could be preparing an ambush while we sit here completely unaware.

These things are too specific for signals, however. *Maybe.*

She nods and keeps her eyes low, scanning the area.

I'm about to settle in for a long three hours when a spot, then five, appear on my grid, still too far away to have distinct colors or sizes.

The amount of time it takes for the dots to sharpen into one small, two middle-sized, and two large spheres, all of varying shades of pale blue, is agonizing. I signal to Cathwell to get ready, but it looks like she's already aware. Her hand is over the compressed weapon strapped on her belt. She looks to me, waiting for me to signal something else.

Follow at a safe distance.

She nods, and despite her peculiarities, I'm glad she's with me.

There's something about her, perhaps the way she carries herself or the way she moves—even with her occasional unpredictability—that is acutely reassuring. That, and I know firsthand how well she can handle herself in a fight.

The people I sensed are headed directly for us, toward the towering tree. I hold my breath; when I can't hear Cathwell exhale, I know she's done the same. The life-deprived bushes on the other side of the giant tree quiver as five people pass through them in no particular formation. They move without speaking, but without too much care for where they step as twigs crack underfoot. They're dressed casually in camouflaged shades of browns and blacks.

Everyone looks straight ahead, which makes me question whether they know we're here and are pretending not to notice, or whether they just aren't wary of being followed. Either way, I wait until they're a full thirty seconds ahead of us before I give the signal to Cathwell that we're to follow.

She falls in line behind me as we stalk the group. We move noiselessly behind tree trunks, through shredded shadows created by the maze of branches overhead. I'm not worried about losing them; as long as they stay within a half-mile radius of me, I'll be able to sense their position.

Cathwell is so silent, I have to continuously glance back to make sure she's still with me. I keep forgetting she's a soldier with years more experience than me.

The rebels proceed without hesitation. This almost feels too easy; after several minutes of tailing them, we still haven't run into any traps. There's been no indication the people we're following suspect they're being followed, either.

Without looking back, I signal to Cathwell. *Be on guard.* I don't risk taking my focus off my internal grid to see if she replies.

Cathwell's presence flashes a sudden violet as someone shoves me from behind. Something sharp slashes my arm. Dust fills my mouth as my face hits the ground.

Instinct and experience compel me to roll out of reach of whatever hit me. I stand in time to see Cathwell leap back from the downward swing of a rebel's sword.

There's a cut close to my elbow, but it's shallow. Cathwell must have noticed the rebel and pushed me out of the way of a potentially fatal blow. I wasn't paying attention. If I had, she wouldn't have had to protect me—*again*.

How could I not have sensed him coming? He didn't appear on my grid at all. That's never happened before.

He's dressed all in black, with shaggy blond hair he lazily flips out of his eyes. "You're the infamous Lai, right?" He bares his teeth in what I think is supposed to be a grin. I hit the red alert on my MMA—and hope the others haven't been caught in a similar trap. "Name's Devin."

He swings his sword easily, carelessly as he speaks, all the while approaching Cathwell.

She doesn't move. Her double-headed spear is already in its extended form. On my grid, her presence is a hammering scarlet. It's not fear she's feeling, like I would've expected, but hurt. Betrayal. But her face gives nothing away, and I don't have time to dwell on it.

I grasp the handles of the knives strapped to my wrists.

The rebel—Devin—charges. Cathwell sidesteps and twirls the shaft of her spear around his sword, attempting to jerk it from his grip.

He pulls free and slashes sideways at her. She jumps back, but he instantly fills the gap. She barely has time to bring her spear up to deflect another blow.

"I heard you were strong," Devin says through their crossed weapons. His expression is wild. "I was told to bring you back alive, but it should be fine if you're missing an arm or two. Don't disappoint me, okay?"

Take her alive? Why would the rebels want to capture Cathwell?

Cathwell meets my eyes. Even though Devin's back is to me, I can't chance taking a shot with her right there.

Then the rebels we were tracking stop. Abrupt surprise radiates through their presences, then hesitation, before they start racing back toward us, their spheres burning with anxiety and purpose. It was a trap.

"Cathwell, we need to retreat," I say. There's no way the two of us can take on six of them.

"Hey, hey, I'm standing right here," Devin says. He brings his sword under Cathwell's spear, then up between her and her weapon. She skips back to avoid the hit, holding her spear in one hand and swinging it in a wide arc. Devin ducks.

There's no chance of me getting a clear shot at Devin. If I attempted to help, the probability of hurting Cathwell instead is high. Our teamwork isn't yet of a high enough level that we could attempt tag-teaming him, either. I'm useless standing here.

The times that I resent my gift's ability are few and far between, but the gnaw of guilt at my being unable to help claws at me now. And as Cathwell and Devin keep skipping back and forth, lunging and dodging, the other rebels are getting nearer.

Calm down. Think. What can I do right now?

We're unable to run, or Devin will cut us down from behind. I'm not able to do anything about him, so I need to handle the other rebels. Even though Devin isn't showing up on my internal grid, they are, which means I should still have the element of surprise on my side.

I begin climbing the nearest tree. I have to make sure I have a good height, but that I can still get down at a moment's notice.

Once I'm in position, I ready my knives and wait for the group of rebels to come within range. I tighten my focus on the forerunner of the group. The wait is agonizing. My palms are wet.

My blade flies.

A light on my grid flickers before disappearing completely. I hear someone stumble and fall before four rebels burst into the area where Cathwell and Devin are fighting—two of the group looking back over their shoulders to ascertain why their comrade tripped. With that distraction, I'm able to take another of them down before the last three realize what's happening and spot me.

They spread out. If any of them are long-range fighters, I'm done for. There's no cover in these dead trees; the most I can hope for is that the branches will deflect whatever attack they throw at me.

My pulse jumps up my throat. I've never been this badly outnumbered before. No plan, no grasp of how strong my opponents are, and here I am, waiting up in a tree.

The rebels below me are circling warily, weapons raised. They don't appear to have anyone with a gift that can reach me up here, but it'd be all too easy for them to avoid my attacks when I'm in clear sight like this, so I'm not able to do anything, either. However, Cathwell won't last long if all of them turn on her.

Do or die. I jump.

The rebels below me scramble back to avoid being hit, but even before I've touched ground, they charge.

I can fight hand-to-hand when it comes to it. But against three opponents with unknown gifts? As soon as I dodge out of their reach, I sprint toward Cathwell. She must guess that I have retreat in mind, because with one final shove at Devin with her spear, she joins me in running.

I hate exposing my back. I'm afraid that any second, I'll feel the harsh, unforgiving thrust of a blade between my shoulders. But we keep ducking and dodging with the rebels' shouts following after us, and nothing strikes me down.

"What's the plan?" Cathwell asks, even as my mind races to keep pace with my feet.

"Run."

"I think we're at that part. What's next?"

I'm about to tell her to just keep running; however, something in the terrain comes up on my internal grid. There's a cliff rising up ahead of us. And at the bottom of that cliff, a cave.

"There's a cave up ahead," I say. "We'll fight there."

Her eyebrows come together. "Won't we be trapped?"

"No one can attack us from behind, and they won't be able to attack us all at once in such a small space."

"Major, this is—"

A knife whistles past. It barely misses Cathwell's ear.

"No time," I say. "Come on."

I take a sharp right and Cathwell follows after me in the same breath.

This is crazy. I know that. But we can't keep running, and this is the best way to limit their movements.

We break out of the trees, into an open space with a short cliff rising up in front of us. I don't hesitate in running straight for the cave, but Cathwell does. It's only when I shout her name that she moves to follow me.

If the rebels hadn't been pursuing us so closely, the cave might have made a good hiding place. But since there wasn't much chance of losing them, they see us duck in.

The cave is smaller than I'd anticipated, the ceiling only about a foot above my head, the width perhaps twice my height. I face the entrance, Cathwell alongside me, but her presence is pulsing violet. Something is wrong. However, I don't have time to figure out what it is before the first rebel appears in the entrance.

I throw one of my knives at him immediately, but he easily dodges and charges. He swings his sword in a wide arc—or he would have, if it hadn't caught on the side of the cave.

I use his falter to rush in, sinking another of my knives into his chest. Warm blood trickles over my hands as he stares at me.

When I rip my blade free, I'm unable to look at him, but push him back into the next rebel trying to enter the cave. I wish I could get rid of the blood on my hands as easily.

"I'm stuck," Cathwell says.

"What?" When I look back, Cathwell is standing there with her spear extended, but not with enough space to swing or effectively use it. The plan I used to restrict the rebels is restricting her as well. At least her presence on my grid is starting to calm down. Whatever was bothering her before, she appears to have put it out of mind for the time being. "It's okay. Stay behind me. I'll take care of this."

I'm beginning to think this will work out somehow. As the rebels drag their friend outside, I can tell they're trying to formulate a plan.

Then five new presences appear on my grid. Shortly after them, coming from the opposite direction, two more. They're all heading toward us.

My stomach sinks. Reinforcements? We can't handle that many, especially if one of them has a gift that could either kill us instantly or smoke us out.

"What do we do?" Cathwell asks. I think she knows about the newcomers as well.

I take a deep breath. It'll be okay. Everything will work out—I just have to think.

But I can't. Between the rebels outside and the ones headed for us, my panic keeps scattering my thoughts like so many startled birds.

"We can't run," Cathwell says. As if she's prompting me.

Her calm sinks into me. I nod. "We'll hold our position here."

"If a strong Nyte comes?"

"There's nothing we can do about that. We'll work it out if it happens and fight as best we can."

"Okay."

She compresses her spear and tucks it into her belt's sheath before coming to stand beside me. She holds out her hand.

I give her a throwing knife, my fingers lingering over hers. "You know, from our training sessions, you appear to be quite good at hand-to-hand combat."

She nearly smiles. "Just a bit."

The rebels outside aren't doing anything. They must be aware their comrades are coming, and it's not as if we're going anywhere. Devin paces irritably back and forth just outside the entrance, but every time he takes a step forward as though he's about to come in after us, one of the others says something and he goes back to pacing.

"So tell me, Cathwell, since we've got a little time," I say. "What's your gift?"

"Secret."

"And do you know that rebel? Devin?"

"No. I've never seen him before."

No itch behind my eyes. She isn't lying. But then why did she feel betrayed when she saw him?

"Then do you know why the rebels want to capture you?"

Her sphere's hue on my grid pales, which is odd, because that's typically what happens when someone grows calmer. "Prisoners of war are often useful for extracting information."

"That's not an answer."

She looks down and away. "Sorry, Major."

The group of five presences on my grid have arrived. From our short distance inside the cave, I can see them regroup with their comrades as they watch us, discussing.

It's hard to keep a steady grip on my knives through my sweating palms. I readjust them. Despite staring the end right in the face, some part of me is still unable to register that I'm going to die here like this. Some part of me thinks there's a way to make it through. I'm going to fight. And I'm going to win.

Two of the new rebels step forward. Cathwell and I stand side by side, blades at the ready.

Before they can so much as take a step inside, they're both propelled back through the air by an invisible force. Seconds later, fire engulfs them. Two lights disappear from my grid.

I can't comprehend what happened until Mendel and Johann come running into view, the former's hand now raised in the direction of the remaining rebels.

The other two presences coming toward us. They were our teammates.

"Why are you so surprised?" Cathwell asks after a quick glance at my face. "You're the one who hit the red alert, aren't you?"

Outside, Mendel and Johann sweep through the rebels, taking full advantage of their unexpected appearance to wreak havoc.

"Why am I not surprised it's you, Erik?" Devin snarls.

Mendel's head whips around so fast I'm amazed it doesn't snap, but he doesn't have time to respond before Devin's sword comes crashing down on his.

"You always were in the way," Devin says. "I guess you disappearing could only last so long."

How does he know Mendel? Earlier, too, he was able to identify Cathwell. Does he have intel on our team? It sounds like he and Mendel have personal history, though. Just what in the gods' names is going on?

"Come on, Cathwell," I say. "Let's go."

"Right."

However, before we can leave, one of the rebels not engaged with

Johann or Mendel turns to face us. Yet she's not looking at us, but somewhere above our heads when she raises her hand.

It takes me a second too long to realize what she's doing.

"Cathwell, run!" I say, but too late. An explosion sounds.

A shudder ripples through the length of the cave, and a heartbeat later, an avalanche of rubble collapses over the entrance.

The noise nearly ruptures my eardrums. I grab the collar of Cathwell's jacket and jerk her back just in time to avoid getting crushed by the wreckage. We both fall in the process. Smaller rocks clatter down on top of us. All at once, the light is gone.

As loud as the noise of the rocks collapsing was, the total silence that replaces it is just as deafening. I can't hear what's going on outside. My eyes take an extended amount of time to adjust, and when they finally do, it's to see dust floating in the now-still air and Cathwell staring at the newly formed rock wall.

"No," she says. She slowly rises to her feet. "No no nonono. This isn't happening."

"Calm down, Cathwell." Pebbles clatter down around us, but I think the rest of the cave should hold. "Mendel and Johann will get us out. It's okay."

"*It is not okay*," Cathwell hisses, surprising me.

I can barely see her, but I hear her as she begins clawing at the rocks, her presence turning a deeper shade of violet by the second, getting closer and closer to black. I grab her wrists and pull her from the rock wall, but at my touch, she flinches back and falls to her knees. I can feel blood on her fingers.

"I need out." She chokes on a sob. "I can't, I can't."

"Cathwell, what's wrong?" Her sudden panic is nearly infectious.

148

I remind myself that the others are just outside the cave, and with Mendel's telekinesis, we won't be here long. They'll have to take care of the rebels first, but our teammates are strong. They'll be all right.

Cathwell starts trembling, which makes everything even worse. I don't know why, but even though the lieutenant is continually distracted and odd, I never thought of her as weak or unable to handle herself. Now, seeing her like this, I wonder what's going on.

"It's okay," I murmur. I kneel and awkwardly hug her, not sure what I should do to make her feel at ease. At first, she tries to squirm away, but when I don't let go, her fingers clench into the back of my jacket so hard I can feel them shaking. She buries her face in my shoulder. "It's okay," I keep whispering, over and over, because I don't know what else to do. I brush her hair back from her face. "We're going to be just fine."

"I know." Her voice is muffled through my jacket. She's still shaking, but her color on my grid has begun to turn a less violent shade.

"Then what's wrong?"

She hesitates, then says, "I . . . I can't handle small spaces." A pause. "Don't tell anyone."

"I don't think anyone would hold it against you."

"Even so."

"But why?"

"It's a weakness," she whispers, so low I can barely hear her. "I hate weaknesses. Especially mine."

"Everyone has weaknesses," I say. "It's only natural."

"Still better that no one knows."

"You really are self-conscious about it. Did something happen to make you afraid of small spaces?"

She stiffens under my arms and I realize that was likely the worst thing I could have said. She was just beginning to calm down, and then I go and ask her about what was probably a traumatic experience. Stupid stupid stupid.

She doesn't say anything right away. "I used to have two best friends. Luke and Sara. They were officers, Nytes. After I was picked up off the streets by Austin, and when I eventually, officially became a soldier in the military, they took me under their wing. They were good people. They were everything to me. And then . . ." Her voice dies away. I don't know what she's remembering, but I have a bad feeling about it. I don't want to press her. If she's having a hard time as it is, she doesn't need to keep going.

"It's okay, Cathwell," I say. "You don't have to talk about it."

She shakes her head. I feel the motion more than I see it, since my chin is resting atop her head, arms still around her shoulders.

"Something strange started happening to Luke," she says. "He would disappear for days at a time, and when he came back, he always looked scared. He would jump at any noise. He would ramble, or talk nonsense. But he would never tell me or Sara what was wrong." She takes a deep breath. "The three of us used to meet in this abandoned storage closet. It was away from all the Etioles and it felt like we had a world to ourselves. One day, when I came for our usual meeting, I opened the door and he was just hanging there."

"Hanging there?" I realize what she means as soon as the words leave my mouth. Oh gods. "I'm . . . but why did he . . ."

"He left a note. It didn't explain like it should've, but it read like it was written by the old Luke, before he started acting strange." Her grip on my back tightens. "When I walked into that room, it shrank.

I was in a tiny box. Suffocating. There was nowhere to go. Nothing I could do."

"I'm sorry," I breathe. I hold her closer to me, feeling her warmth through my clothes. "I'm so, so sorry." I wish there was more I could say than some stupid, meaningless words of apology, but what *can* I say? How do you reply to something like that?

"Soon after that, I went to prison," she ends lamely.

Again, I don't know what to say. But I need to say something, because I hate feeling useless like this. I want to help her.

"Are you scared now?" I ask.

"What?"

"Right now. How do you feel?"

A pause. "Better than before."

There's no itch behind my eyes to say she's lying. She's still shaking, but not as badly as before. "Don't worry," I say. "I'm here. And I already said I won't leave you, remember? I promise."

"You shouldn't make promises you can't keep. We're on the verge of a war."

"Well, with you watching my back, it seems like I'll probably make it out all right. If your protecting me doesn't end up killing me first, that is."

I can feel her smile against my chest. "If you'd take better notice of your surroundings, I wouldn't have to protect you so much."

"Ouch. We can't all have razor-sharp attention like you."

"You could at least try."

I laugh. It's good to hear her act like her normal self, even if she isn't all the way back yet. Perhaps by talking about Luke, she somehow came to terms with her trauma a little. I wonder if she's ever confided in anyone about his suicide before. But that reminds me of something else. "The other friend you talked about," I say. "Sara, was it? What happened to her? I don't know any Nyte in Central by that name."

Cathwell stiffens once more under my touch. I realize my mistake too late.

"Sara left," she says very quietly.

"Is she . . . alive?"

"Yes."

She still isn't lying. But then where did Sara go? Why wouldn't she have remained by her closest friend's side, especially when she needed someone so badly? I've pushed my limit for asking personal questions, however, so I cast about for some other topic.

"What about you?" Cathwell asks before I can think of something. "How did you end up in the military?"

"Me?"

She nods.

No one has ever asked me about my past before. It's disconcerting. "I met General Austin at an event my father hosted. He told me if I ever wanted to join the military, I would be more than welcome."

"And you wanted to join the military?"

"Well, no. Actually, at the time he said it, I never thought I'd even consider taking him up on his offer."

"So what changed?"

Against my will, memories of Father come back to me, more feelings than any vivid recollections. Constantly being brushed aside, concentrating on nothing but my studies and responsibilities as his heir to please him, and always being presented with *Can't you even do this much right?*

The night I stood outside his room and overheard his conversation with our maid.

"I realized I was never going to be good enough for my father," I say. "That there was no point in me remaining home any longer." If one could even call it such. How can a place you were only ever rejected be a home?

When Cathwell doesn't reply, I realize I wasn't very clear in my explanation. Should I tell her everything? She told me, after all, even though it must have been painful.

"My mother died when I was born," I say. "And my father is the head of one of the larger underground farm corporations. I was raised as his successor. He hired all sorts of tutors to teach me everything from chemistry to finances to religion."

"And piano?"

I smile. "And piano." I absently stroke her hair. "When I was still very young, my father and our maid realized I was a Nyte. I was too strong, too fast to heal. After that, Father became distant. Well, more so. He only spoke to me when we were in public and he had to pretend we were close, like I was normal. It only became more strained between the two of us as the years passed."

"He didn't disown you for being a Nyte?" Cathwell asks. I can feel her heartbeat nearly against my own. It's much slower than before, calmer, and yet it makes mine pick up speed. "That's what most people in power do, isn't it?"

"I don't think he wanted to hand the company over to anyone

else," I say. "He didn't trust the people working under him. At least with me, he knew I would do whatever he wanted." The memory of how easily I would comply with whatever he said makes my stomach turn. He could have told me to bring him back a live three-headed Feral and I likely would have attempted it.

"So what made you decide to join the military?"

The same words that have haunted me for years come to mind. I close my eyes. I already decided I would be completely open. Cathwell did the same for me, and if it made her feel better, then perhaps it will me as well.

"One night, I overheard my father talking to our maid," I say. "I'd gone to ask him about a job. But something made me stop outside his door, and I heard him say it was my fault Mother died. That it was because she gave birth to a demon."

It feels silly when I say it out loud. I'd been living under his constant disapproval all my life. Why should one more thing like that affect me? And if I'd really thought about it, it should have been obvious he'd thought I was responsible for her death. In a way, I was. She died giving birth to me. Yet somehow, hearing the words, and the broken way he said them, and the awful way in which he really and truly believed them, glass ripped through my chest. I knew I couldn't stay in that place any longer. I couldn't stay near him. "The next day, I called Austin."

"I'm sorry." She hugs me closer, pulling me to her this time, so that I'm the one being comforted now. "I'm really sorry."

I wonder if she struggled to think of something better to say than an empty apology and failed the same way I did. Gods. Why do either of us even have to be sorry? What are we apologizing for?

We stay like that in silence, hugging each other tightly, the only sound that of our own breathing. Her heartbeat keeps time against mine. I have never felt closer to a person before, nor more sad.

I'm unable to tell whether it's relief or disappointment that comes to me when cracks of light begin to appear in the rock wall. The cracks gradually turn into holes of sharp sunshine, and then a wall of it, completely free of debris. I stand and help Cathwell to her feet as Johann and Mendel come to meet us, a little cut up and bruised, but none the worse for wear.

"You okay?" Johann asks. "Are you hurt anywhere?"

I didn't even think to check Cathwell for injuries. I quickly scan her, but she only shakes her head. Apart from her bleeding fingers, she appears unharmed. And other than the cut on my arm from Devin's initial attack and a few scrapes from the cave-in, I'm likewise unhurt.

"We're okay," I say. "Thanks for getting us out of there."

"What are teammates for?" Mendel asks. It sounds strange coming from him, but I don't say anything. I do owe him for a second time.

"What happened to that rebel?" I ask. "Devin? He seemed to know you."

Mendel hesitates, but Johann says, "He and some of the others got away. We can talk about it later. We should get out of here before anyone else shows up."

I try not to look at the bodies of the rebels he and Mendel fought when I say, "Yeah. Let's go."

15
LAI

KITAHARA FILLS THE others in on what happened as we write our reports together in one of Central's many meeting rooms. The task is tedious, but one I'm used to, and it goes by faster with all of us. Kitahara keeps glancing at me, and for some reason, I catch myself sneaking looks at him, too.

I said way too much when we were stuck in that cave. Regret should be worming its way through my stomach, and yet, it's something else. Something like relief.

Our hands brush against each other and we both jump. Ugh, I'm losing it.

"So Cathwell managed to hold her own again?" Johann asks. **She handled herself last time, too. Maybe she's more capable than I thought.** "Pretty good for someone who's been out of practice for two and a half years."

Mendel's eyes don't leave his papers and I don't offer an answer. It's Kitahara who says, "Perhaps she practiced on her own. If General

Austin was aware, then it's no wonder he called her back. She's a great fighter."

I smile, then shake my head and frown. Seriously, what is wrong with me today? "Your intuition was good since you knew something was wrong, but you need to pay more attention to your surroundings," I say. "Don't rely on your gift too much."

Kitahara blinks and looks down at the freshly bandaged cut on his arm. "Sorry. It was my mistake."

"What about that guy you were fighting?" Mendel asks. "Devin, was it?"

My lip curls. "Don't know." I couldn't read his thoughts, which was deeply disconcerting, but I'm almost glad I couldn't. I'd hate to see what was going on behind those violence-crazed eyes.

And that group of rebels we'd been tracking. When I listened to their thoughts as they first appeared, they were at ease. Just passing through. They didn't know anything about the ambush or the part they were going to play in it until they got the message to double back and help Devin. Ellis knew I'd be instantly aware of a trap if anyone in on the plan actually knew about it. She sent those rebels out clueless just to counter me.

But what really hurts is the knowledge that if neither Kitahara nor I could use our gifts on Devin, he must have a power crystal from Gabriel. One of the Order's original members. Someone who was an older brother to all of us. Someone I can't imagine turning his back on us to fight with the rebels.

He wouldn't. He's better than that. I *know* he is. Surely he couldn't have changed that much in the last two and a half years. Right?

"Did he say anything?" Mendel asks.

It takes a second to come out of my thoughts and remember he's talking about Devin. "Words."

"You know what I mean," Mendel snaps. **Why did he know my name what did he mean do I know him why.**

"Calm down," Kitahara says. "He didn't say anything of importance, just his name and some threats." But even as he says it, he looks at me. **Why did he attempt to take Cathwell with him?**

I don't meet his gaze.

Mendel's jaw locks. He signs off on the bottom of his papers, shoves them to Kitahara, and leaves without another word.

"Did a Feral jump him or what?" Johann asks. **Kitahara and Cathwell are being weird today, too. What's with everyone?**

I have to bite back a comment about "being weird today." If even Johann has picked up on something, I really must be acting odd. And not in the usual way.

Kitahara only shakes his head. "I don't know. He's been acting strange ever since we returned—no, even before that. Then again, you were oddly cooperative yesterday as well."

Johann looks up from her papers to find Kitahara watching her with a neutral expression. If I wasn't a mind reader, it'd be hard to tell what he's thinking.

"I haven't been any different from usual," Johann says.

"You followed orders without objecting once and didn't nearly kill a teammate," Kitahara says. "You've actually been getting along with everyone."

I can feel the flicker of fire in Johann's thoughts as strongly as if she'd summoned physical flames. "Are you saying I wasn't good enough before?"

"I'm only saying you weren't as willing to work with the team previously." Kitahara's tone is as neutral as his expression, merely stating a fact. It makes it hard for Johann to fuel her anger. "I didn't mean to imply anything negative. But why the sudden change?"

Cathwell coming into my room, telling me she knows my secret. "I just decided a change was necessary." Johann crosses her arms, daring Kitahara to contradict her. He raises an eyebrow and Johann remembers he can sense lies. Guilt replaces the earlier fire in her thoughts, but she says, "Any problems with that?"

"No. I'm rather glad for it, actually." I can hear the sigh Kitahara's holding back.

"I'm done with my report," Johann says, another lie. She knows it's done half-heartedly, but she doesn't want to work on it any longer. That, and all of us are getting on her nerves, which I take some offense to. I've barely even spoken.

But again, Kitahara doesn't call her out on it. He only shakes his head. "You're free to go. I'll contact you again when I've received further orders."

I watch Johann exit and then lean back in my chair. "Guess that leaves the reports to you and me, then, huh?"

"You can go if you want," Kitahara says. "I can take care of this."

"Is that what you always did before?" I ask. "In Eastern? You told the people you worked with you'd take care of things and then they left you to do all the work?"

He frowns at me. It's different from the looks he gave Mendel and Johann. "What makes you think that?"

"It seems like the sort of thing you'd do," I say. He opens his mouth, maybe to protest, but I wave away whatever he's about to say. "I didn't mean that as an insult. But you don't need to take everything on by yourself. We'll do it together, like a team should."

He stares at me over the tops of his glasses for a long moment. "Okay." His happiness is practically tangible. He likes the idea of being part of a team. It's a shame he got placed on such a radioactive one. "Together, then."

That afternoon, Johann goes looking for me. Her thoughts are so loud with their strength and intent, I can hear them three floors away. Well. Guess I'd better go greet her, then.

She goes a few different places searching for me before I catch up to her. Our room, the mess hall, then to Mendel and Kitahara's room to see if I went to pay either of them a visit.

By the sounds of the thoughts, it's Mendel who answers the door. He and Al are obviously talking, but I can't hear what they're saying, only what they're thinking.

Why's Mendel been so surly since yesterday I thought he was more laid-back.

Ugh I really don't want to deal with Johann right now. Why can't he take a hint and go away?

What the hell I just asked if Cathwell was here what's with the attitude.

If this guy doesn't shut up and leave he's going to find himself stuck in the ceiling.

I round the corner just in time to catch Johann's next words. "You're the one who's been acting like a malfunctioning Watcher ever since we got back. You keep snapping at everyone—even Cathwell, who's barely paying attention half the time."

Despite still being some distance away, I can see Mendel's bright green eyes burn as he gets right up in Johann's face. **This idiot doesn't have a clue.** "Don't talk to me about Cathwell. She's—"

I cough. "Hello."

Mendel and Johann both spin around to face me. The former reluctantly backs off. He straightens his collar while looking steadily past my shoulder. "Cathwell. Johann was looking for you."

"I know."

"Can you come see me after he's done with you?"

"But I can see you right now. You're right there."

Mendel shuts the door.

I turn to Johann. "You needed something?"

Her original purpose in trying to find me returns and her energy sparks up again. "I've never really seen you fight, and I need to know my teammates' strengths," she says. "Train with me today."

I consider her request. There're so many soldiers out and about, all their thoughts melding together to pound in my head like so many marching feet, that it's a struggle to stay focused on what she said. Eventually, I nod. "All right."

I follow Johann to the training hall and to a semi-empty space in the center of the room. The other soldiers make way for us. We get a few stares, but at least they're trying to be discreet today. The few gifted soldiers present give us sympathetic looks.

There are enough people that I have to keep my hands moving

all throughout our warm-up stretches to have something to focus on and avoid being overwhelmed by everyone's thoughts.

Once we've finished, Johann doesn't waste any time getting started. "You ready?"

I nod. "What are the rules?"

"We'll start with hand-to-hand combat," she says. "For now, let's say the first person to land a blow wins. Any complaints?"

"Are gifts prohibited?" I focus my gaze somewhere past her shoulder. "I'd rather not burn to death, but it would be inconvenient for me if they were against the rules."

Some Nytes have gifts like superhuman scent or the ability to attain perfect balance. Nothing significant, certainly nothing that could turn the tide of a war. Since I've never talked about my gift or used it with Johann's knowledge, she assumed mine was something of that sort. Her assumption doesn't change, but she does add the fact that my gift is useful in a fight to her list of mental notes about me.

I'll try to figure out what it is during our spar so I need her to be able to use it. "Gifts are allowed. Don't worry, I can control my flames to do exactly what I want." She flexes her hands. "So if I wanted my fire to give off a lot of heat, but not actually burn, then I could make it happen. Don't worry about getting hurt from that."

I smile thinly at Johann's implication. Just because her fire won't hurt me doesn't mean I won't get hurt.

Not that it matters anyway. Johann doesn't intend to use her gift, at least not the first round. She wants to see what I've got without anything getting in the way of her assessment.

"Are you kidding? There's no way Lieutenant Cathwell will lose." It isn't until I overhear this that I realize a small crowd has gathered. They give us a sizable berth, but they've still formed a distinct circle around me and Al.

Someone whispers, "Isn't it a bit odd? A well-practiced soldier fighting against someone who's been stuck in prison the last couple years?"

I can almost hear Johann fighting the urge to whip around and make everyone scatter. As it is, her fists clench at her sides.

Someone else replies, "Haven't you seen her training in here? Doesn't seem like she's lost any practice to me."

"My money's on Johann. Don't care who this Cathwell is, no one ever lost to the sergeant major before."

"You weren't here three years ago, were ya?"

Johann charges. Partly because she's impatient to start, partly to block out the voices of everyone around us.

That's fine by me. I wait until the last moment to sidestep, eyes focused elsewhere in the crowd as I do.

Johann wheels around, leg extended, intending to strike me across the back, but I jump over it and land with a little bounce beside her. Her elbow is still moving with the momentum of her kick, so she aims for my chest. I lean back. She barely misses me.

Johann doesn't hesitate in throwing her attacks at me, but I've had so much practice reading others' movements that I don't need to read her thoughts to know how she'll move. The way her muscles shift, the direction her feet face before she attacks, how sometimes her eyes will flick certain places. She can feint, use one attack to lead into another, or throw out any other combination of tricks she likes, but I still dodge it. Every time, I do it just barely, intentionally. My steps are more bounces, my movements light.

I don't attack. I hold my hands behind my back, arms straight, unchanged since the start of the match. Part of it is just because I like messing with her, and doing it in a way that she'll know that's my intention. Part of it is payback for nearly frying me on our first mission.

This is no spar. This is evasion practice. "What are you doing, Cathwell?" It's the first time Johann's let up on her rapid-fire attack pattern. "I thought you agreed to a fight with me, not a dodging contest."

"Aren't they relatively the same?"

Johann falls back a few steps, enough that I can't reach her in a single stride. "Are you too scared of humiliating yourself to fight me seriously?"

"Not particularly."

"Then you're afraid to lose."

"Like I'd lose to you," I say before I can help it. I clamp my mouth shut. Idiot. Who falls for shallow taunts like that?

The crowd is dead silent. Whereas before there was low chatter, now no one speaks.

"Yeah?" **This should be better.** "Prove it."

I attack first this time.

Johann waits until I'm practically on top of her before she sidesteps, mimicking my first move from earlier, but it was easy enough to guess she'd do that. I pivot around with her as she moves, leg whirring at her neck.

Her arm jerks up with barely enough time to block me.

I can't hide my surprise that my kick didn't connect—there's no way she should've been able to block that quickly—but it doesn't stop me from immediately switching legs to launch another. Johann ducks and swings her foot at the ankle that's keeping me standing. I hop-jump above it, about to come landing back down on her leg until she quickly retracts it.

I pull myself down, knees bent, and use the momentum to aim an uppercut at Johann's chin. She propels herself back, but the movement throws her off balance and she falls flat on her back.

As my fist comes flying at her stomach, her arms swing up to deflect my blow again.

Her reaction time is unreal. No matter how clearly I can read her movements—and eventually, her thoughts—despite knowing how she's about to move, for some reason, I can't get into her defense. Fighting as a telepath is an art I perfected years ago. The speed with which I can read my opponent's thoughts and moves can keep up in almost any actual battle. So why is it so hard to do anything against her?

Johann has noticed I underestimated her. Or rather, that I thought too highly of my own abilities. I let my frustration show too clearly on my face.

Did she think it wouldn't take this long once she got serious? This arrogant—

I messed up. In a lot of ways. As soon as I lose my footing in one of my more reckless attacks, Johann drives me back with a quick series of punches. She doesn't risk a kick, correctly guessing that they're my specialty and it could create an opening. I duck and weave through all her hits. At least dodging is one thing I don't have to doubt my abilities in.

She's good. But I'm starting to get the hang of how she moves.

I need to end this quickly, but without underestimating her anymore and without being reckless.

For a long time, we just keep punching and kicking and blocking, neither of us managing to land a solid hit. The soldiers around us, when I think to listen, have stopped calling bets.

Sweat runs into my eyes, burning them, but I can't waste a moment to wipe it away.

Johann and I pull apart, both of us panting. My eyes rake over her, searching for an opening, the key to her movements, anything that will put an end to this.

"You're good," Johann says between breaths. **Good enough for my team.** She might have told me she accepted me when I blackmailed her, but she didn't mean it until now. For obvious reasons. Threatening someone doesn't exactly get you points with them. "How do you manage that when you haven't fought in years?"

"I never said I didn't practice." I'm struggling to control my breathing. My fists are still up, as are Johann's, but I really just want to end this. I haven't had a practice match this long or intense in ages. It's shown me just how low my stamina has become.

I hadn't wanted to use this since it's not always successful, but I force my mind to empty of everything except Johann's thoughts. I breathe out deeply, then in, then out. My back straightens. My foot inches forward as I change my stance slightly. A low pounding resounds in my head. Every fleck of thought that runs through Johann's mind echoes in my own simultaneously. I can nearly imagine I *am* her, I'm so synced in to her thoughts. But my body stays my own, and waits for the commands that will counter my—Johann's thoughts. Her movements.

Warning bells go off in Johann's head that something has changed, but she can't tell what, and she can't defend against what she doesn't know. Even though she'd decided not to be the first to attack this time, the unease of knowing that *something* about me is different makes her itch to move.

She runs at me and twists the side of her hand, bringing it down like a blade across my shoulder. Or she would've. I leap clear above her and land lightly on her extended arm, foot already wheeling toward her face. She ducks—barely—and jerks her arm out from underneath me.

Even before she moved, I'd twisted so that when I hit the floor, it's my arms supporting me, leaving my legs free to attempt a kick straight to Johann's stomach.

Her arms coil around my ankle, trapping it, but I have enough momentum that I'm able to bring my other leg around and slam it into Johann's chest before she can react. She hits the ground.

When I extract my mind from Johann's, I register the silence.

Then someone says, "Looks like you haven't lost your touch after all, Lieutenant," and a huge round of applause goes up. Whether it's for me or Johann, I can't tell. I'm just surprised they're clapping for us at all.

Someone whispers, "Thank the gods those demons are on our side."

When I offer a hand to Johann to help her up, she looks at me with surprise. She grabs it, and then I'm the one who finds myself surprised.

"What happened at the end there?" Johann rubs her chest in slow, small circles where my kick connected. I should have held back, but she was too strong for me to be able to afford that. "Something about you changed."

I shrug noncommittally. Tapping into someone's thoughts that deeply is disorienting, and not something that always works in a fight. Maybe with Johann as my partner, it's a skill I'd be able to refine. But I don't know that I'd ever want her to know just how much I'm in her head for me to be able to fight like that.

Probably her gift. I'll have to ask her about it when her guard's down.

"Okay," Johann says. "Let's take a break, then go again. This time, with weapons."

16
LAI

JOHANN IS AN incredibly difficult and worthwhile opponent. I knew she had a short temper—I hadn't expected she would leave it out of her battles. She fights with a calm head, and reacts without emotion. Sometimes taunts get to her, but so far we've been too engrossed in our fights to talk much, even for the sake of distracting each other. If anything, the longer we go on, the cooler she becomes. Frustration seems to make her more focused, not less.

We practice hand-to-hand, with weapons, with gifts—she actually uses her fire after the first round—and without.

It was hard enough to win without her shielding herself in a wall of heat. In a real battle, she wouldn't even have to fight. She'd only need to call out her flames and her opponent would be killed instantly. No matter my fighting ability, I would lose in a serious battle without question.

I'm starting to understand the Etioles' resentment of us.

We've been at it for a few hours when Johann finally says, "Do you want to stop here?" She's just won after another round in which we were allowed to use our gifts. We're both out of breath, and though I'd never admit it, all I want to do is lie down on the cold ground. My muscles ache and throb, and my mind is sluggish from extended concentration. Johann is much the same.

"Sounds good," I say.

As Johann goes to get some water, a black butterflies drifts into view. It flies purposefully as ever toward me.

Oh, come on. What is it this time?

They're never anything good, but I hold my hand out to it anyway. Its message echoes through my head. *Cut it a little close this time, didn't you, Lai? You're getting sloppy.*

I frown and wave my hand through the remains of the rapidly disintegrating shadow messenger. Ellis is about the last person I want criticism from.

I try to put it out of mind as Johann returns. After doing some cool-down stretches, we fall in line together and head back to our room. This time, none of the other soldiers stare at us as we pass. They'd dwindled away as our spars continued, and now they don't risk eye contact.

"You're a lot better than I thought you'd be," Johann says. "Where'd you learn to fight?"

"Before I joined the military, I was living on the streets," I say. "I learned how to fend for myself there. And then when I came here about eight years ago, Austin, and then another Nyte, taught me." The memories of my training sessions with Sara lie heavier than usual on my chest. I shove them somewhere I won't have to think about them. "What about you?"

"I always got into fights when I was a kid, but I didn't really learn how to hold my own until I joined Sector Eleven's military." Her lips curl in an uncharacteristically wry smile. "Sector Eleven is different from Eight. It was do or die, and I sure as hell wasn't about to die."

I catch flitting memories from Johann of getting shoved down stairs, finding herself cornered by other soldiers, being pinned to the ground. I shudder inwardly. "Because you were a Nyte?"

"There was that," Johann says. "But it was also because I looked like a girl."

"But you are a girl." Despite the fact no one's around, I keep my voice low.

She shakes her head. "Like I said, Sector Eleven is different from Eight. Women can't join the military. We're seen as weak. To get in, I had to pretend to be a boy, and I wasn't very good at pretending back then."

"Why join the military at all?" I ask. "It sounds like a lot of trouble."

"I wanted to get stronger, and I needed their information," she says. **And I had nowhere else to go.**

"Information? What would you need that for?"

She hesitates. "There's someone I'm looking for. I thought if I joined the military, I could find out where he was."

"Oh. Wait, but how did the military not know you were a girl?" Surely that would have come up in the medical examinations or some other mundane way.

"I think they did know, but Nytes are rare in other sectors and Nytes with strong gifts even rarer. They knew they could use me, so they let me in."

I had heard there were sectors that looked down on women and denied them certain rights—I've even met women from those sectors through the Order—but it's hard for me to personally imagine. It's bad enough getting abuse as a Nyte, let alone for anything else. I wonder what that must have been like for Johann growing up. To be hated not only for being gifted, but being a girl, too.

"But you're in Sector Eight now," I say. "Why keep up the pretense of being a boy?"

"You must know how hard it is for a Nyte to move from one sector to another," Johann says. "It was hard enough getting permission from Sector Eleven's Council without telling them I'd been lying about my gender for seven years. And if I'm found out lying now, I might just get sent back."

"I doubt the Council here would let you return even if you wanted to." We come to a stop in front of our door. "Is that why you came to Sector Eight, then? To escape from everything?"

"No," Johann says quietly. She hesitates again, an oddity even just the one time, before unlocking the door. She doesn't continue until it's closed behind us. "I came here because I found out my brother had come here."

"Oh. Is he the person you joined the military to find?"

Johann seems to withdraw inside herself as she rummages through her drawers for clean clothes. "Yeah."

I know better than to pry this much. If I really wanted to know, all I'd have to do is lean in on her thoughts. But I want her to tell me. She wasn't the only one who had a change in opinion about her sparring partner. "Can I ask why?"

Johann pulls out a wrinkled but clean pair of black pants and a plain red shirt. She stares at them for a moment before sighing and dropping them on her cot. "He killed our parents. So now I'm going to kill him."

The words hang in the air, a wall between us. Johann continues to stare at the messy clothes on her bed. Her expression is impossible to read. "I used the military's information system to track my brother to Sector Eight. Two years ago, when I thought I was strong enough to kill him, I followed him here. But now his trail is gone. There are no records of him currently living in this sector, but there aren't any of him moving to another sector, either. He must be here, but I don't know how to find him anymore."

I don't know what I was expecting her to say, but it wasn't that. I had known about her search for her brother from listening to her thoughts, but not the reason behind it. Now I wonder if I shouldn't have asked about it at all. *Idiot, you of all people should know better. You did know better.*

"I'm sorry." The words ring empty, but I don't know what else to say. It's that same feeling of knowing there's nothing you *can* say as I felt back when I was with Kitahara in that cave-in.

Johann shrugs with one shoulder. "It was nine years ago."

I want to ask why he killed them. How she knows about it and why he didn't kill her, too. There are so many things I want to know, but I'm not going to lean on Johann's thoughts for the answers, and I'm certainly not going to ask the questions aloud. Not unless she wants to talk about it.

"Well, you don't have to pretend to be a boy when you're with me," I say.

She looks up at me.

"I mean, when no one else is around, of course," I add quickly.

"Unless you don't want to. But I already know your secret, so you don't have to keep up the act around me. You can use your normal voice or take off your binding or say or do whatever you want." At her continued silence, my babbling gets out of control. "And, you know, I can speak Gervaic a little, too. That's Sector Eleven's main language, isn't it? I'm not great, but I've kept up practicing, and I think we could hold a pretty decent conversation. I mean, if you wanted to."

She continues to stare at me, skeptically at first, but then with something almost like surprise when she realizes I mean it. Maybe I'm imagining it, but her shoulders seem to loosen fractionally. "*Danvu*, Cathwell." *Thank you.*

"You can call me Lai. If you like."

She gives me another measured stare, but this time, it's accompanied by a smile. "All right. Lai it is."

17
LAI

MENDEL TAKES FOREVER to get back from meeting with yet another information broker. I'm leaning against the wall across from his and Kitahara's room when he finally returns.

His shoulders are slumped as he walks down the hall, hands shoved in his pockets. The meeting must not have gone well. Sure enough, when I listen in on his thoughts, it's to hear that the broker couldn't find out anything about Mendel's past.

"What do you want?" Mendel asks as soon as he notices me.

"So touchy. Sorry your meeting didn't turn out like you'd hoped."

It takes a moment for him to process how I knew where he was and what happened. Then he remembers my gift, and the frustration that was simmering in the back of his thoughts flares up. "Is that all?"

I lift my chin and look down at him. "I hope you don't think I would waste my time going around giving condolences to everyone who's had a bad day." He opens his mouth, but before he can reply, I say, "I'm here for our deal. You've held up your side of the bargain so far. Or would you rather I leave?"

All the anger in his thoughts deflates. It isn't replaced with the anticipation he had when I first told him I'd try to help him get his memories back.

"Well?" I ask.

"Let's go." Mendel unlocks his door and walks inside. When I don't follow, he raises an eyebrow.

I shake my head. "Not here. Kitahara could come in at any moment."

He doesn't protest like I expected him to, but silently follows me as I lead us away from modern Central and into the walkways that link to the more disused building in the back.

I know Mendel is too caught up in his thoughts to pay attention to where we're going, because he nearly runs into me when I stop.

The usual clean halls are gone. There are no high, narrow windows. There aren't any Watchers around, either, as I open one of the doors and wave Mendel inside an old meeting room turned storage room.

Crates are stacked everywhere, rusty filing cabinets filling the spaces between. The tiles are cracked. Dust coats everything.

I climb onto a stack of crates and take a seat facing Mendel.

She really does like putting herself above others. One day, when I don't have to stay on her good side to get her to help me, I'm going to find out about her past and even the playing field. I should have asked Mark to dig up something on her.

"He wouldn't have found anything anyway." I cup my chin in my hand, watching him.

Stupid mind reader. "So how's this going to work?" he asks.

A few days ago, the night after my conversation with Al, I

managed to sneak out to the Order to pick up Peter's power crystal and check the specifics of his gift one more time, among all my other usual tasks. When I first asked him telepathically if he could help me out, I was worried he'd say no—it's a personal thing to ask for a Nyte's power crystal—but he was happy to be able to assist. I should've known. I can't rely too much on his constant eagerness to help, though. He has enough to do as it is.

"I got a power crystal from the friend I told you about," I say. "His gift works on a question-and-answer basis. I'll ask a question, and any relevant memories that answer that question should appear. We'll both see them, so, sorry, but you won't be able to keep anything in those memories secret from me."

Not that I could've anyway with her annoying gift.

I smile but don't comment. "Do you want to choose the question? They're your memories, after all."

He looks surprised, or maybe skeptical, that I'm leaving the decision up to him, but he doesn't say anything. Instead, he wonders what kind of question he should ask. His thoughts wander back to our recent run-in with that group of rebels, and the one, Devin, who recognized him. **Why did he know me?** *How* **does he know me?** Even now, the rebel's words gnaw at his thoughts.

"Do you want to ask how you know Devin?" I ask.

"I'm not going to waste my time asking about some rebel." **Maybe it'd be better if I didn't know anyway.**

"It could be dangerous not to know."

"Can you just let me decide on my own, without prying into my thoughts?" **Would she just get out of my head already? It's not like I control every thought that crosses my mind. It was better**

when she was pretending to be some weirdo and I didn't know.

I open my mouth to reply to that thought, think better of it, and close it without saying anything.

I'm surprised she's passing up a chance to screw with someone.

My nose scrunches at *that* thought, but I keep quiet. Unlike with Fiona, Mendel and I aren't close. By any definition. If I get under his skin too much, it could end up making things worse for me later on.

Mendel returns to considering the question he wants to ask. He wants something that'll be broad enough to bring up as many memories as possible. But he also doesn't want to see anything mundane or pointless that won't give him any clues to go off from here. Something that'll hit the most important parts of his life.

He takes so long I start to get bored and he starts getting frustrated with himself.

"You know, we can do this more than once," I say. "You don't have to worry so much about picking the one perfect question."

"Fine," he says. "Ask what my life was like before I lost my memories."

A broad question. I don't know if that's good or bad.

"All right, then." I heave myself off the crates and walk over to Mendel. He tenses, but I don't pause before drawing a sky-blue crystal out of my pocket and setting both it and my palm against his forehead. "His gift works through touch, so both the crystal and I will need to be in contact with you. Are you ready?"

He hesitates, which surprises me. Then again, he's been full of hesitation about all this since I first made the deal with him. Our recent encounter with Devin has only made him warier of his past. But finally, his eyes meet mine. "I'm ready."

I take a deep breath and close my eyes. Focus on the crystal in my hand until I feel the thrum of power connecting from it to me. I've never heard Peter ask his questions aloud before, but I do it now both to put Mendel at ease and to feel more solidly in control.

"What was your life like before you lost your memories?"

A barrage of images instantly floods my head.

I stand overlooking a city blanketed in darkness. The night is broken only by lanterns strewn throughout the maze of streets below. Next to me, a girl with pale blue eyes leans against the balcony railing. "The night is approaching," she says.

I'm in a woodshop that isn't Central's, poring over a model of a building. My hands move slowly, carefully around it.

As I walk away down a dark hall, Devin says, "You know, I used to respect you."

My eyes snap open as soon as the images stop. There were other scenes as well, blurring behind the ones that mainly stuck out to me, but they were all hazy. Impossible to make out.

Mendel opens his eyes, too. "What gives, Cathwell? Why'd you stop? And why were those memories so broken up like that?"

"I stopped because that's all there was." I could tell as soon as the power from the crystal cut off that no other memories would appear for us. "That was all our question dug up. But that's . . . not how it usually goes." I drop my hand from Mendel's forehead.

"Whenever my friend uses his gift, he always sees whole, clear memories play out. I don't know why it was so fragmented like that."

"I couldn't make out many details, either," Mendel says. His eyes drift to the crates behind me. Thinking. "That girl's face, the city, the places. Everything was so blurry. Why?"

I shake my head. "I don't know. Like I said, it isn't normally like that."

His eyes cut back to me with annoyance. "That's not exactly helpful."

"What, you think I'm doing this intentionally?" It's a struggle to hold back my irritation. Though whether it's aimed at myself for not being able to follow through on my promise yet or Mendel for being Mendel, I can't tell. "At least there was some success."

"Yeah, if that mess is what you wanna call *success*."

"Hey, it's better than nothing, isn't it? Now stop complaining and pick your next question. Maybe if *you'd* picked something less broad, the results wouldn't have been so bad."

"*Fine*. Then ask how I lost my memories."

"Fine." I shove my hand and the crystal against his forehead. This time, we're glaring at each other when I say, "How'd you lose your memories?"

The memories come slower this time, as if they're being dragged to the surface of some deep lake.

I wake up to see someone I don't know staring down at me. I sit up so fast I nearly headbutt him, but he jerks back to avoid me. He's got dark brown hair long enough that it almost obscures his eyes. I don't trust people whose eyes I can't see. I think.

I enter the bar for the first time with enough fake confidence to take on a
pack of Ferals. I know this district is anti-Nyte, but when the information
broker's messenger told me to meet him here, I couldn't think of a good
reason to ask for a different place. I'm not worried about being discovered
because of getting hurt. I know my way around a fight. I'm worried this
guy won't help me find out about my past.

Again, the thread of power connecting me to Peter's power crystal cuts off, and again, the images end along with it.

The memories were a little longer this time, and in focus, which is a plus. But they were both from after Mendel actually lost his memories.

When he opens his eyes, he looks even more annoyed than before. "How the hell do either of those things that *I still remember* answer how I lost my memories?"

I throw my hands up in the air. "I don't know, Mendel, okay? Maybe the power crystal is malfunctioning. Maybe one of us did something wrong. We'll just try it again."

So we do. We try again and again and again, but every time, we either draw out memories Mendel still possesses, or else scraps of memories even shorter and more indistinct than our first attempt. They're so blurred as to be useless, and sometimes there isn't even sound to them.

Mendel is the one who finally says, "Stop—just stop, okay? This isn't working. It's just getting worse the more we try."

"This shouldn't be happening." I glare at the crystal, as if that'll get it to clean up its act. "My friend's never mentioned anything like this before."

"Maybe you just can't control it," Mendel says. Surprisingly, the irritation has left his voice as he switches over to going at this more logically. "Not all gifts are easily used, right? Have you ever tried using this one before?"

I hesitate, not wanting to admit that he may have figured out the problem before I did. "No. I haven't."

"Then it's probably that. You just can't use the gift right, so we're getting these crappy results."

He waits for me to reply, and I know what I should say. I should suggest I bring my friend to meet Mendel in person so that the Nyte himself can try accessing his memories. But I don't trust Mendel. He might be working with the team now because he wants my help, but that doesn't mean I want to get Peter involved with him. Especially not now that Mendel obviously has some sort of past ties with the rebels. Besides, this isn't something I can just volunteer Peter for without even asking him first. I'm not *that* bad of a friend.

"Well?" Mendel asks when I don't say anything.

I sigh. "I'll try seeing what I can find out. I'll talk to my friend, too. Just give me a little time to figure things out."

"And I should just trust that you're going to follow through on that?" Mendel asks. He crosses his arms. "I should just *trust* that you're actually going to try doing something else now that your first plan has fallen through?"

"Well, yes."

"No offense, but I don't have any reason to trust you."

"Nor I you."

He blinks in surprise, then catches himself and smiles ruefully. Being able to read his mind, I know him better than anyone here. I know what a liar he is. How he'll do or say most anything to get what he wants. And he's fully aware of that.

"Look," I say, "I know this isn't ideal. But I'm not about to sign my friend up for something he isn't even involved in. I don't want to make him feel pressured to help for something that I started, either."

His face remains neutral, but internally, he's surprised by the amount of consideration I'm giving my friend. Somehow, he hadn't expected it. Without consciously thinking about it, he'd thought I was like him—alone, and willing to use what I can to get what I want. When he realizes he was wrong, he doesn't know how to feel about it. It throws me off guard, too.

"I'm going to see what other options we have, and talk to my friend in the meantime," I go on. "Maybe he'll know what happened with his power crystal. Maybe he can tell me how to use it properly. But I need you to give me some time to work all that out. Please."

He takes so long to answer I think he's going to say no. But he says, "Fine. Just don't keep me waiting too long. If you do, who knows if I'll be able to keep my mouth shut with all these secrets of yours."

"If you do, I don't know that I'll be able to keep *my* mouth shut about the fact that you're missing your memories and you think you might have been associated with the rebels," I say. "Or about that anti-Nyte bar you go to to meet your information brokers, and how for months you've watched fellow Nytes get beaten up without lifting a finger to help them." His eyes meet mine, defiant, neither of us giving way. "You may know my secrets, Mendel, but don't forget that I know yours, too."

He glares at me but says nothing.

I turn on my heel and head for the door. But for some reason, I find myself pausing with my hand on the doorknob. This isn't how I want to leave things. I turn around to face Mendel head-on when I say, "I *am* trying, Mendel."

He looks at me with something almost like regret. **I really wish I could believe that.**

18
JAY

THE FAILURE OF our last mission weighs heavy on my mind over the following weeks. Perhaps it was unavoidable given that it *was* an ambush, but I'm unable to stop thinking about what I could have done to turn it into a success. I pore over the reports on the rebels' movements in the area and pinpoint all the flaws in my last plan before going to train. I need to become better.

Once I've finished in the range, I head to the mess hall for lunch and happen upon Cathwell and Johann. They're sitting across from each other at one of the many long tables placed end-to-end together to form neat rows down the room. Both of their presences radiate a brilliant, happy yellow hue.

They're having a strange argument about drinks when I seat myself next to Cathwell.

"That stuff is going to be the death of you one day," Cathwell says as she indicates the soda placed before Johann. Her left hand taps a furious, inconsistent rhythm atop the table.

"Better than drinking milk straight," Johann says with a wrinkled nose. His tray is piled high with food, most of it meat. He wolfs it down between words. "I don't know how you can stomach that poison."

"I don't know how you can go through life not being able to appreciate the glorious state of being that is milk." Cathwell jabs her fork in Johann's direction to emphasize her point, and a piece of fruit flies off the tip. She continues quite gravely. "This is why we can never truly be friends, Al. We shall always border the edge that separates the milk drinkers from the milk haters."

"That's a little harsh, isn't it?" I ask. It's entertaining simply to watch them while I eat, but I want to be a part of their conversation as well. Ever since Cathwell and Johann began training together almost two weeks ago, they've been getting along famously. Johann was the last person I expected to get along with the lieutenant, considering his impatience and initial loathing of her being placed on the team, but I can't locate any trace of that now. It's a bit lonely. The fact that they room together and refer to each other on a first-name basis only makes the feeling worse.

"It's not harsh," Cathwell says. "Milk is delicious. Al is crazy."

"You're the one who's a weirdo," Johann says. "That alone means I win."

"Hey now. This and that have nothing to do with each other." Cathwell waves her hand ambiguously.

"How did you two even get on this subject?" I ask.

"I asked Lai what her favorite food was," Johann says. "Apparently what one of us loves, the other hates. We were just seeing if it was the same with drinks when you came."

"So far, the answer is yes," Cathwell says.

"Only because someone doesn't like soda."

"Soda kills you."

Their intimacy makes my chest tighten. It takes an extended period of time for me to recognize the feeling as jealousy, and then yet another to realize why it's plaguing me. All the years I was at Eastern, and all the years I spent at home prior to that, I never had any friends. Work was continuously my highest priority. First, trying to meet my father's expectations, immersing myself in my studies as heir to the company, doing everything to a T. When I entered the military, it was hardly any different. Executing a mission perfectly, filling out reports over and over until I was satisfied with them. Even disregarding the fact that the majority of soldiers are Etioles who likely wouldn't take well to me trying to talk to them, I never even attempted to. Seeing Johann and Cathwell get along so well, I'm envious of something I've never had.

Cathwell is watching me. I hope she didn't ask me something when I wasn't paying attention, but Johann is eating without a care, so I suppose not. I clear my throat. "So is there anything you two both like?"

"Bread," Cathwell says. She holds out her pinkie to count, considers, and frowns. "Yeah. Bread."

"That's it?" I barely suppress a laugh, but it's mostly at the expressions they're both wearing.

"Well, Al doesn't like sweet breads," Cathwell says. "So cinnamon rolls and glazed bread are out. Which is sad, because those are the best."

"You just have too much of a sweet tooth for your own good," Johann says. "Which is why I find it odd that you don't like soda."

Cathwell shrugs. "Sugar fuels the brain, but acid kills the body."

Johann shakes his head. He tosses the last of his food in his mouth and stands. "I'm going to go pick up a few things in town before I have to start guard duty. Anything you guys want?"

"I'm good," Cathwell says. "Thanks."

Johann turns his attention to me, but I say, "That's okay, but thank you for the offer."

He snorts. "You don't have to be so formal all the time, you know."

"Yeah yeah," Cathwell chips in eagerly. A bit *too* eagerly. "You can call us by our first names, too."

Johann lifts an eyebrow at that, but merely says, "Yeah, why not? We're all teammates. Honestly, we really should be using each other's first names by now."

Cathwell beams at him, then at me. "See? If even Al says so, then it's fine."

"Hey, what's that supposed to mean?"

"Nothing, nothing."

"I've never actually called anyone by their first name before," I say.

"Never?" Johann asks incredulously. His and Cathwell's looks of surprise are so prominent I wish I hadn't said anything. "Come on. What about siblings?"

"I don't have any."

"Childhood friends?"

"None."

"Okay, then you definitely have to start calling us by our first names," he says. "I won't answer you until you do."

"Me too," Cathwell says.

"Why?" I can't understand why they're making such a big deal out of this.

"Isn't it obvious?" Johann asks. "It means you're close to someone if you call them by their first name. It's like you don't consider us friends. You're the one who wanted the team to work well together, right? We'll work together better if it's our friends we're looking out for in battle instead of just some people we're assigned to work with."

I'm not quite certain what names have to do with that, but I don't dissent.

Johann shakes his head, checks the time on his MMA, and says, "Sorry, I have to go. See you guys later."

"Bye, Al," Cathwell says. She gives me a pointed look.

"Oh, uh, talk to you later," I say. When they both continue to stare at me, I awkwardly add, "Al."

Johann nods and appears satisfied. Once he's gone, it's just me and Cathwell.

I'm not certain what I should say to her. Following our last mission's report-writing session, our meetings have been sparse. Our shifts are continuously opposite, and lacking any new missions from the Council, we haven't had any need to seek each other out regardless. I wish I had a reason to approach her occasionally, though.

I look up from eating to see Cathwell watching me with that same expression from earlier. She hastily looks away when our eyes meet and thrusts a forkful of chicken in her mouth. She swallows it so fast she begins coughing and I have to hold back a laugh. There's something funny about Cathwell being the one to act awkwardly for once.

"I nearly died over here and you're laughing?" Cathwell asks once her throat's cleared. "Some friend you are."

"Oh, I'm very sorry."

That appears to have been the wrong thing to say. Her expression drops. "I was just joking. You know we're friends, right? You don't have to be so serious and polite about everything. And if you ever want to talk, you don't need a reason to do it. You can just come find me."

"Now who's being all serious?" I attempt to say it lightly to divert attention away from this topic, partly because it suddenly did become serious, partly to deflect from how spot-on her words are.

Perhaps I really am too easy to read. I don't want her to be kind to me merely because she noticed my negative feelings. How pathetic.

Her lips tighten. Her focus appears to be elsewhere as she takes another bite of food, then another. Irritation flicks over her face one heartbeat, quickly followed by triumph, followed up once more by irritation and a roll of the eyes. Her presence keeps consistent beat with her change of emotions. I wonder what's going through her mind right now.

Finally, she turns back to me. "Are you busy tonight?"

The question takes me off guard enough that I answer without thinking. "No."

"Good. Come out with me."

"Um, okay. Where to?"

"Secret."

"Uh."

Her voice drops so only I can hear. Not that there's anyone else around us regardless. "We're going to be out past curfew."

"What?" I say, perhaps too loudly, because she gives me a disapproving look.

"It's not going to be very secret if you start shouting about it."

I lower my voice to match hers. "That's breaking the rules. Why don't we just go to this place well before curfew?"

"Because we can't. It's after curfew or not at all."

I shake my head. "We can't."

"Why not?"

"I just told you, it's against the rules."

"So?"

"So? We could face severe punishment—or worse, we could be suspected as rebel spies."

"So then we won't get caught."

"You—"

"Do you trust me?"

"Whether I trust you and whether I'm going to sneak out is—"

"Do you trust me?" she asks once more, and this time, I catch the weighted undertone. Her eyes are suddenly serious, all her typical playfulness gone. Her presence on my internal grid beats a slow, stable orange. Expectant. Waiting.

I hesitate. There are a multitude of things I could say in response, and a number more I want to ask, but I don't give voice to any of them. I realize all at once that the destination isn't necessarily important in why she's asking me to accompany her.

I consider her question seriously. I think about how she's saved me twice on the battlefield now, how capably she handles herself. I think of the things she told me and the things I told her in that cave-in, things she'd likely never told anyone before, things I'd definitely never told anyone before. I think of how she stayed with me to help finish the reports when the others had left.

Our eyes meet. "I trust you," I say.

"Then meet me outside the used bookstore a couple blocks south at ten." I'm unable to read her expression as she stands with her tray and smiles a small, private smile. "See you then, Jay."

I know I told Cathwell I trust her—and I do—but trusting her and risking everything I've worked for all these years are two incredibly different things.

It's getting nearer and nearer to ten, and I've still yet to decide whether or not I'm going as I take notes on the last scouts' report in my room. Again. Mendel is gone, likely to the woodshop. He's perpetually there.

I wish I had my own haunt to escape to; this room feels smaller with each passing day. Mendel's tottering stacks of furniture don't help.

I lean back in my chair. For possibly the first time since I joined the military four years ago, I feel lonely. And bored. I haven't felt like this since I was studying under the tutors Father hired to teach me. It's not a feeling I would have liked to replicate.

What am I doing? I don't have time to be bored. I don't even have a reason to be. I've always done my work without a sense of it being tedious. There's nothing I would even rather do. I don't keep up hobbies. Whenever I have spare time, I spend it training or reading up on military tactics. Whatever is necessary to ensure I can execute my job without error.

So why do I feel as if there's a gaping hole in my chest?

My MMA beeps. *9:30.* I stare at the time as though it will give me an answer. *9:31.* I can't go. It's far too risky. *9:32.* What will Cathwell think of me when I don't show up? She asked me to trust her. *9:33.* She'll understand if I don't come. If we truly are friends as she said, then she won't hold this against me. *9:34.* What comes next if I don't go?

The sudden thought makes me panic. I imagine sitting here for the remainder of the night, alone, senselessly checking through this report once more. Tomorrow, facing Cathwell, whatever her reaction might be.

And then I look behind me. All the weeks dragging into months straining into years. What have I actually accomplished since I entered the military? I left because I wanted to be happy. Can I honestly say that's what I am now? It's all too easy to imagine my future in the upcoming years. Ever the same. Stagnant.

9:40.

I stand up.

Agitation scorches under my skin, but I manage to keep my pace to a walk as I go through Central, out the front doors, and into the streets. And then I run.

I don't need to. I'm right on time. Cathwell will think I'm strange if she sees me like this. But still, I run all the way to the front door-step of the bookstore we're meeting at.

She appears surprised to see me running—or perhaps surprised to see me at all—but the look easily melts into a smile. She laughs as I skitter to a halt in front of her.

"That excited to see me, huh?" she asks.

I know she's merely teasing, yet I feel my face warm. "I just felt like running a bit."

"Sure, sure."

"Where are we going, anyway?"

She skirts past my awkward attempt to change the topic and starts striding down the sidewalk. I follow beside her. "It's secret," she says with a tilt of her head.

"Still?"

"Still."

The sector is silent. Too-dim streetlights cast an eerie glow over the road. From somewhere in the distance, the rowdy singing of a bar drifts toward us.

"I'm glad you came," Cathwell says. She faces straight ahead, but her eyes dart to me and then away once more. "I was worried you wouldn't."

"I almost didn't."

"What changed your mind?"

I'm not certain how to answer, so I don't. She doesn't press.

As we continue on, the red-bricked buildings give way to white marble apartments with elegant balconies and low, sweeping door-ways. They're not as haphazardly designed as in the previous districts—although they still have a minimum of eight floors—but rather, ornately decorated and carefully constructed. The streetlights are twisted wrought iron, one stationed along every corner. The shop windows gleam back with our reflections.

These are the homes and shops that belong to the affluent—the most gifted scientists and engineers, the District Committee members who run the sector's fundamental operations, and the traders and merchants who've worked their way up over time. And, much farther west, Father's home.

Everything is neat and orderly. The occasional tree or small garden appears every so often, but for the most part, this district is as bare of greenery as the previous one.

We've been walking in silence for an extended amount of time before I finally work up the courage to ask, "Why did you really invite me out tonight?"

Cathwell keeps staring straight ahead and I can't tell whether or not she heard me. I don't repeat the question.

She leads us down a side street. The land slopes downward slightly, and the streetlights that were so bright and plentiful in the last district slowly decrease in number. Through the looming buildings, a small sliver of the sector's only lake is visible in the distance, shimmering in the moonlight like beaten silver.

We finally come to a halt in front of a large warehouse that looks much like all the others around it. The stone is worn and the structure appears abandoned. High windows rise overhead, the majority of which are boarded up. Flyers, most of which are torn or ripped, indiscriminately cover the lower floor of the red-bricked building. A simple pair of double doors offers up entrance.

Cathwell finally turns to face me. "I invited you out tonight because there's something important I want to share with you."

"Something important?" I ask. She's suddenly very close. "Out here?"

She nods. "Have you ever heard of the Amaryllis Order?"

"No?"

"Good." She smiles and takes a step back. With a twirl of her hand, she presents the run-down building before us. "Welcome to Regail Hall, home of the largest peace coalition of the gifted and ungifted. Also known as home of the Amaryllis Order."

19

JAY

I MERELY STARE at Cathwell. What is she talking about? A peace coalition? Housed in this decrepit warehouse?

I recall the various times she's reached out to thin air as if something was there.

"I'm being serious here," Cathwell says with not just a touch of irritation. She turns to the building with a certain look of fondness I'm not able to imagine ever possessing for such a run-down place. "It might look like this, but that's so it doesn't attract attention. It wouldn't be much of a secret hideout otherwise."

"But it doesn't even appear to be in use." My eyes linger on the traces of faded graffiti and dirt. "If the District Committee saw a building like this, wouldn't they do something about it? Renovate it, tear it down?"

"They can't. One of our members owns the building, so they can't complain about how it's used. On the records, it's written off as a storage building—and it is. Just not for what they think."

Cathwell closes her eyes, and when she opens them once more, the fondness is still there. "Regail Hall is home to many of our members who've been displaced in the struggle between Nytes and Etioles. Here, everyone is family."

She's not lying, but it's hard to accept her words as fact. I can't imagine *anyone* living in this warehouse, let alone an entire organization. "You said this is a secret hideout. Why the secrecy?"

"Not everyone is enthusiastic about the idea of Nytes and Etioles getting along," Cathwell says. "We don't want our members to be targeted. And since the rebels intend to go to war against the sector, it'd be safest if they don't have any idea where we are. Or that we even exist. Not until we're ready to defend ourselves, at least."

Once more, I merely stare at her. "I'm sorry, *what?*"

"Let's get inside before someone sees us. We'll talk more there." She doesn't await my response before approaching the doors. I don't have much choice but to follow.

Cathwell thrusts a heavy-looking copper key into the door's lock and slips inside without turning on the lights.

Musty air promptly slams into my face as I step through the doorway after her. I can feel the large expanse of space around us. It's only thanks to the filtered moonlight falling through the few windows not boarded up that I don't run into any of the towers of crates stacked around the room. There appears to be nothing else here. Is this truly the home base of a secret peace organization?

We come to a halt before a stack of crates only two tall; Cathwell easily pushes them aside to reveal a trapdoor.

Well. That wasn't what I was expecting.

With a silver key perhaps half the size of the first one, she unlocks the door and drops through the opening. The echo of her boots hitting stone reaches me seconds later.

I waver at the edge. I can see a dim light, but not the bottom.

Cathwell's voice ricochets up. "There's a ladder if you don't want to jump."

My lips press together. I jump.

The fall isn't as far as I anticipated; my feet meet solid ground once more fairly quickly. A warm, golden glow cast from lines of lanterns on either side of us illuminates a winding hallway of carved-out gray stone. Another surprise.

Cathwell tugs a cord, and the *thud* of the trapdoor hitting concrete and automatically locking back in place resounds through the tunnel.

For a heartbeat, I worry about her fear of small spaces, but though her presence has violet tremors around its edges, ultimately, she's calm.

She proceeds down the tunnel. "The Amaryllis Order was founded around five years ago with the aim of bringing about peace between the gifted and ungifted. When the rebels came into existence two years ago, our focus shifted somewhat to take the threat they pose into account, but our ultimate goal remains the same."

Every noise is amplified down here. The sound of my breathing alone reverberates around me. I lower my voice so as to avoid the echoes when I ask, "What do you mean your focus has shifted somewhat? Shifted in what way?"

"If the rebels *do* go to war against Sector Eight, we're going to protect as many people as we can," Cathwell says. "You'd be surprised how good our information networks and collection of technology are." She appears immensely pleased by this. "We're not ready just yet, but when we are, I think we'll be able to do more than hold our own."

Gradually, the tunnel turns into a hallway, becoming more rectangular in shape, splitting off in several directions. We remain on the main path. We encounter no one else.

Cathwell's fingers have started tapping against one another behind her back. I wonder where she got her fidgeting habit from, and what purpose it serves. Her presence isn't anxious in any way on my grid. What brings it on?

The farther we go, the more the path slopes downward. When I check my grid for our position relative to ground level, we're nearly four stories down.

Merely by glancing at the multitude of diverging paths, and seeing all the passageways and doors off those, I can get a fair idea of how extensive this place is. More than likely, these tunnels already existed long before the Order moved in, much like the military's underground tunnel network. But how did the Order find out about them? And how is a tunnel system this huge not logged into the military or Council's records?

For the first time, it strikes me how serious all this is. What the organization that inhabits this place could be, what it could do. The fact that Cathwell is a part of it.

"Just what is the Amaryllis Order?" I ask.

"You'll find out soon," Cathwell says. "Very soon."

The hallway lets out into a cavernous room. It isn't gradual; we go from a hallway only a few feet above our heads to a space that towers at least three stories high. If I'd thought sound ricocheted in the hallway, it's absolutely thunderous in here. The walls and floor are of the same gray stone as the halls. There are no fanciful decorations. A stage is positioned far off to our right, but that's the only thing in the room.

There are rail-less balconies on two different levels, the first perhaps twenty feet up, the second, forty; from those balconies, wide openings lead back into what I assume are more passageways. A stone ramp circles the entire room. It begins from the floor and leads all the way to the highest level. Bright lanterns hang along it at intervals— enough to illuminate the whole room. People gather along the edges of the balconies, wearing all different colors and styles of clothing.

The crowd on the ground floor is much the same. The brilliant golds, purples, and reds of Sector Ten blend with the muted grays and browns of Sector Two. Men and boys wear traditional wraparounds that hang off one shoulder, or elaborate robes displaying embroidery from either Sector Twelve or Thirteen. Women and girls lift pleated skirts that reach past their ankles as they walk, jumpsuits in varying pastels, plain pants and shirts.

There must be at least one person from every sector here. It appears the rebels aren't the only ones who've been gathering forces from outside Sector Eight.

"How many people are in the Order, exactly?" I ask.

"Mm. Maybe about a thousand?"

A thousand people assembled in one place. Not only the number but the diversity of it astounds me. No, even more than that, the fact that everyone here appears *happy*. No one seems to be alone, and there is no clear split of Nytes on one side of the room and Etioles on the other. People pass to and from groups, hugging, kissing on the cheek, exchanging bows, handshakes, and all sorts of greetings like it's one big family reunion. And nearly all of them are smiling or laughing.

I suddenly feel dizzy. Is this truly happening? How in the gods' names can this place, all these people, actually exist? How does no one else know of this? It seems impossible that such a momentous thing could remain secret for so long.

"How is this possible?" I ask.

"Desperation," answers a voice from behind.

I turn to see a group of five people approaching us. The person who spoke is one of a set of gangly, freckled twins. Cathwell raises a hand in greeting. Her presence on my grid glows happily when she says, "Paul. Everyone. This is the guest I told you about earlier, Jay Kitahara."

I can't sense any of the newcomers with my gift. Alarm bells start ringing in my head, but before I can say anything, Lai whispers, "Don't worry if you can't sense them. I'll explain later, but they're safe."

Her words are hardly reassuring. However, if she trusts them, I'll hold off on my suspicion until she can explain things to me properly.

The twin who spoke before, Paul, smiles as familiarly to me as Cathwell did him. "Welcome to Regail Hall. I'm Paul Wood, and this is my brother, Peter."

His brother jerks his chin up by way of greeting. "Yo."

"It is good to meet you, friend of Lai," says another of the group. "I am Tristao Clemente. But please, call me Trist. All friends do." He's a tall, dark-skinned man perhaps in his early twenties. His face is full and broad and he has limbs that appear thick enough to break a person in two. But most of his face is taken up by his huge smile, and the bass of his voice is full of warmth.

"Fiona Seung," the only girl of the group says. She has short, wavy black hair, golden-brown skin, and a lifted chin. The look she gives me is cold. I wonder if I've already done something to upset her. She nods to the last of their group, a boy who looks barely older than twelve; small and pale, with short, messy blond hair and slightly hunched shoulders. "This is Syon."

"It's a pleasure to meet all of you," I say. I hope I can remember all their names. But my attention is still halfway caught on not being able to use my gift on them and halfway on what Paul Wood said previously. "What did you mean before?" I ask him. "About this being possible because of desperation?"

He offers a timid smile. "Most people here have hit rock bottom at one point or another. They want something to hope for. And when we're at our lowest point, we're more receptive to things we might've previously rejected—especially concerning others who have felt our pain. Nytes aren't the only ones hurting from discrimination."

He nods to a woman passing by, at least ten years too old to be a Nyte. Long gashes wrap around her arm. I initially mistake them for a tattoo. Then I see that it's a burn mark, only, too neat to be an accident. Someone intentionally scarred her like that.

She disappears into the crowd.

I'm about to ask how people find this place when a boy and a woman approaching us wave to the twins' group. "Hey, it's been a while!" the boy says. "How've you been?"

"Oh, you know, same as usual," Peter Wood says with a grin. "Just saying hi to a guest."

The pair comes to a halt before us. The boy is squared-faced, bronzed, and muscular, perhaps fifteen. The woman's skin is a beautiful sepia, almost completely covered by colorful, elaborately embroidered clothing; a scarf of brilliant scarlet wraps around her head. I'm unable to estimate her age, merely that she isn't young enough to be a Nyte. These two, I can sense; their presences glow a welcoming orange. They scan me, though not as if they were analyzing a threat, which is the look I'm accustomed to.

"Welcome to the Order," the woman says with a small smile. "I do hope nothing too awful has brought you here."

"Oh, uh, no," I say. I look to Cathwell for support, but she merely nods to me encouragingly. "Nothing like that. Just, um, looking." Do people only come here when something bad has happened to them? That's a depressing thought.

"What a whimsical reason," the boy says. "I hope you don't make all your life decisions like that."

"Is coming here a life decision?" I ask. "It's just a group advocating equality, isn't it?"

That was the wrong thing to say. Both their eyes harden, but it's the woman who says, "This is everything to many people here—the place they live, work, and find peace. Please do not treat it so lightly."

The fierceness with which she says the words takes me aback. And scrapes my lungs with guilt. I'd thought this place appeared as if out of a fairy tale, but for everyone here, this is their reality, their last sanctuary. This is no simple organization—it's an entire society.

"Sorry, Captain Amal, we haven't explained things to him yet, so he doesn't know much about this place and everyone here," Paul Wood says quickly.

Amal looks me up and down once more before she shakes her head. "No, I spoke too defensively. My apologies. I wish you well and hope you decide to join our cause." She dips her head, and then she and the boy move on to another group of people.

"Sorry about that," Cathwell says. "I should've warned you, but don't talk about the Order as some kind of club when you're around its members. There's a lot at stake for the people here."

No kidding.

"No, I'm sorry," I say. "I didn't mean to insult them or this place."

"There was no insult meant," Clemente says. He claps a hand on my shoulder and my knees nearly give out. "Your intentions were not bad, so please do not be sorry."

His sincerity is clear, but it does nothing to move the uneasiness in my stomach.

"By the way, Lai," Peter Wood says as he turns to Cathwell. "Did you find out any more about that, uh"—he glances at me—"conversation from last time? About the experiments?"

Cathwell's presence immediately darkens. "No, nothing yet. I'll keep looking into it."

I don't know what they're talking about, but it obviously isn't anything good.

Seung glances at her watch. "Lai, we need to get going. The meeting will start soon."

"You say that like they'd start without us," Cathwell says. She pokes Seung's cheek as she passes her, to which the other girl responds with a scowl. Cathwell stops next to Peter Wood. "Oh, and I need to talk with you later, Peter."

"Me?" Peter Wood asks. "Why's that?"

"It's about the person I told you about before—the one I needed your help with. Things didn't quite work out with your power crystal, and I wanted to see if you might know the reason why."

"That's weird. But yeah, sure."

"Thanks," Cathwell says. She turns to me. "Paul and Peter and Syon are going to stay with you during the meeting. If you have any questions, you can ask them."

"What about you?" I fight to repress a sudden wave of panic. Left alone in a hall packed with strangers in a place I know nothing about? No matter how friendly everyone here might appear, I can't think of a worse situation.

"Don't worry, I won't be far," Cathwell says. "I help with keeping an eye on the crowd during Order meetings. For that, I have to go, but I want you to watch this. I want you to understand what kind of group we are."

Her words are careful and somehow fragile. When I look up at her, intending to ask how she's been assisting with meetings when she's been in prison for two and a half years, I realize she's watching me. Searching.

This is something incredibly important to her. These people, this place. And she's chosen to share such a treasured secret with me.

"I understand," I say, however much I don't want to. "I'll pay close attention."

The smile she gives me is the most genuine I've ever seen from her. My heart kicks.

"Thank you," Lai says. "I'll be back soon." She begins departing with Clemente and Seung, then appears to think of something and turns back around: "By the way, don't worry if you can't sense me with your gift."

She vanishes into the throng of people before I can ask what she means.

Okay. Okay. Now what?

"So, you're Lai's teammate?" one of the twins asks. I think it's Paul Wood. "She's told us a lot about you."

"She has?" My surprise must show more than I intended it to, because the twins exchange a mischievous grin. Syon merely watches us.

Peter Wood throws an arm around my shoulder, an unfamiliar gesture I have to physically force myself not to flinch away from. "Of course she has. How could she not? She obviously thinks pretty highly of you if she invited you here." He directs his focus toward his brother. "Well, she doesn't talk about you as much as Paul talks about his dear Joan, but then, I don't think anyone else talks about another person that much."

"*Peter*," Paul Wood says, horrified. "We only just met him, you don't need to go talking about stuff like that."

"What, did you want to tell him about her first?" Peter Wood asks with a laugh. "We would've been here all night."

"That's not true and you know it."

"Riiight."

Just as I'm thinking I couldn't feel any more out of place, I notice a tug on my sleeve. I look down to see Syon holding on to it, a notepad in his other hand. In possibly the prettiest handwriting I have ever seen, it reads *Peter's just jealous.*

"Oh." I'm not certain what to say. "That's, uh, nice."

The Woods peer over my shoulder at Syon's notepad.

Peter Wood bristles defensively. "Don't go telling him lies, Syon."

"I don't see any lies," Paul Wood says. Now it's his turn to laugh. He must notice my discomfort, however, because it quickly slips into a more shared smile. "Sorry, you must be feeling overwhelmed by everything."

"A little," I say, which is a gross understatement.

Syon tucks his notepad back in his pocket. Peter Wood notices my attention follow it and says, "Syon's mute, so he uses the notepad to communicate with people who can't sign. But he usually chooses not to. He must've taken a liking to you."

Once more, I'm not certain what to say. I've barely even said anything for him to have been able to take a liking to me.

I'm saved from having to respond when Syon looks up as though someone has called his name. All the lanterns save the ones illuminating the stage dim to embers. The hall begins to quiet.

The lanterns must be controlled by a Nyte to dim like that. That would explain quite a lot. The Order can't have too much access to electricity; if they used it all the time, the high bill would be too conspicuous not to warrant an investigation. But what kind of gift controls them?

My wonder at the underground lighting system comes to an abrupt halt as Seung, Clemente, and a young woman I don't recognize walk out onstage. The crowd falls silent.

My stomach plummets. "How important are Seung and Clemente in the Order, rank-wise?"

Peter Wood answers. "Fiona and Trist are second only to Walker, leader of the Amaryllis Order." His grin from before returns. "Just in case you were wondering, there are also eight captains under them, two of who are me and Paul. And Syon is what we call a Helper, someone who supports the Order in a huge way but doesn't have a position of leadership. Usually by choice. Lai's a Helper, too, by the way."

Of course they're all high-ranking. Of course I've been making an awkward fool of myself to the very leaders of the Order.

But what truly surprises me is how important Lai appears to be in the organization. I didn't realize how deeply she was involved. It's unexpected, given that she's been in prison these last few years.

"This meeting of the Amaryllis Order is now in session," the young woman, Walker, I presume, says. She doesn't have to raise her voice; her lightly accented words reach us all the way in the back of the hall. The acoustics in this place are astounding.

I try to use my gift to sense her emotions and pinpoint how her presence appears on my grid, but as with the others, she doesn't appear at all. And when I try to locate Lai, she, too, is nowhere to be found. Just as she said. But how is that possible?

"Why doesn't my gift work on the three of you or the people up there?" I ask quietly as those up on stage each give a short greeting. I realize, belatedly, that perhaps I shouldn't have admitted to attempting to use my gift on the very leaders of their organization.

"We all have power crystals that neutralize other Nytes' gifts," Paul Wood whispers back, seemingly unconcerned. "It's to protect ourselves and the information we carry, especially during meetings when everyone is gathered in one place."

But that can't be right. Since our last mission, I've been thinking about that rebel Devin and how we couldn't use our gifts on him. He didn't appear to have any starlight armor that would've canceled out our gifts. The more I considered it, the more convinced I became that Devin either has the ability to cancel out other gifts or else possesses a neutralization power crystal. Each Nyte's gift is unique; there can be only one person with the gift to cancel out other Nytes' gifts, and thus only one Nyte can make a power crystal with that ability—which means that whoever made the Order members' power crystals is working with the rebels.

But that doesn't make sense. Isn't the Order working *against* the rebels? Just what is going on?

"Our first order of business today is updates on the military and the rebels," Walker says.

Seung steps forward. "We've caught word that the High Council has been performing some sort of long-term experiments. It seems they are somehow attempting to take full control over the gifted. For the time being, we are assuming they're making a weapon. Our informants are searching for more details, and we will keep you updated as we learn more. If you hear anything of interest related to this, please let us know."

Bursts of conversation flare up all around us as everyone voices their concerns. Seeing the Etioles just as worried as the Nytes takes me by surprise. Are the ungifted here truly that concerned for us?

"That can't be true, can it?" I ask.

"It's information Lai herself gained for us," Paul says. His eyes are downcast as if out of respect. "It can be trusted."

Lai did? How could she have learned that? When would she have even had the chance?

I want to ask more, but based on what Seung just said, I doubt I would receive any substantial answers.

As Seung goes on to talk about the little progress the military has made in finding out more about the rebels, I'm unable to prevent my attention from wandering over the mass of people assembled here. This place, these people, their very existence is every idealist's dream. No one is arguing. No one is glaring at one another. There's not a trace of the usual tension that inevitably arises when Nytes and Etioles are present in the same room.

All at once, a deep sense of longing rises within me, so strong it takes me aback. I've always wanted to see the gifted and ungifted get along like this, as equals, without any apparent effort. However, without realizing it, I must have dismissed that desire as impossible somewhere along the way. I'd try my best to do what I could, but I knew I would never live to see the day Nytes and Etioles would truly get along.

But I was wrong.

My attention snaps back to the stage when Seung says, "Our own scouts have been able to locate two smaller rebel bases. We're keeping an eye on them in the event the rebels start moving, but nothing of import has happened yet. We will keep everyone updated on this matter as events occur."

"If you know something as important as enemy locations, why not share that information with the military?" I'm not certain which of the twins I'm directing the question to.

"Why should we?" Peter Wood asks. "The military may be willing to use Nytes, but that doesn't mean they like us or treat us well. A coalition of Nytes and Etioles? They'd try to rout us out and label us as part of the rebels so they could stay in control of the gifted. What we work hard to learn is our own information."

I don't pursue the topic, but that doesn't mean it doesn't bother me. I know from all the looks I receive at Central, from the way people avoid me in the hallways or the mess hall, that the military tolerates us merely because we're useful. However, if the Order shared its information with the military, we could put an end to the rebel threat all the sooner.

"That is all for our outside news," Walker says when Seung steps back. "Now then. Home reports, Trist?"

Clemente steps forward with a clipboard in hand. "Earlier today, Captain Jair Lovell separated a fight between Gregor Fijk and Remy Fontaine in the marketplace."

"Will all three named please step forward?" Walker asks.

Now my interest is piqued. What's all this about home reports? Are these people going to be punished and made an example of before the entire organization? No one appears overly concerned, however. It must not be punishment, or at least not a drastic one.

I expect to see perhaps a middle-aged man and a boy who's at most nineteen step up with the named captain. Instead, two older men step up, led by a deeply tanned man who's probably in his late twenties. None of them could be Nytes.

"Jair," Walker says once all three men are standing before her on the stage. "Please give me your account of what happened."

"Of course," Captain Lovell, the youngest of the men, says. "I was patrolling the southern region just after noon when I passed through the marketplace. Someone informed me of a dispute over by the butcher's, so I made my way there to find these two arguing over a chicken."

"There's been a shortage of meat," one of the men says. He throws his hands out in appeal. "I got there first, and was getting ready to—"

"Whose turn is it to speak?" Walker asks, quiet and cool. She doesn't even look at him. The man shuts his mouth, and Walker waves for Lovell to go on.

"The butcher told me it looked like they grabbed it at the same time and began a spat over who had it first," Lovell says, as if there was no interruption. "It was the only one in the store."

Walker nods to the man who spoke previously. "Gregor. Please tell me your side of the story in the most unbiased manner you can."

"I came into the store and went to see if there was any meat to be had," Fijk says. He speaks more cautiously now than when he interrupted the captain. "My girls, they love chicken."

The other man, Fontaine, opens his mouth, but just as quickly snaps it shut, likely recalling when Fijk spoke out of turn. His presence radiates fury.

"So I find the first chicken I've seen in weeks, and just when I lay hands on it, this here man tries to rip it out of my possession," Fijk says.

"Remy," Walker says. "Your side, please."

"With pleasure," Fontaine says. He elegantly twists his hand in front of his chest, a gesture of respect I used to see presented to my father dozens of times when I was younger. I think it's from Sector Fifteen. "My wife and I finally saved enough money to buy meat since coming here. Our anniversary was approaching, and we agreed to indulge ourselves for once." Now it's Fijk's turn to be infuriated. "Just as I was about to purchase the chicken in question, it was rudely taken from me and this gentleman declared that I had stolen it from *him*."

No one in the crowd speaks. Walker has her hand over her mouth, thumb hooked under her chin; her eyes are downcast as she thinks. Finally, she looks to Lovell. "The butcher couldn't determine who had it first?"

"I'm afraid not."

"And neither of you can differentiate as to who claimed it before the other?" Walker asks the two men.

"That'd be me," Fijk says in the same heartbeat Fontaine says, "I did."

Walker's air is cold. "You're sure that's your answer?"

Following a quick glance at each other, they both nod.

I'm not quite certain what's going on. When the mention of a fight came up, I was anticipating a genuine *fight*. Not this quarrel over a chicken. I'm unable to comprehend how this matters, or why anyone cares. Give half the chicken to each of them and send them on their way. It feels a waste of time to discuss it at a meeting of everyone in the Order. This isn't even an argument between a Nyte and an Etiole.

"I see," Walker says. "Lovell, please make sure that neither of these men are allowed to go into the butcher's for two weeks' time. The chicken can go to someone else."

Now start the murmurings in the assembly, though not, I notice, of disapproval. As all three men descend from the stage, I ask, "What just happened?"

"Walker does this every meeting," Peter Wood says. "She's only in Regail Hall for these assemblies since she's out gathering intel, allies, and living her normal life the rest of the time. She doesn't even come to the organizational meetings with Fiona, Trist, and the rest of us." He shakes his head. "So whenever there *is* a meeting, she handles the domestic problems that come up."

"Well, not all of them, of course," Paul Wood says from his brother's side. "We have a normal court led by Trist for that. But she handles enough cases to remind everyone why we're here, and that fighting among ourselves isn't acceptable."

"She's pretty fair with her verdicts," Peter Wood continues. I wonder whether they switch off like that a lot. "Which is part of the reason everyone loves her. She doesn't differentiate between Nyte and Etiole, so no one can really complain."

"Though they don't have to stay to watch her trials if they don't want to," Paul Wood says. "It can get a little boring after a while, but people usually hang around."

"So which is she?" I ask. "Nyte or Etiole?"

"No one knows," Peter Wood says, but even without being able to use my gift on him, I know he's lying. *Someone* must know aside from Walker herself.

Paul Wood is watching the stage, where three new people have been summoned. "She has another power crystal in addition to the neutralization one. A crystal with the ability of illusions from Fiona. The illusion is set to make her appear about nineteen, so that she could look to be a Nyte, but isn't necessarily one. Since she's trying to get discrimination to fade, she hasn't revealed what she is. This way, people can't say she's biased one way or the other."

"If she's attempting to eliminate prejudice, then she shouldn't let whether she's a Nyte or an Etiole stop her," I say. Lying can't be okay. The Order should've demanded answers from her by now. Why haven't they, after all this time?

"Everyone's scared," Paul Wood says quietly. "They want someone to believe in, someone similar to them who knows their suffering. That doesn't work both ways. Most people who first come here hate the kind of people who hurt them to begin with. It takes time for them to adjust. They project onto Walker whatever they want to be true. It's another reason for her illusion. Since everyone knows that isn't who she really is, they can imagine whoever they like. It's comforting."

I'm not certain I've ever been so desperate for something that I would outright lie to myself about it to make myself feel better. That doesn't sound as though it would end well in the long run.

But no. That's not true. I lived my entire childhood like that. Believing that if I worked hard enough, if I did everything just as I was taught, then Father would come to accept me. I must have been aware all along it was pointless. But I wanted that delusion badly enough that I was willing to lie to myself for years.

There are a few more domestic problems similar to the first. Occasionally it's Nyte against Etiole, sporadically Nyte against Nyte, but generally Etiole against Etiole; likely due to the fact that there are simply more of them. There are always more Etioles.

The problems are rather mundane. Minor property damage. Accusations of stolen food. If nothing else, I gather the Order isn't doing very well on rations.

Only once is there an Etiole with a problem against a Nyte for no other reason than him being a Nyte. The instant they step foot onstage, a silence so complete it has weight falls upon the hall. You could hear a speck of dust drop. Everyone stares at the Etiole.

She holds herself with straight-backed pride, but I can sense her anxiety on my grid. It swirls like a storm in response to the muted aggravation in the room. She doesn't look at the Nyte beside her.

Walker looks them both over carefully before her gaze settles on the Etiole woman. "Has Leo wronged you in some way, Maya?"

The woman gazes coolly back at Walker. "His kind killed my husband and only son. You know that, Ms. Walker."

The Nyte, Leo, maybe thirteen or fourteen, keeps his eyes trained on his feet. His presence sputters a nervous indigo.

"I do," Walker agrees. "But that isn't what I asked. Has *Leo* done anything to wrong you?"

"Only his demon brethren," the woman says.

Anger ripples through the crowd, along with a few shouts. The woman's presence tightens in on itself, defensive, hating, and so, so alone.

Despite myself, I feel a twinge of sympathy for her. She lost so much, and in her quest to find someone or something to blame, she's ended up bearing the furious attention of everyone in this room. She's in the wrong. But at the same time, I feel like I can understand her anger and loneliness.

Walker's voice only softens in response to the woman's words, a fact that I respect. "Maya, I know this is a hard time for you. And I understand full well that it must be difficult to look at the gifted with an open heart after what happened to your family. But not all gifted are the same, just as not all ungifted are the same. I would ask that you reconsider your feelings toward them. Please."

"Ms. Walker, I am forever indebted to you for giving me a place to call home after I lost everything to Nytes," the woman says. "But you can't make me feel something I don't. I told you that when you first invited me to come here. I'm not going to take that back now."

"I know," Walker says. "I have no wish to force anyone to feel or believe what I do. But I would like it if you would merely give others a chance. Not everything is so black and white." At the woman's silence, Walker continues. "To that end, you will be shifted from your current duties to volunteering in the school for three months. You will assist both the gifted and the ungifted students who attend. While there, please do your best to get along with everyone."

Silence descends once more upon the crowd as the Etiole and Nyte make their way off the stage. From the overwhelming mix of emotions on my grid, I can't tell what the general mood of the hall is.

"What kind of punishment is that?" I ask the twins. "What's the point?"

Peter and Paul share a glance. It's Paul who answers. "Whenever there's someone who hates so broadly like that, Walker always sends them to the school. All the kids go there together, whether they're Nyte or Etiole. And for the most part, they get along just fine. They don't discriminate between gifted or not like adults do. Often, being around that kind of atmosphere, and being around kids in general, can help alleviate such blunt hatred. Not always, but often."

"A lot of people here have worked at the school at some point," Peter adds. "Plenty of our members have been in the same position. With enough gentle pushing in the right direction, they usually come around."

I look at the crowd once more. The mix of people, of emotions.

What kinds of experiences has everyone here had? How many of them were once so hateful?

I find myself relieved at Walker's "punishment." Without meaning to, I somehow ended up hoping for a good outcome for the Etiole woman. I've seen firsthand in the military how harsh consequences can sometimes merely make a problem worse. But I imagine the woman can find no true self-pity or resentment in such a sentence. Walker showed concern, understanding, and fairness. She didn't try to force anything on the woman. She merely gave her the chance to change.

Again, that feeling of deep yearning rises within me. *This* is what I've always wanted. This sense of unrestrained empathy, understanding, and patience. *This* is what I've always been searching for and never believed could truly exist between Nytes and Etioles.

From the stage, Walker begins speaking once more. "Friends, family. I ask you to remember why we're all here, what we're working for. I ask you to show compassion and understanding to those who are different from you, and even to those who hate. Pain takes time to heal. Prejudice takes time to dissolve. We must be patient and persevere, for that is the only way to win this war of hatred. It is difficult, but we can do it. One step at a time. One person at a time."

The air in the room and the presences on my grid immediately lighten. People turn to those around them and smile. A few people even clap before Clemente calls for the next two people to come to the stage.

By the time Walker has settled the last domestic report, it's two hours past midnight. If I had known it would take this long, I would have taken a nap earlier. I suppose I was still thinking I wouldn't come then. Now I'm glad I did.

"Thank you, everyone, for coming tonight," Walker says. "I know it's been hard waiting these past few years. But we must first be strong in our beliefs within our community before we try to spread them to others. Our time will come to openly advocate peace between all people. At that time, I hope you will stand together with me."

Cheers resound in the hall as though the sound were a living thing, and in the same heartbeat, Syon and the Woods usher me into the hall I entered from previously with Lai. "What's the hurry?" I ask, but I allow them to lead me along regardless.

"We need to get to the conference room before everyone starts to leave the main hall," Peter Wood says. "It'll get way too crowded after that."

I'm shepherded down the hall until it turns into a tunnel once more; then I'm led through so many snaking corridors that I lose my sense of direction. I can't imagine ever knowing this maze so well as to navigate it when all the hallways look exactly alike.

We eventually reach a small door at the end of one of the halls. Inside, there's a wooden table with perhaps fifteen mismatched chairs centering the space; filing cabinets line two of the walls. Maps cover the other two, much like in Central's meeting rooms. Tacks and strings haphazardly cross over them in patterns I don't understand.

Walker, Clemente, and Seung are already seated at the table; how they succeeded in getting here before us is a mystery. In any case, having the three leaders of the Order gathered together before us makes me uneasy. I don't see Lai, either.

Paul Wood must notice my unease at her absence, because he whispers, "Lai always stays behind after meetings to talk with the information division. She isn't here in person very often, so she has to make the most of it when she is. She should be here soon."

"Thank you," I murmur back.

Walker stands, and now I can finally see her clearly. She's lean and tall, wearing a regal black coat and uniform trimmed in silver with matching knee-high boots. Her thick, dark red hair is clasped at the back of her head, ends sticking up, and a wave of bangs falls across her forehead. I have to remind myself that this isn't how she truly appears; it's merely an illusion created by Seung. Still, I didn't anticipate that I'd be meeting the actual leader of the Order. My gut twists.

"It's a pleasure to meet you," Walker says with a small smile. Her voice carries the lilt of a western accent.

I give a small bow of my head, both knowing and feeling that I need to be polite to this person. "The pleasure is mine. Thank you for allowing a stranger like me to attend one of the Order's meetings like this."

Walker waves her hand for me to lift my head. "Not at all. We are always looking for those who might wish to take part in our cause. From what Lai has said, it sounds like you would be a good match. Tell me, what did you think of the meeting?"

"You seem to have a very organized system," I say carefully as I straighten. "Your followers appear to respect you a great deal, and the harmony of this group is unbelievable. You have an amazing community here."

Walker's entire expression brightens as she claps her hands together. Such an honest reaction takes me aback. "I was hoping you would like it. Then, will you join us?"

I know she mentioned joining only a few heartbeats ago, yet still, the direct question rips the floor out from under me. Me? Join the Order?

"I am already a part of the military," I say. "I don't have any time to commit to anything outside of that." Nor am I certain it wouldn't be considered treason. Recalling the information the Order has but won't share with the military, I wonder if my merely being here and knowing all this isn't treason in and of itself.

"We would never ask you to do anything you didn't want to," Walker says, unperturbed by my response. "Nor anything you felt you couldn't do. We would ask only that you come to the meetings to stay up to date."

"Then why ask me to join at all when you would gain nothing from it?"

Walker smiles that small, quiet smile from before. "It isn't about gaining or losing anything. We just want people to support the idea that the gifted and ungifted can live together in peace. And if you, a person in a position of power, were to assist in spreading that idea when we finally go public, I think it would give it more weight. That is all."

My heart is pounding. I know—I *know* I shouldn't, but I ask, "If you're truly about peace, then why do you all have power crystals from someone who's helping the rebels?"

Silence falls like a solid thing into the room. No one looks at anyone else. Walker closes her eyes, but when she looks back up at me again, her gaze is unwavering. "An old friend and one of the original members of the Order gave us these crystals. He left us some years ago and we have not been in contact since. I doubt he knows anything of what our group has become since then. We suspect he has joined the rebels, but our investigation is still ongoing."

I wish I was able to use my gift to sense whether she's lying, but everyone in the room is still under their respective crystals' protection. Walker doesn't *appear* to be lying, but I grew up in the company of enough politicians and businessmen to know you can't trust appearances.

"So?" Walker prompts. "Will you join us?"

I'm not certain what to say. My first reaction is *yes*, which is frightening. I have no desire to betray the military in any way, and not merely because I don't wish to face the consequences of an action like that. I've given everything I have to them these past many years. I've always believed that though wrong in some ways, they are ultimately fighting for the good of the sector.

But then I saw the people here. I felt that choking longing to be a part of such an empathetic community. The idea that I could be seen as a person and not merely a Nyte, and that I could learn to see Etioles in the same way, is a realistic one here. A place where patience and understanding rule over hatred, where you're encouraged to be sympathetic over dealing blind justice.

I've never felt so strongly that I wanted a group to thrive. To *succeed*. I look at the people here, and I think that they're attempting to do true good. When I compare them with the military, it feels obvious who's in the right. Who I should side with. Who I truly *want* to side with.

And when I think of that, I wonder what it is I'm doing. What I've been doing all these years. Much as when I was back in my room at Central debating whether or not to meet with Lai, I think of my time in the military. The never-changing state of things, the stagnating, constantly unfulfilled me.

Deep-rooted desire pulls against duty pulls against doubt pulls against loyalty in my chest. I know only what the Order has chosen to show me. They're suspicious in more ways than one. But then again, if what they said about the High Council really is true, they and the military, who work under them, are no less so. No matter what, I need to be careful.

However, I can't deny the incredibly strong feeling that *I want to be a part of this*. Isn't peace between the gifted and ungifted what I've always wanted? Isn't that why I'm fighting to protect the ungifted now? It's true I can fight in the military, but what about here, where they're fighting in a way that reaches deeper than physical blows? In the way I always wanted to fight?

I want this.

I joined the military because I felt I had no other place to go. But now it isn't like that. I can choose something I want merely because I want it, because I feel it's something right; not because I'm trying to please anyone or because I have no other alternatives. I can make my own choice. I can choose to go after something I want.

I close my eyes. When I open them again, everyone is watching me. "I want to join the Order."

20
LAI

THE AFTERNOON AFTER Jay decided to join the Order—a fact that still makes me bounce with every step—I tell myself I won't go meet him. That I'll train with Al or makes notes on last night's meeting. And yet I somehow find myself standing outside his and Mendel's door.

What am I doing? There are a million other things I need to be working on right now. And yet . . .

I knock. "Jay? You home?"

The door immediately falls open under my hand. On the other side, Jay looks a little flustered, his hair messy, cheeks slightly flushed. "Lai. Hi."

Just the sight of him makes me happy. And he called me Lai.

"Hey," I say. Suddenly words are hard. "I just thought I'd stop by. And maybe see if you wanted to hang out?" I could kick myself.

But if Jay notices my awkwardness, he doesn't point it out. In fact, he seems to be struggling with the same problem. "Yeah! I mean, uh, yeah. Sure. What did you want to do?"

"I was thinking we could play piano together." It's something I've been thinking about since yesterday. When Jay came to the realization he was stuck, and once I gathered that from his thoughts, I started wondering if there was anything I could do to help.

I know what it's like to not have a goal in life from my time on the streets. Every day, all I was concerned about was how I'd live on to the next day, and then years passed without me realizing. It felt like there was nothing I could do, nowhere I could go, no way I could change. Then Austin gave me purpose. He tried to do the same for Jay, but it didn't change him any.

I really think the Order will be good for him—and for my own selfish reasons, I'm thrilled he joined. But I want to give him more than that. He's been there for me every time I needed him, even when we were at a disadvantage in battle, even when he didn't understand what was wrong. He never abandoned me. And now, when he's feeling lost and lonely and disconnected from the rest of the team, I want to do something for him. Something personal, something he'll enjoy.

And then, when I was thinking about what I could do for him, I remembered all the times he tried to talk to me about piano. How a small part of him would light up when he mentioned it.

"Piano?" Jay repeats. The offer is met with an internal mix of uncertainty and enthusiasm. It's been a long time since he last practiced, and he's afraid of embarrassing himself, but he wants to play.

I can relate. My years in the prison were mostly spent sneaking out to help the Order. The lonely piano in the corner of my room would constantly draw me to it, but it's been some time since I played anything seriously.

"I'm pretty awful these days," I say, partly to reassure him he's in good company, partly to cover myself ahead of time. "But if you wouldn't mind that, then I think it'd be a nice break from everything related to war."

After a slight pause, Jay smiles. "Only so long as you don't mind practicing with someone who hasn't played in years."

I smile back. "I think I can handle that."

Central's music hall is usually deserted this time of day. Most soldiers are either eating lunch or out running errands around now, so it's the perfect time to practice without drawing attention to ourselves.

The room itself is a pretty good size, everything adjusted for the best acoustics. Two grand pianos crouch in opposite corners of the room while racks upon racks of music line the back wall. The right wall is nothing but floor-to-ceiling windows that look out upon the sector. There's a hallway to the left that leads to private practice rooms, and beyond that, the locker room for instruments. Music stands and chairs litter the center of the space.

I haven't been in this room for over two and a half years, and yet it hasn't changed in the slightest. A wave of nostalgia rushes over me.

Jay walks into the room with his mouth slightly open. "This place is huge! Eastern's music hall was little more than a dorm room with a baby grand piano shoved inside."

"I'm glad you like it, then." I've never known anyone other than Mom who was interested in music. Luke liked to come and hear me practice, but he never played himself. He didn't even know how to read music.

I sit at the closest piano, a pitch-black one I used to play frequently.

It was my escape when I first came to the military. Back when I avoided everyone. I'd been tired of being judged as a Nyte, and I certainly didn't want others to know about my living on the streets for nearly two years. They didn't need any more reasons to be disgusted by me.

But Sara and Luke were different. Maybe because both of them were also Nytes, but even once they found out I was a telepath, that I ran away from home, that I stole for years, they still accepted me. They were okay with me being next to them.

Jay sits beside to me on the bench, fingers laced together in his lap. "What should we play?" he asks. His heels tap against the wooden floor in alternating beats.

"Whatever you want." A few pieces come to mind, but all of them are more difficult than I can handle right now. Besides, Jay should decide.

He only too eagerly makes his way to the racks of music. He rifles through the sheets like a boy at a candy shop searching for the largest piece. I wonder if he's ever even been inside a candy shop, what with that dad of his. I guess he never got the chance to be a kid.

"Okay," Jay says, bringing me back to the present. He's sitting next to me on the bench again. I didn't even notice him walk over. "I think I've decided. Do you know Bashir's sonata?"

"Number twelve?" I look over his shoulder at the piece he chose. He's clutching it like a trophy, but carefully, so as not to wrinkle it. "Sure, I know it. It's pretty popular." It's a mid-range piece, as far as skills go, so it shouldn't give me too much trouble. Probably.

"Then let's try it." He carefully props the sheet music up in front of us. "How do you want to do it? Should we play together on different octaves, or one at a time, or split the parts between bass and treble since it's been a while?"

His enthusiasm makes my chest warm. "What do you want to do?"

He half smiles at me, inwardly realizing his overexcitement and feeling embarrassed by it. "How about at the same time on different octaves?"

I'm not entirely sure that's a good idea since we'll be overlapping like crazy, but maybe that's the point. Maybe he doesn't want to focus on anything stylistic and just wants to have fun with it. He was never able to do anything like that in the past. If nothing else, it'll be a ridiculous display. Good thing no one else is here.

"All righty, then." I poise my hands over the keys, making the gesture large and overdramatic. "Count us off, Major."

"One, two," Jay breathes. His eyes are shining. "Three, four."

We come in at the same time, but that's about where our luck ends. I continuously find the keys a split second too late as my fingers' habitual memories take over and the treble and bass lines blur into one in front of me.

Jay is even worse off. He stumbles over the notes, often hitting two at once. The keys' placement is probably fuzzy for him after so many years. At least I had the piano in the prison to practice on, however infrequently I actually did.

Our elbows keep knocking into each other, and when it's not our elbows, it's our hands or wrists or fingers. The melody is buried by dozens of wrong notes, and I'm pretty sure we're not even playing at the same tempo. It couldn't be worse if a hundred Ferals were clawing at glass. I'm surprised my ears aren't bleeding.

When we hit a rest and Jay plays straight through it, I start laughing. And then I can't stop. I laugh until my stomach hurts and I can't play, and then Jay bursts out laughing, too, and we're both incapacitated for a ridiculous amount of time given how unfunny the situation is.

When I can breathe again, I say, "That was terrible."

"We didn't even get to the second page."

"That might be a good thing."

"The gods would have struck us where we sat."

"Only if we hadn't already killed them with our demonic noise."

And then we start laughing again. I can't remember the last time I laughed like this. Not since Luke and Sara.

Jay is the first to recover this time. "I haven't played seriously since I left my father's home a million years ago. The person who taught me there was so uptight; all he cared about was technique and style. I don't think he could even hear the music."

I feign a shudder. "That sounds awful. My mom taught me how to play. I was the worst, but it was fun because she didn't care." Looking back on it now, those were probably the happiest moments of my childhood. "I would sit in her lap on the bench, and she'd put her hands over mine. That was when I was really little. When I got a bit older, and better, we would play simple pieces together."

I'm suddenly struck by how much I miss Mom. I wonder how she's doing. Better, probably, now that I'm gone.

"Your mother sounds like a warm person," Jay says softly. His head is bent as if in prayer as he traces his fingers over the keys.

I want to tell him it's okay he never met his mom. That she would have loved him even though he is a Nyte. That his dad is a coward and a sorry excuse for a parent. Mine was, too.

But I don't say any of these things. They wouldn't do anything for him in the end.

"I'm glad you're a Nyte, Jay," I say. "Maybe you aren't because of how things went in life, but I don't think you'd be who you are today if you weren't born a little differently."

His eyes fall. I put a hand on his shoulder.

When he looks at me again, it's over the tops of his glasses. They're skewed slightly. "Hey, Lai? Will you tell me a secret?"

"A secret?"

"Yeah. Anything is fine. I just . . . Do you remember when you asked me if I trusted you?"

"Of course I do. It was only yesterday."

He smiles slightly. "Yeah. Yeah, I suppose it was."

I make sure to meet his eyes when I say, "I trust you, Jay." I kick my heels against the ground. "How about this one, then? Me being in prison was my own choice. I never committed any crime. Austin just helped me pretend I did so I could get sent out there. It was all fake."

His head snaps up. "What?"

"Yup."

He stares at me as I flex my fingers over the keys but don't touch them. "But why?"

I flip to the next page of the piece and move my right hand along with the treble line without actually playing the notes. The keys are cool beneath my fingertips. "I wanted to leave the military to help the Order, but of course the military would never let a Nyte just go. So I left in my own way and then snuck out of prison to Regail Hall as often as I could. If I had been in the military, I wouldn't have had time to do what I needed to."

He's silent for some time. "Why bother? Why care so much about the Amaryllis Order? You've never struck me as someone who was so passionate about nondiscrimination between Nytes and Etioles. Yet you went to such lengths for it." He's still struggling with his own decision about joining the Order. He doesn't think it was the wrong choice, but he's not sure how to feel about how it may or may not have affected his loyalty to the military. "And after all that, why come back to the military?"

"I mean, why not, right?"

"Lai."

My breath slides out between my teeth. I know I shouldn't be talking about this at all, but when it comes to Jay, I just can't help it. I *want* to confide in him. It's been so long since I've met anyone like that. Fiona doesn't count. Even though we work so closely together, and we're there for each other when need be, we've never really gotten along outside of work. And Trist and the twins and Syon, I love them, but I've never wanted to go to any of them about my personal problems.

I might consider Al, but she's too honest, and too reckless. She could accidentally spill my secrets. Plus, if I'm being honest with myself, I really want her to like me. Telling her more about myself would ruin any chance of that. Mendel is far too similar to me for my own liking, not to mention his perpetual suspicion rules him out as someone who would honestly listen. As does the fact that I don't really trust him. Besides, I want to tell *Jay*. He's self-conscious and too much of a perfectionist, but he's earnest and honest and straightforward. My total opposite.

"The Order was founded by Luke," I say, trying to make the words light, but falling flat. "He was an idealist, you see. He really thought Nytes and Etioles could get along. But he died before the Order could become anything. Then Walker took over and made it really something." I look down. "Since it was Luke's dream, I'd do anything for the Order. Even pretend I committed a crime to leave the military. The reason I came back is because I thought it'd be better for the Order for me to be inside Central, where everything is happening. Where I can get information."

I chance a glance at him. He doesn't *seem* mad.

"You said you'd do anything for the Order since it was Luke's dream," Jay finally says. "Were the two of you . . . ?"

I laugh, but it doesn't sound right. "No. I mean, *I* had feelings for Luke, but he only ever saw me as a little sister. He and Fiona were head over heels for each other."

"And the Nyte who gave you all neutralization power crystals? What was he like?"

I hadn't thought my heart could drop any lower, and yet, here we are. I can't hold back a sigh. "Gabriel. He was like an older brother to all of us. Always watching over us, always gently scolding us when we'd do something wrong." I laugh. "Actually, maybe he was more like our mom."

"And you think he went to the rebels?"

"I could never imagine him joining their cause. He's too . . . *good* for that. And yet all evidence seems to indicate otherwise."

He doesn't say anything right away. Then, partly to change the subject, partly because he wants to know, he says, "May I ask what your gift is? I still have no idea."

"It's a rather revolting thing, really." I trace my finger over the sheet music, outlining the treble clef, not looking at him. "I'd prefer not to say if I don't have to. It sort of drives people away."

"I'd still like to know," Jay says.

I start playing the treble line on the piano for real now, using the right amount of pressure to make the notes hang between us. It isn't a slow section, but I play it that way.

He gently grips my wrist and lifts it so I can't play. I stare at it as the notes fade. "You don't have to tell me if you don't want to. But know that I won't leave you. I already promised you that, didn't I?"

Telling Mendel I could hear others' thoughts wasn't hard. I needed something from him in return, and it was fun messing around with him. Jay is different. I have nothing to gain by telling him, only things I could lose. He might not trust me anymore, which wasn't a problem with Mendel because he didn't trust me to begin with—he doesn't trust anyone.

But I don't know that Jay would mind like others would, either. He knows what it's like to be isolated because of his gift. He knows what it means having to struggle to please others. It's made him more accepting. If anyone was going to put up with me after they found out I could hear their every thought, it would be him.

I finally look at him. "I'm a telepath."

I wait for the flash of betrayal, the disgust, or the running through of past thoughts he had while I was around, analyzing them, but the only thing I get from him is blank surprise. **Oh. That's certainly a difficult gift to admit to others. No wonder she hasn't wanted to share it with us. Wait, is she—are you reading my thoughts right now? Oh. Probably. Well, it's good to know for future reference.**

"Okay," he says. "Okay."

"Okay," I say. Our eyes meet, and he doesn't look away. I'm not sure if he understands. The thoughts are all in his head, but he isn't connecting them like he's supposed to. He's not *reacting* like he's supposed to.

Then again, he's very aware of how important this is to me. He knows how he reacts could hurt me if he's not careful. He's always considerate of others like that.

"Thank you," he says. "For trusting me."

A thought crosses his mind, and now he really *does* take the fact I can tell what he's thinking to heart. He looks down. What little I can see of his face is red.

I lean over to cup his cheek in my hand. Our eyes meet and hold. And then I kiss him.

I've never kissed or been kissed by anyone before. I don't really know how it works. I always wondered what it would feel like, always knew I'd be awful and awkward at it. But somehow, with Jay, I don't mind.

His lips are soft against mine, and when they part, there's a warmth that fills me. His hand comes up to hold my cheek. I both want to read his mind and am terrified to know what he's thinking.

His hand, still on my wrist over the keys, shifts to tangle his fingers through mine. He grips them tightly before pulling back first. We watch each other for a long moment.

He turns to the sheet music, but with a smile intended for me. "Well. Let's give this piece another shot. Try not to sound like you're skinning a Feral alive this time, okay?"

21
LAI

TWO DAYS AFTER Jay and I played piano together, I'm tasked with the most unfortunate role of messenger.

I find Mendel working away in the woodshop, as usual, but unlike usual, his thoughts are distracted from the work at hand. Something happened recently. Something with Al.

I knock on the woodshop's doorframe. He doesn't hear me the first time over the wood saw, so I do it again when it's stopped, and he looks up, startled.

He opens his mouth with the intention of telling me to get out. Instead, he says, "You have to wear goggles when you're in the woodshop."

"The general is calling us."

"Another mission?"

"He didn't say any specifics." A disturbing fact, but one I couldn't change.

"I'll be right there."

When I don't make any move to leave, he raises an eyebrow.

"Something happen recently?" I ask.

"Odd of you to care."

"You are my teammate, you know."

"Since when does that mean anything?"

"What happened with Al?"

He sighs and sets his goggles on the bench next to him. I think I hear a muttered "Stupid mind reader" before he stands and starts cleaning up the wood shavings from his time on the saw. "Not that it's any of your business," he says, "but we got into a fight."

"When *aren't* the two of you in a fight?"

He pauses in his sweeping long enough to give me a sarcastic, "Ha ha."

I throw my hands up in fake apology. "All right, so what was the fight about?"

"Something stupid." He half shrugs. "Does it matter?"

"Clearly it does."

"Johann asked me about that rebel, Devin," he says. The admission comes on so suddenly I'm not sure he meant for it to come out at all. He bites his lip but continues. "He said I wasn't taking the rebels seriously enough and we started fighting. Then he asked why a rebel knew me personally. I think he'd been waiting to ask for a while. But when I said I didn't know, he just . . . dropped it."

Al, waiting to ask something serious? And then dropping it so easily? That sounds unlike her. But then I think of when we spoke of our pasts and her hesitation during that conversation. I wonder if she had already gathered that Devin was a touchy part of Mendel's history. She doesn't know about Mendel's missing memories, and Devin certainly didn't talk to Mendel like a friend, so maybe she thought they had fought before. I doubt she suspects Mendel having potentially been a rebel himself given that she let the matter go. And if she didn't think Mendel was a threat, then she wouldn't dig where she wasn't welcome—especially since that often invites digging in return.

"Does that bother you?" I ask. "That Al let it go?"

He shakes his head. "No. I guess it's just . . . I wasn't expecting it." He struggles for a moment with the words. "I wasn't expecting him not to pry. I didn't think he'd trust me enough not to ask any more."

"Isn't that a good thing, then? That Al's trusting you? What is it you're so bothered about?"

Cathwell is the last person in the world I want to talk about this with.

I cross my arms. "You got someone else to talk about this with?"

He throws a half-hearted snarl my way. But we both know the answer to my question, so he goes on. "When someone looks like they have a connection to the enemy, normally you push to find out what kind of connection it is so you don't end up with a knife in your back."

"So you're worried Al's not taking this seriously enough?"

"I'm worried he shouldn't trust me." The words are so quiet I almost miss them. When he speaks again, his voice is back to normal. "I don't trust him. I don't trust anyone here—you especially, in case you had any doubts. It feels wrong for him to not be at least a little suspicious of me."

"Feeling the responsibility of someone placing their trust in you?" I tease. "That certainly is a heavy thing to bear."

He doesn't snap a comeback this time. Instead, he bends down to sweep his small pile of wood shavings into a dustpan, taking his time to think while he does it.

Finally, he asks, "Have you ever trusted someone who doesn't trust you in return? Or the other way round?"

He asks the question with a rare seriousness, and so I consider it seriously. It's difficult. "I've had people trust me who I didn't trust," I finally say. "Or I guess, it's less that I didn't trust them and more that I didn't choose to share everything with them."

"And it didn't bother you at all?"

"It's rare that I find someone I'll tell everything to."

He picks up my meaning immediately. Telling someone you can hear their every thought is a big leap of faith to take. It's not something you do for everyone who thinks they trust you.

But it's not the answer he wanted. His thoughts on the matter are still uneasy, and it's difficult for me to understand why. Shouldn't Al putting a little trust in him be a good thing? There's something more going on, something I can't understand.

"There's actually something else I wanted to talk to you about, too," I say. "I spoke with my friend about his power crystal."

His thoughts instantly pick up, though with a sobering edge of wariness. "And?"

"He doesn't know why his crystal acted like that." I struggle to get the next words out, because I really, *really* don't want to say them. "But he offered to use his gift on you himself to see if we can get better results."

"Really?"

I try not to let my unease show as I nod. I don't like Peter going out of his way for me for this. I don't know that I like him and Mendel meeting, either. I don't think Mendel means any harm to anyone—for now. But what if it turns out he was a rebel? What if he goes back to them? The less he knows about me and anyone related to the Order, the better.

But I made a promise to Mendel, and I don't break my promises.

Mendel's silent as he finishes cleaning up the room and putting the tools back in their places. He doesn't speak again until we're exiting the woodshop. "You really were serious about helping me get my memories back, weren't you?"

"No, I just said it for kicks," I say. This part of Central Headquarters isn't as tidy as the rest. Paint droplets trail the concrete floor, and water stains ruin every surface. The air is humid and damp, despite the fact there's no water around. "Of course I meant it. I don't waste my time on things I have no intention of following through on."

Mendel rolls his eyes. "Yeah, because your actions always give me so much reason to believe what you say."

"I told you before, I don't lie. If I say I'm going to do something, I'm going to do it as best I can."

"People always lie."

"How can you really know? Maybe you just think everyone lies because you always lie."

He doesn't answer.

We don't say anything else on the walk to Austin's office. By the time we arrive, everyone is already there. Al sits on the very edge of one of the chairs in front of Austin's desk, akin to a Feral poised to pounce. Jay stands next to her, hands clasped behind his back. Austin sits at his desk.

"Ah, good," Austin says as Mendel and I enter. "Now we're all here."

I hesitate before going to sit in the chair next to Al. Mendel comes to stand behind me. Al seems to share the feeling that something is wrong, because her eyes are searching Austin's, looking for the source of the problem. Jay looks equally uneasy even as he smiles at me in greeting. At least we all seem to be on the same page.

"I've called you all here for an important announcement," Austin says. His eyes are unusually serious. "The rebels have contacted us. They want to arrange a negotiations meeting."

For about three seconds, everyone is too shocked to speak. Al is the first to say, "*What?*"

"It came as quite a surprise to us as well," Austin says. He holds up an envelope for us to see: faded cream in color, someone's signature scrawled across the front beneath the words *For General Austin*. I recognize the signature instantly. Ellis.

Fury and shock spike through my blood like white-hot fire. There's no way Ellis wants to negotiate anything. The rebels' aim has always been one and one alone: to destroy the sectors and all the ungifted living within them.

Jay's eyes snap to me. **Are you okay?**

Right. His gift. Of course he'll notice if I get angry. I need to keep my emotions in check.

I nod infinitesimally to him.

But Jay isn't the only one to notice my anger.

Who's Ellis? Mendel asks me internally, thinking that he might as well try to communicate by thought since he assumes I'm always reading his mind anyway.

242

He doesn't expect me to reply in his head. *The rebels' founder and leader.*

Why is this my first time hearing such an important name?

Probably because you never tried to learn anything about the rebels.

Cathwell—

Austin starts speaking again, sparing me from having to continue with Mendel. "This letter was left in my inbox yesterday morning. Someone must have snuck in and left it." Austin seems to grit his teeth here. "Regardless, it requests a meeting between Nytes only. An emergency meeting of the High Council was called, and it has been decided that the four of you will represent the military in negotiations."

"Wait, you mean you're actually going through with this?" Al asks. "Isn't this obviously a trap? Request some of the military's strongest soldiers to come alone, then ambush and kill them. If they really wanted to negotiate, they would ask to meet you directly, or set up a line of communication."

"The Council said we cannot assume they have the technology to communicate with us in such a way," Austin says. "That it would be only proper to meet them face-to-face in a show of goodwill. We can't start off trying to gain peace with them by outright saying we don't trust them enough to meet in person."

"The rebels don't want peace," I say. It's hard not to spit the words out one by one. "They want to annihilate the ungifted. You know that."

"I do." Austin holds my look. "I told the Council it was almost certain the rebels were plotting an ambush, but they insisted on going through with the peace talk. They decided we shouldn't plunge head-long into a war that might otherwise be prevented by diplomacy. The matter is out of my hands."

"Diplomacy?" I can't contain the venom in my voice, seeping into my bloodstream, the air in my lungs, my anger poisoning everything inside me and threatening to spill out. I feel Jay's eyes on me. I tell myself I need to calm down, but I can't. "You know how Ellis is. The Council is sending us straight into a trap. We can't go through with this meeting."

"I have protested and provided as much evidence to my case as possible. I was ignored." He closes his eyes, and I imagine him pacing back and forth behind his desk despite the fact he's completely still. "The requested meeting date is in four days. You are scheduled to head out in three. There is little time in which to convince the Council to back out."

"Even if we had more time, convincing the Council seems unlikely if they've already set their sights on this," Kitahara says. I feel his eyes still on me, worried, but unable to do anything right now.

Austin shakes his head. "The Council thinks if they send all of you, you're more likely to be safe. Or at least take down a good number of them with you. Either way, I will continue to work on convincing them. In the meantime, they have stated you are all on standby in order to prepare for this meeting."

"What if we refuse to go?" Mendel asks quietly. The way he says it, and the fact that it's the first thing he's said, takes me by surprise. "We do have a choice in the matter, don't we?"

Austin's jaw clenches. "The Council has informed me that any who refuse to take part in this meeting will be court-martialed and

244

charged as a traitor without question." When no one speaks, he says, "That's all for now. As soon as I get more news, I will contact you again. You are dismissed."

I'm the first one out of the room. I'm so agitated by Ellis's letter and the imminent ambush that I can't calm down, can't think straight, can't put words together correctly.

"Cathwell, wait up," someone says from behind me. Mendel. "Tell me really. Who's Ellis? Why did you get so mad when you saw that name on Austin's letter?"

I stop, but he doesn't, so he ends up a few strides in front of me and has to turn around. My hands are clenched into fists at my sides, digging into the fabric of my pants. I glare at the ground, afraid of what I might say if I look at Mendel directly. Behind me, I hear footsteps as Jay catches up to us.

"Who wouldn't get angry hearing that name?" I ask. "Ellis is manipulative and cold and unrelenting. She formed the rebels solely for the purpose of killing thousands of people, and she won't stop until she gets what she wants. The Council are a bunch of fools to believe she could actually want peace when her goal is to wipe out the sectors altogether."

"You talk like you know her well."

I flinch and brush past him.

I must've hit it right on the mark. He almost follows after me, and I don't know what I would've done if he had, but a soldier coming from the opposite direction hails him. I make sure I'm long gone before they finish.

22
JAY

MENDEL IS ALREADY in our room by the time I return from the training hall. I'd considered going after Lai following our meeting with Austin, but she was so upset and appeared so very *not* willing to talk with anyone that I decided to let her be for a while. Besides, I needed to vent out my own frustration at the situation first.

My roommate is at his desk. His presence on my grid appears neutral, focused, although there's an undercurrent of anxiety. Understandably. He's sketching away at something, as he typically does when he's not in the woodshop. The soft scratching of lead against paper fills the space. Eraser shavings coat his desk, and I wonder how he can stand to not brush them away.

"We haven't talked lately," I say after we exchange greetings. He shrugs in that way that means he may or may not have even heard me. "What did you and Lai talk about after the meeting with Austin?" I was only able to catch the tail end of their conversation before Lai fled, and I wonder whether their talk had something to do with how upset she was.

Mendel spins around in his seat to point his pencil at me accusingly. "Since when did you start calling the lieutenant *Lai*?"

Oh. Right. "Since she asked me to," I say, well aware that that's stretching the truth since she asked me an extended period of time ago and I've only just recently acquiesced.

He shakes his head and resumes his work.

"So?" I ask. "What did you and Lai talk about?"

"Nothing important."

There's no itch behind my eyes to say he's outright lying, but the tone of his voice says his words aren't entirely true, either.

Okay, so being straightforward isn't going to work. I need to go about this more delicately.

I peer over his shoulder to get a glimpse of what he's sketching. The drawings are disorderly and overlap, layered in different-colored pens, but it appears to be a design for . . . a box? I've never seen him draw anything save furniture or buildings before. The design is intricate, with tiny detailed patterns and twisting curves.

"Hey, can you not breathe down my neck?" Mendel asks. He slams his sketchbook shut and glares at me, his presence flashing an irritated pink, but I'm not certain why. It's not as though this is the first time I've looked over his shoulder to see his drawings.

"Your work is amazing," I say. "You like designing, right? It's my first time seeing you work on something other than furniture."

"It doesn't hurt to broaden your skill set," Mendel says, though not with hostility. I choose to take that as a good sign.

"What's the box for?" I ask. He stiffens, and I wonder whether it was a bad idea to ask. I had assumed he'd say it was merely for fun, as with all the furniture he previously made with no special purpose. I suppose this one is different. "Sorry, you don't have to answer."

"No, it's fine," Mendel says. "I . . . happened to talk with another officer earlier. An Etiole." He pauses. "I've been trying to pawn off some of this furniture on the other soldiers, and she came to pick up a chair today. We started talking, and eventually we got to the topic of the potential war with the rebels. She told me she thought about dying a lot when she's standing on the battlefield. When she asked if I did, I said no. I didn't. What about you?"

I recall the many times over the past four years that I've been preparing for a mission. It wasn't generally death that hovered over my mind, but whether or not we could execute our given job properly. My teammates now are strong enough that there's no need for me to worry about them, and I'm not generally involved in close combat myself. The few times I have been, it was typically against small numbers, with someone fighting beside me and not enough time to consider it. The last mission was an exception.

"I suppose not." It likely doesn't help that I never became overly involved with anyone at Eastern, nor was I ever part of a team prior to this, so if someone died, it was sad, but not a personal loss. I wonder whether I would feel the same now, to lose any of my teammates. I shudder. "What does that have to do with the box?"

"She said it'd be nice to have something to leave behind for the people she cares about after she's gone," Mendel says. "Something for them to remember her by. And I thought it sounded kind of poetic. I decided to make this box with that in mind, but . . ." He trails off. I haven't the faintest idea what he's thinking.

He doesn't appear willing to pursue that line of conversation, so I say, "Lai is fully convinced Ellis will ambush and kill us."

Mendel snorts, but at least he appears engaged in our conversation once more. "Not that she'll explain why. I swear, she needs to be less secretive."

"Is that why you followed her out of Austin's office?" Come to think of it, it's strange how regularly he confronts her directly, without appearing to care about her distractedness getting in the way. Actually, he confronts her a lot more than seems normal. Almost as though he's aware of just how in-the-know she is.

"More or less," Mendel says. "Did you talk to her, too?"

"I'm planning on it." I decide to go a little further. "She can be hard to talk to sometimes, though. I wonder if she's even aware of what's going on around her half the time."

"If only you knew," Mendel mutters.

"What do you mean?"

"Nothing. She can just be weird is all."

"Why are you lying?"

He stiffens. "What?"

"Just now. Why did you lie?"

"I didn't lie."

"Mendel. You can't lie to me without my knowing, although I appreciate the effort. I'm aware you know something about Lai that you're not telling me. Seeing as how we're heading to our possible deaths in a handful of days, I'd be happy if you could be open with me. Or at least not insult me by trying to convince me of a lie."

Mendel's eyes narrow as he watches me. His presence pulls in on itself. "I don't see why I have to do anything you say. You can be our leader or whatever else you like, but outside of military operations, I don't answer to you."

"I'm not saying you have to," I say calmly. "I'm merely asking you not to look down on me by telling me things we both know aren't true. I doubt you'd be happy about it if our positions were reversed."

He pauses. For someone who gets annoyed at even the smallest of things, he must know what I said is true. "Fine. Fair enough."

"So how is it that you're always able to talk to Lai normally?" I ask. Being direct really won't work. In that case, I'll make it appear as though I'm asking for his help. It'll make him feel above me, and he'll be much more likely to talk than if he feels as though I'm demanding answers from him. "She seems to stay on topic much more often when she talks with you. What's your secret?"

His irritation still remains, but sure enough, his presence swells. His voice, however, is careful. Careful not to lie. "It just took some talking out between the two of us."

"Really? What kind of conversation was that?"

He hesitates. "Well, we had it while playing cards, so I guess you could say it was pretty relaxed."

"Another lie?" I ask mildly.

Mendel scowls. I wouldn't have anticipated he was this bad at getting out of things without resorting to lying. "*Fine*," he says. "We made a deal, and it was obvious she could pay attention when she wanted to."

"A deal?" That wasn't what I was expecting. That wasn't what I was prepared to hear. I had only been trying to see how much he knew about Lai and maybe get a hint as to what had upset her so much following our meeting with Austin. "What kind of deal?"

However, Mendel has realized his mistake. He's watching me with once more narrowed eyes, more cautiously than he's ever looked at me. "Did you do that on purpose?"

"What kind of deal, Mendel?" I ask. "How much has Lai told you?"

"How much she's told me?" Mendel repeats. "How much has she told *you*?"

This conversation is going in circles. "Tell me about your deal. Tell me what you know and I'll tell you what I know." So long as it isn't something Lai hasn't yet told him.

Mendel examines me carefully one last time. Then he tips back in his chair and hooks his feet under his desk to steady himself. "I lost all my memories from before four and a half months ago. Cathwell promised to help me get them back in return for me cooperating with the team. That was our deal."

I examine him closely, but he doesn't appear as though he cares in the least about what he just said. My gift didn't detect any lies, so he's undeniably telling the truth—but how can he be so nonchalant about saying he doesn't remember who he is? He doesn't even appear bothered that I now know, although when I check his presence, it beats an irregular pattern born of nervousness.

How did he come to join the military? I'm not able to imagine them taking in someone who has absolutely no recollection of who they are. Not to mention, Mendel already has a relatively disagreeable personality as it is. Why would he even agree to join? There are so many things I want to ask, but I've already pushed much further than I meant to.

At least now I know why Mendel began complying with whatever

I said on our second mission. What about Johann? Did Lai make a deal with him, too? Much as I try, it's difficult to imagine the sergeant major being persuaded into anything.

"I'm sorry about your memories," I say quietly. "I didn't know."

He waves me off. "You weren't supposed to."

"Then why tell me? You didn't have to answer my question."

He appears to consider his words before answering. "Earlier, you used your gift to gauge my emotions and push me into telling the truth out of irritation, didn't you?"

I don't answer.

He laughs, once, short. "You're better than I thought. Or worse. So? What do you know about Cathwell?"

"I know she's the type of person to do whatever she feels she needs to in order to accomplish her goals," I say, thinking of the Order and her time in prison. That seems a safe thing to admit to. "I know she cares a lot about establishing peace between the gifted and ungifted."

At that, Mendel laughs once more, this time with venom. "*Peace?* Cathwell? The only thing she cares about is running around manipulating people into doing what she wants."

"Isn't that a little extreme?" It seems a huge, unfair statement to make when Lai isn't even here to defend herself.

"You just don't know her well enough yet," Mendel says with hard eyes. "I don't know if she's told you about her gift, but she's been using it to dig around into our personal lives to find something to hold over us. I have a feeling she did the same to Johann. If she hasn't done it to you, it's only because you're already playing the role she wants you to just fine. You can't trust her."

I want to object. I want to say he's mistaken, and that he only thinks that way because Lai needed his help and offered him a deal in which he'd benefit more than if he refused. That he didn't have to accept, and he could've done whatever he desired, no matter what Lai said.

However, I recall just how many secrets she's been keeping and still keeps; how she pretended to commit a crime to leave the military, how she's been hiding the Order and its information all this time, how she's been pulling strings behind the scenes for over a month now. If I hadn't spoken with Mendel, I wouldn't have even been aware of that last fact.

But more than feeling suspicious, I feel hurt. Lai's been going behind my back all this time, manipulating our teammates? And she told Mendel about her gift. She trusted him with her secret before she trusted me. Mendel, who she's always at odds with, who blatantly doesn't care about anything. Does Johann know, too? He and Lai are so close. Did she only tell me so that everyone on the team would finally know?

I'd thought that moment in the music hall was a moment of truth, of openness. But now I wonder whether it was anything at all.

I discover I'm unable to say anything in response.

I hear Lai before I see her. She's playing a piece I barely forget the name of, one of those that I'd feel silly not remembering once someone told me the title. It's slow, dark, and low, picking up in pace and intensity as she enters a thundering crescendo. I watch her back from the doorway; I know she's aware of my presence, so I wait.

Her shoulders curve and straighten as her hands glide deftly over the keys to punch them flat. It's a piece she appears to be quite familiar with, because she doesn't falter when she transitions into the faster-paced section. She sways with the music.

When the piece finally comes to a close on a low, prolonged note that balances in the air between us like a shield, even though her posture doesn't slump, something about her does. For once, I don't check my grid to see how she's feeling. I don't want to.

"I see you've been talking with Mendel." Her words shatter the spell and displace that last, firm note that was ringing in my ears. She doesn't turn around to face me.

Of all the things swirling in my head, I'm not certain which I want to say most. I settle on, "Why?"

"You'll need to be more specific. I have different reasons for different things I've done."

"Why did you essentially blackmail Mendel into working with the team? Did you do the same to Johann, too?"

She shakes her head, still not looking at me. "I didn't blackmail Mendel. I made him a deal and he took it. It helped everyone involved, so I don't see how it's a bad thing." She hesitates. "I *may* have actually blackmailed Johann in the beginning, but things have changed. Johann is working with the team willingly now."

"Ignoring the fact that you actually *blackmailed* one of our teammates, if you didn't think the deal was so bad, then why didn't you tell me about it?"

"Come on, Jay, how could I have told you that?" Lai asks, and now, finally, she turns around on the bench to face me. "What was I supposed to say? 'Oh, hey, by the way, I pulled some strings and got the others to work with the team, so you don't have to worry about that anymore.' Yeah, that would've gone *great*."

"You shouldn't have been messing around with people like that to begin with," I snap. The words come out more strongly than I meant them to, but I don't pull back. "You shouldn't have gone behind my back and—that isn't how a team works. Everyone has to *want* to work together. You can't just manipulate everyone into doing what you want them to."

Her eyes flash and she stands. "Maybe in a perfect world, Jay, but we're on the verge of a war, in case you hadn't noticed. We didn't have time to wait around until everyone *wanted* to get along with each other—if ever that happened. I gave them a reason to want to make the team a success, and guess what? *It. Worked.*"

"It shouldn't have been through manipulation and secrets. How is there supposed to be trust in our team like that?"

We glare at each other for long heartbeats, neither of us backing down. But I already know Lai is stubborn. I can't make her see something as wrong if she doesn't think it is.

"I'm not saying what I did was morally right," Lai says. "I'm just saying it needed doing." She turns her back to me once more. "Not everything good in life can be accomplished by honest methods."

"The end justifies the means," I say. "That's really what you believe?"

She doesn't answer.

I had thought, before, that Lai's willingness to do whatever it took to accomplish her goals was an admirable thing. I liked that about her. However, now, hearing some of the ways in which she's set out to accomplish what she wants, I wonder. I wonder what other under-handed things she's done that I'm not aware of. I wonder if Mendel was right when he said she can't be trusted.

I sit next to her on the bench.

"Lai, why are you so on edge about Ellis?" I ask.

"Who isn't?"

"I meant, why are you so *personally* on edge? As soon as you saw that envelope from the rebels' leader, your anger was instant and incredible. Why?"

Her fingers glide over the keys, expression distant. "Can we not talk about this?"

"That depends. Do you know something you're not telling us that could hurt the team?"

Her eyes flash to me. "You think I would intentionally put the team at risk?"

"I think you have a lot of secrets you're not telling us. And that's fine; you have every right to withhold whatever personal information you choose. Unless it puts the rest of us in danger."

She doesn't say anything.

"Our odds of coming out of this meeting alive are already bad," I say quietly. "I don't want to walk in blind if there's a way to be better prepared beforehand. If there's something you know that could help us . . ."

Lai doesn't answer for a long time. Her hands, for once, are still in her lap. Her focus appears a million miles away, though not in her typical distracted sense. Her presence is withdrawn, subdued.

I've just about given up on receiving a reply from her when she says, "Sara Ellis left the military two and a half years ago. Two years ago, she formed the rebels. Ever since then, she's been using her gift of shadow manipulation to communicate with me and try to convince me to join her—or even just to taunt me." She won't meet my eyes.

"That's why Devin tried to take me with him on our last mission. And the rebel with ice powers on the mission before that. Ellis's gift is pretty intricate. And dangerous. I'll explain it to everyone in detail once we're all together."

I don't know how to answer. The way Lai spoke of Sara before, the possibility that she had gone to the rebels *had* crossed my mind. However, I was hoping for something different. I certainly hadn't anticipated that she'd gone on to found and lead the rebels.

I nearly say I'm sorry. But that isn't right. "Thank you," I say. "Knowing the details of the rebels' leader's gift will help us tremendously. We can go in with a better plan of attack."

She says nothing in response, and I'm not certain where to go from here. No wonder she was so angry when she saw Ellis's letter. No wonder she didn't want to talk about it. No wonder she's so anxious about this meeting. Will it be the first time they've met since Ellis left the military? What kind of communication have they had in the last few years? Will Lai be able to properly fight against someone she was once so close with?

I don't want to pursue the topic, but nor do I want to leave like this—especially not when we'll be heading out to meet the rebels so soon. Was it really only just a few days ago we sat in this same spot unable to stop laughing?

"Do you want to practice together?" I ask. "I mean, I don't know about you, but I could really use it."

She looks at me out of the corners of her eyes and offers a slight smile. "Don't lie to me, Jay. You know I need the practice as much as you do."

23
LAI

AL STANDS BESIDE me as we wait for Jay and Mendel in one of the many open spaces in the training hall.

My talk with Jay last night weighs heavy on my mind. When he honestly wondered if I could be trusted, it cut me more than I expected. More than it should've. Who cares whether or not he trusts me? Maybe he shouldn't. And why should I care anyway?

And yet, I do.

When Jay and Mendel arrive, we all stretch together. I take the chance of everyone being half distracted to say, "Before Ellis founded the rebels, she was an officer in the military. Her gift is shadow manipulation. She can observe anything or anyone touching a shadow that connects back to her own. She can also communicate through shadows by turning them into butterflies, or have those butterflies hide in someone's shadow and keep watch over them. But the last one can only be done with the person's permission. And it takes a lot of effort, but she can travel through connecting shadows, too. The farther the distance, the harder it becomes for her."

Everyone listens silently. Surprisingly, no one questions how I know so much about her gift, or what my connection to her is. Not out loud, anyway.

That will be a difficult gift to deal with. I'll have to take it into account when I make our plan.

So that's why she was so mad yesterday when she saw that letter. For her to know that much, they *have* to know each other.

What's this all of a sudden? I won't complain about more info but why didn't she say something sooner?

No one comments as we continue stretching, and honestly, I'm glad. It's bad enough having to think about my reunion with Ellis without having to answer a bunch of personal questions about my relationship with her, too.

But mostly, I feel relieved to have warned everyone. I don't want to talk about my past with Ellis. I don't want to cast even more suspicion on myself than I already have. But as soon as Austin told us about that meeting, guilt born from my silence settled in my lungs. It's not like the military doesn't know about Ellis's gift. It isn't as if the others couldn't have found out the details of it from the new files we were given earlier this morning that included intel on some of the rebel members. But my personal involvement with her made me feel responsible for telling them. And now that I have, a small weight I didn't even know existed has gone from my shoulders.

Once we've finished, Jay says, "Okay, let's start. We'll begin with a two-on-two, no gifts, since we're still not used to coordinating with one another yet."

If anyone has been more on edge than me in the past twenty-four hours, it's Jay. His eyes are somewhat bloodshot, and he's developed a habit of tapping his heel when he's been standing in one place for too long. It's mostly to due to his stress over the rebel "meeting," but it's got a lot to do with Mendel and me as well.

"Why no gifts?" Mendel asks. He shoves his hands in his pockets. "It's not like we won't be able to use them at the meeting."

"I wouldn't be so sure about that," Jay says. He taps his heel. "None of our gifts worked on Devin. And who knows how many others have a power crystal with the same neutralization gift? Besides, what if you reach the limit of your gift in the middle of a battle? Are you going to push yourself until you have a fallout, or are you going to fight?"

When Nytes overuse their gifts, it takes a toll on their bodies and puts them in a state of extreme exhaustion. We can barely move, let alone defend ourselves. We try to avoid getting to that point since it would practically spell our death—whether through the fallout killing us or someone attacking us.

Mendel doesn't seem to have anything to say to Jay's points, so he drops his hands to his sides and waits for the major to go on.

"I know we all have our differences," Jay says. He doesn't look at me, but his thoughts are on his conversations with both Mendel and me last night. "But we're setting out in a matter of days. If we really are walking straight into a trap, then we *need* to be able to work as a team if we want to make it out alive."

No one objects—probably because we're all thinking the same thing. Even Mendel seems to take Jay's words to heart, rare as that is.

Jay thinks, hand over mouth, before saying, "Hand-to-hand, first person to hit the ground loses for their team. Lai and me against

Mendel and Johann." He looks up at Al's stuttered beginning of a protest. "You two need the most work in coordinating with each other. You work well together in the actual heat of battle, but you never stop fighting outside of missions. You need to be able to work together at all times, not only when our lives depend on it."

Now Al is the one who can't argue against him.

I have to hold back a laugh. Mendel's respect for Al has gone up a little since she didn't push about his past, and she's picked up on that from the more tempered way he's been speaking to her. They've graduated from spitting fire at each other to tolerating each other, but that's about as far as they've gotten. A little challenge like this will do them good.

I pat Al on the shoulder on my way to Jay. I'm given a scowl in return.

As Mendel makes his way to Al's side, I overhear him say, "Look, I know we're not exactly the best of friends, but I really, *really* don't want to lose. Especially not to Cathwell."

Lai? Why her especially? Even if she is a little distracted, no one would blame him if he lost against her. She's strong. "I never go into a fight intending to lose," Al says. "Just try to keep up."

Al's inward praise of me makes me unexpectedly thrilled. I have to push down the feeling as Jay smiles at me, and then I hesitate. Are we okay after last night?

But there's no lingering anger or frustration in Jay's thoughts, nor in his voice when he asks, "You ready to go?"

"As ever," I say. It still hurts. Even though Jay seems back to normal, the sharp cut of that lapse in which he didn't believe in me stings. But I don't want him to know about that, and I definitely don't want to linger over it. It's easier to put it out of mind and act like nothing was ever wrong.

Jay turns back to the others. "Ready?"

By way of reply, Al stands with her feet shoulder-width apart, hands raised, and keeps one eye on Jay and the other on me. **I just need to watch, analyze, react.**

Mendel stands slightly behind her, less enthusiastic about the whole thing, but ready to put up a fight.

Jay and I are completely still. I catch Mendel take a step before freezing, probably hoping to attack first and then thinking better of it, but he's already moved. Jay shoots forward, and I follow close behind. Al moves to block him.

Mendel had the same idea. He and Al slam into each other, and only barely recover their balance in enough time to defend themselves. But now we've cut them off from each other. Jay and I are back to back, with Mendel facing Jay and me facing Al.

I wait and watch out of the corner of my eye as Jay lashes out at Mendel, who ducks and misses the punch. He catches Jay's knee with one foot and yanks upward to try to catch him off balance. But I step back to support Jay's weight, so that he falls against me and uses me to spring a kick on Mendel.

At the same time, Al charges at me, knowing she needs to get me away from Jay, but I easily deflect her punch with a firm guiding hand. I don't let her go around to help Mendel, either. No matter how she tries to sidestep past me, I'm there to block her.

The thud of someone hitting the ground tells me we've won even before I see Mendel on the floor.

I grin and exchange a high five with Jay. He returns the gesture with some surprise, like he's never done it before. He probably never has. I make a mental note to do it more often with him in the future.

"You let yourselves get divided too easily," Jay says with a glance between Al and Mendel. "After that, it was only a matter of time."

Al wants to blame Mendel for not trusting her to take care of Jay's attack, but she knows that's wrong. Jay was aiming for Mendel. Of course he would move to defend himself. She should've gone for me and tried to separate me from Jay, like we did them. Mendel's eyes meet hers and he's resisting the same urge to blame her for their failure. But surprisingly enough, he doesn't.

"Let's try again," Jay says.

We have another go. This time is hardly any better for Mendel and Al. The two of them put up a stronger front at first, but then Jay slips between them and I come around Al's back, and like Jay said, it's only a matter of time after that.

"Don't let us through," Jay says. He offers a hand to help Mendel up off the ground, and the corporal surprises me again by accepting his help.

What's gotten into him? His sudden decency is suspicious.

Not that it makes him fight any better. After his and Al's third failed match, and Mendel hits the floor yet again, Jay rubs his eyes. "Okay, let's try something else. Johann, Lai, you two work together against me and Mendel. Try to think of how your partner will move and act accordingly. You can't just fling yourself headfirst into a fight when you have someone else's back to watch as well as your own."

"You're focusing too much on victory," I say to Al. The corner of my mouth quirks into a smile as I switch to Gervaic. "*Focus on keeping us alive instead.*"

"*What do you mean?*" Al asks, also switching over.

I tilt my head. "*When we're in a real fight, you and your teammates' lives are more important than defeating the enemy. This is no different. Make sure you're always in a position to defend, and offense will come with it. Never leave your partner undefended. As soon as you do, you're just as vulnerable.*"

"*I don't need anyone watching my back to survive,*" Al says. "*I'm perfectly capable of looking after myself.*"

"*Perhaps when you're in a one-on-one situation,*" Jay says. I didn't know he was even paying attention to our conversation, let alone that he knew Gervaic. I should have expected it from the former heir of a company with business partners in multiple sectors. "*Once you're outnumbered, your back is wide open.*"

"In a language everyone can understand would be nice," Mendel says as he crosses his arms.

Al feels a little bad for him. Even though she enjoys being able to talk in Gervaic after so many years, she switches back to Efrain so he doesn't feel left out. "Realistically, if I was in a situation where I was outnumbered, I could just use my fire." She snaps her fingers and a tongue of flame hovers over them. "There wouldn't be any problem."

"What if you're close to a fallout?" Jay asks. "And there's still the matter of the Nyte who can cancel out others' gifts. If you come up against that person, or anyone who has their power crystal, you won't be able to use your flames."

Internally, Al grudgingly admits he has a point.

"We should get back to work," I say. "We're here to train, after all."

So Al and I take up our positions opposite Jay and Mendel. I don't move. Al knows from experience that I never strike first, but since Jay acts by the same philosophy, either she or Mendel will have to start. If Al goes in, she knows I'll have her back. But she also wants to stick to my don't-move-first policy.

After a long silence, Mendel charges, Jay falling in line behind him, and Al darts forward to block him. I follow close behind, as before with Jay, and when Al deflects Mendel's punch, I fly past her to intercept the major. Al shifts automatically so that her back is to me, like what Jay and I did in the first match, but Jay's already slipped past to stand beside Mendel.

Mendel isn't weak, but he's not a difficult opponent. Not for Al. It would've been easy for her to take him down if he were alone, but every time he messes up or Al is about to knock him down for good, Jay steps in. When Al beats Mendel back, Jay is right behind him. He uses Mendel's retreat as a chance to attack as well as a way to cover his partner. And when the major senses that he's in trouble, unlike Mendel, he has no problem backing away.

I linger at Al's back, waiting for a chance, making sure Jay and Mendel can't sneak up on us. Al must know I'm here, because she falls back somewhat to regroup.

This time, Jay leads the attack. He's faster than Mendel, though not much stronger physically. His blows are predictable, and while they push Al back, she's in no danger of being hit. Mendel darts from around Jay toward Al, but I bolt forward to kick his feet out from under him. He slams to the ground for the fourth time.

"Our win," I say.

"You didn't even do anything until the end," Al says with a frown.

"I didn't need to do anything until the end. Sometimes waiting for your chance is the best course of action."

Al rolls her eyes, but she doesn't object.

"Why am I the one who keeps getting knocked to the ground?" Mendel mutters as he stands and brushes himself off. "I'm not that weak, am I?"

"Surely not," I say, and am rewarded with a glare.

"You just need to be more patient," Jay says. He's clearly trying to hold back a smile. "You have to make sure your way is clear before you go for the attack. You knew Lai was waiting for an opening; you should've tried to draw her out, not gone straight for Johann."

Mendel seems to actually listen closely before nodding once. Even more to my surprise, he's the one who says, "Okay, let's try again."

24
LAI

BY THE TIME we finish training two hours later, we've each had mixed results of wins and losses. We all teamed up, and while I had a difficult time partnering with Mendel, it was a surprise for all of us that the worst pairing was Jay and Al. Neither of them could tell what the other was thinking or predict their partner's movements. I think the two of them were more surprised than anyone to discover that they couldn't work together effectively, although they did improve a lot during our practice. Even Mendel and I reached a fair enough level of teamwork.

"Okay, let's stop here for today," Jay says with a clap of his hands. He looks exhausted, probably because he's been leading the group and trying to give pointers even while he was working just as hard as the rest of us. He really is a good leader. "We'll have one more training session like this tomorrow afternoon. We need to work together as well as possible before we meet the rebels."

No one says anything out loud to his statement, but we're all thinking about it. About our chances of survival, and how all of us want to increase those odds. For possibly the first time since our team was formed, everyone really is on the same page. We all want the same thing and we're all willing to work together for it.

"That's all," Jay says. "Rest well and let me know if you need anything."

When Mendel and Al break off to talk, I turn to Jay. "You'd better rest up, too. You look like you didn't sleep at all last night."

"Who among us did?" Jay's eyes won't meet mine.

I slip my fingers through his and squeeze. "We'll make it through this somehow."

"Yeah. I just need time to sort everything out in my head." He lets go first.

"Well, if you have the time and mindset, the Order is having a smaller meeting tomorrow night. I'd love it if you could come."

"The night before we head out?"

"I've relayed the meeting with the rebels and its details to Fiona and the others already," I say. "But I need to be there to help sort things out. Just in case . . . well, you know."

The lines around his eyes tighten. "Yeah. Yeah. Unless something comes up, I'll go. I did say I'd attend the meetings, after all." **And I want to see more of what the Order is about.**

I smile. I'm glad he's taking the Order seriously, even if he does still feel a little unsure about the whole thing. "All right. Do you want to play piano together tonight?" Maybe it would help him relax a bit.

He gives me a tired smile, but a genuine one. "Yeah, that sounds nice. I'll meet you in the music hall, okay?"

"All right."

He kisses me gently on the forehead when Al and Mendel aren't looking, and then heads out with a wave over his shoulder.

Once Al also leaves, I catch up to Mendel before he can disappear.

He looks skeptical at my wanting to talk to him, but doesn't say anything. He really has been odd today.

"So I heard you and Jay talked," I say.

"Did you *hear* that, or did you snoop around our heads and find out about it?"

"A bit of both. Enough of the latter to see that you made the mistake of confusing Jay's kindness for weakness."

He grimaces. "If that's all you wanted to say, I'm leaving."

"Actually, I wanted to talk to you about the matter we discussed before."

What is she talking about?

"You don't have a very good memory, do you?"

"Shut it," he says. **It must be about my memories, then.**

I grin. "Now that's more like it. You've been so weirdly polite today I'd started to think you actually believed your own act."

"You gonna tell me what this is about or not?" he asks. He acts irritated, and even his thoughts are irritated, but secretly, he finds my blatant disregard for his attempts at politeness relieving. He's been trying to be nicer to everyone to try to become closer to us—of his own volition—but it's a lot for him. He'd never admit it, but he likes the fact that I prefer his unaffected self.

"Tomorrow morning, we're going on a little trip," I say. "Meet me at the front gates at six."

* * *

I'm much less enthusiastic about the next conversation I need to have. It was something I'd been thinking about even before the rebels wanted this "peace meeting," but now, it's become necessary.

Al is in our room, having just finished taking a shower after our joint training session. She looks up as I walk in and grins. "Hey, nice work today. I think our pair had the most wins in the end."

I try to smile back and fail. Words aren't coming, and in the pause, Al realizes something is wrong.

"Don't worry about the meeting," she says gently, incorrectly guessing the cause of my anxiety and making me feel even worse. "We're the strongest there is. We'll be all right."

I shake my head. "Thank you, Al, but that's not what I'm worried about." Another pause. "We need to talk."

Al frowns as she plops down on the edge of her bed. **Did something happen? She looks really upset.** "All right, shoot."

My fingers tap against my leg. I walk to Al's bed and sit beside her. Wait, maybe I should've sat on my own bed to put some distance between us. If she tries to hit me, can I dodge in time? Should I even try? I'd probably deserve it.

"You of all people being this quiet is weird," Al says. **Well, weirder than usual.** "What is it already?"

"I'm a telepath," I say, because I have no other way to say it. "It's—that's my gift."

Al is very still and very quiet beside me. I can't find it in me to look at her head-on, so I keep my gaze on my feet. The practical part of me says I should read Al's mind to know what she's thinking, and so that I can maybe come up with some good lines of defense beforehand. But I'm too scared.

270

"I can hear others' thoughts and put my own thoughts in other people's heads—mostly to pass on messages," I go on. Her silence is unnerving, and I find it makes me unable to shut up. "I might have to use it on our next mission to talk with everyone secretly—so the rebels don't overhear our plans or anything. I just wanted to warn you ahead of time. I mean, I should've told you before now, but I just . . ."

"Is that how you knew I was a girl?" Al asks quietly.

I don't know how to answer. "I just wanted the team to work."

"So you used your gift to *blackmail* me?" Al demands. She's standing now. Her hands are balled into fists at her sides, and for a moment, flames flicker around them. They're not nearly as frightening as the fire in her eyes, though. "You looked into my head, found my weakness—my most important secret—and used that to manipulate me? When else did you take what I was thinking and use that to your advantage? Have you—has anything about you been honest all this time?"

All at once, the anger in her voice gives way to hurt, and that at last pushes me to read her thoughts. She thinks of how we talked about our pasts after our first spar together, all the times we joked around and hung out, how she trusted me with things she'd never told anyone. The first person she'd confided in since her brother killed their parents.

Her thoughts, now laced with betrayal, rip at my chest. I pull back from her mind and force myself to meet her eyes. It's hard. I don't want to. I'm scared of losing my friend.

"I'm sorry," I whisper. "I know I used your thoughts against you, and I'm so sorry. I never meant to hurt you. I've never lied to you, and you're still one of my important friends, and I—I never knew when I should tell you about my gift. I was afraid you'd hate me once you knew, and then time passed, and it just got harder and harder."

"Am I supposed to feel *sorry* for you?" Al asks. "Sorry for the girl who threatened me into doing what she wanted, who's known whatever thought crossed my mind and never even told me about it?"

"I'm not asking you to feel sorry for me. I just wanted you to understand why I didn't tell you sooner."

"Because you're a coward."

"What was I supposed to do?" I ask, standing up myself now. My hurt makes way for an anger I've pent up for so long I nearly forgot it existed. "Am I just supposed to tell every person I meet that I know everything they're thinking as soon as I meet them? Am I supposed to push people away before I even have a chance to earn their trust? Or at what point is it acceptable to tell someone I've been in their head the whole time without hurting them?"

"Maybe they wouldn't be so hurt if you didn't use what you heard against them," Al says. Her voice is nearly a shout. "*Maybe*, if you cared a little more about the secrets you heard that weren't yours to know, people wouldn't feel so betrayed!"

"Oh, so it was fine when you thought I knew you were a girl by sight alone, but as soon as you find out it was because of my gift, it's a problem?"

"It was always a problem! But it was a more acceptable one when you knew on accident instead of intentionally going through my head looking for something to hold over me."

"As if you never use your gift to your advantage! You never hesitate before using your flames. I'm sorry mine is more *personal* than useful on the battlefield—"

"That's not the point!"

"Then what *is* the point?"

"That the person I thought was my friend has been stabbing me in the back this whole time!" Al is breathing hard. She rubs the heels of her palms over her eyes. I almost think she's crying, but when she lowers her hands, she just looks tired. "Can you get out? I want to be alone."

I almost say no. I almost say let's talk this out. But then, just behind Al, I catch sight of a single black butterfly. Why now, of all times?

And all at once, everything is too much. The fight with Al, with Jay, the rebels, Ellis. I don't want to deal with any of it. I'm *tired* of dealing with all of it. I can't.

I don't say anything as I walk out the door.

25
LAI

ALL THROUGH PLAYING piano with Jay, I can't stop thinking about my argument with Al. Jay notices my distraction, but says nothing. His mind is on our fight from the previous night, and I can't help but feel that all I ever do is make things worse for the people around me. It would've been better if I'd never told anyone anything.

Al is pretending to be asleep when I get back. I don't call her bluff.

The next morning, I'm ready and out the door before she wakes up.

The halls are already busy with soldiers starting their day. My gift wanders through everyone's thoughts, but for the most part, there's nothing of particular interest. Only worries about the upcoming meeting with the rebels.

But just as I'm about to reach Central's front entrance, I latch on to some *very* interesting thoughts.

Why'd the Councilors even want us to bring this stuff all the way out there?

Could've at least told us what it was for.

Ugh and I thought I was getting a promotion when they summoned us.

I search for the people the thoughts belong to, but with all the soldiers around, and my inability to track thoughts to a precise location, it's impossible. But as generally useless as those thoughts alone were, I recognized the place they were thinking about—the place they're headed to transport whatever it is they're carrying.

I try to focus in on the thoughts, but they're already fading as they move farther away, and it's not long until they've disappeared altogether.

Okay. Okay. So the Council has some soldiers running secretive errands. Could it be related to their experiments? I don't know what they're transporting, but I do know where they're headed. It could be the first hint I've managed to find since overhearing those Councilors' conversation so long ago. I can use this. But for now, I continue on my way.

As expected, Mendel is already waiting at the gates when I get there ten minutes early. He looks up as I walk toward him, but before he can say anything, I hold a finger to my lips. I jerk my head for him to follow me out of Central's grounds and into the streets. They're fairly busy for this time of morning as everyone heads out to work or to run errands. Without our uniforms, and once we're far enough away from Central, we don't attract too much attention. We're less obviously Nytes once it's not readily apparent we're with the military.

Still, I don't take any chances. We take a few back-alley detours and pass through some less savory districts before we finally reach our destination: a small, weathered shrine tucked into a corner of the lakeshore.

The building is round and simple, a rare thing for a shrine. The white stone walls are worn but solid. A wooden door sits somewhat crookedly in its frame, but well-kept flowers bloom along the path leading up to it and along the windows' ledges. It's obviously well cared for, even if it is near on ancient.

I don't know which god it's supposed to be dedicated to, only that the sole shrine maiden charged with watching over it is a member of the Order who's said we're free to use the shrine whenever we wish—so long as we don't do anything unholy there or damage it or insult the god it's dedicated to in any way.

I'm not really sure what actions count as unholy or offensive, but hopefully trying to get a Nyte's memories back through the help of another Nyte's gift doesn't qualify as either.

"A shrine?" Mendel asks skeptically.

"We're going inside."

"We're wha—hey, wait!"

Despite his doubts, he follows me. Not that I gave him much choice.

The inside is as bare as you would expect from seeing the outside. A plain offering box sits at the back of the room underneath a small, high window, but other than that and the other windows placed at intervals throughout the single circular room, there's nothing.

Well, nothing but Peter Wood, who's standing and staring at the light streaming in from the window. It gives him a look of consideration and thoughtfulness rarely displayed by this twin. He blinks and looks up at the sound of our footsteps like he's coming out of a trance. "Yo. You made it."

I wave in greeting, then gesture to Mendel. "This is Erik Mendel, the one I told you about last time. Mendel, this is Peter, the one whose power crystal we tried to use. He's agreed to assist with trying to get your memories back."

"Thanks for all your help," Mendel says cautiously.

The last traces of whatever Peter had been thinking about so deeply before disappear as he dons his trademark grin. "No problem. If it's for a friend of Lai's, I'm happy to do what I can."

Mendel's thoughts stir uneasily at the mention of being a friend of mine, but I just say, "Thanks, Peter. I owe you one."

He waves my words away. "Don't mention it. You've saved my skin dozens of times before." He stretches his arms out before him, flexing his fingers like one might before exercising. "You ready to go?"

"How does it work?" Mendel asks. His eyes are narrowed, but at least he isn't showing as much suspicion as before. "Is it the same as your power crystal?"

"Pretty much," Peter says. His usual excitement is back, though I'm not sure now is exactly the time or place for it. His enthusiasm is making Mendel uneasy. "We have physical contact, I ask a question, and then we'll both see the parts of your past that answer that question. At least, that's how it usually goes. Forehead's best since that's where the memories are and all."

"Of course." I can tell Mendel is fighting the urge to back away from Peter. "Obviously."

"We'll start with something simple, like how you lost your memories," Peter goes on. He flexes his hands again and puts one palm over Mendel's forehead. Mendel tenses, but if Peter notices, he doesn't give any sign of it. "Once we see the memories that answer that question, we'll go from there to choose the next one."

Mendel looks to me, and I give what I hope is a reassuring nod. I never know how he'll interpret any gesture I show him.

Peter doesn't give any warning before he uses his gift, but since I'm in Mendel's head, I see the effects of it. His thoughts whir in and out of cinematic strips of events and people and places from memories before Central, filled through with black holes as if someone had taken scissors to the images and cut out the main parts. There are no faces, no sounds, no distinctive features to any of the rooms or buildings or streets I see except for the fact that they're all either dark or dimly lit.

As soon as it started, it stops. Peter frowns and slowly pulls his hand back.

"What was that?" Mendel asks.

"A bunch of holes," Peter says.

"Is that . . . normal?"

Mendel glances to me, but I'm watching Peter. The two of us communicate through looks about what just happened.

Mendel is being quite distracting, though. **It must be nice to constantly know what's going on.**

"It's like someone deliberately messed up your memories," Peter finally says. "Axed the important stuff and left a bunch of useless info behind."

Mendel's usual guarded expression melts into one of pure panic, and it takes long, scrambled seconds for him to regain it. "Does that mean I can never get them back? If it was a Nyte who erased them—"

"No," I say. I'm still watching Peter. What he saw and what I saw from inside Mendel's thoughts are the same, but I got a different read from them than either of them did. Mendel has no experience with the feel of thoughts or memories, and Peter isn't used to pin-pointing incongruities within them. "I don't think they've been erased. Just blocked. From the looks of it, they wanted you to remember again at some point."

"So you think a Nyte did this?" Mendel asks.

I nod, once. "That kind of memory damage isn't accidental."

He'd never considered the possibility that someone might have intentionally messed with his memories. He'd always assumed it was because of a blow to the head, since he was already injured pretty badly when he first woke up in Central's care.

But why? Why would someone cut off all his memories from him? Did he see or hear something he shouldn't have? Not that I would wish Mendel dead, but it would've been safer to kill him had that been the case. Unless his death would've been more suspicious than his loss of memory. No, then why would they take out everything he remembers and not just the thing he wasn't supposed to know about? More than being surprised that someone intentionally did this to him, I can't fathom why they would have.

"I'll have to come up with something else." I sigh. "This is prov-ing harder than I expected."

"Do you *have* anything else?" Mendel asks. "How do you get around the work of a Nyte's gift?"

"I'll come up with something." My eyes slide to the ceiling. "I always do."

"If Lai says she'll get something done, you don't have anything to worry about," Peter says. He gives Mendel a grin that the corporal doesn't even try to return.

"Thanks," he says.

"Buck up, we'll get there!" Peter gives Mendel a solid thump on the back that just seems to make him more depressed. "We're already a step further than we were five minutes ago."

"One step forward, two steps back," Mendel mutters, but if Peter heard the words, he chooses to ignore them.

"Sorry to leave so soon, but I've gotta be heading back," Peter says. "Busy times these days."

The reminder of everything that needs doing in the Order before our meeting with the rebels tomorrow forces me out of my thoughts. "Thanks for taking the time to come out and help, Peter. I really appreciate it."

"Anytime," Peters says. "You just let me know if there's anything else I can do."

"Will do."

When he's gone, it's just me and Mendel alone with our thoughts in a place that might or might not have a god condemning us as we sit in its place of worship.

For once, I don't lean in to hear Mendel's thoughts. So I have no idea what he's thinking or why he says it when the words come out of his mouth. "Hey, Cathwell. You think we could ever be friends?"

"Us?" I ask in surprise. "Highly doubtful."

I don't realize how harsh the words are until Mendel doesn't say anything for a long time.

Shit. That was uncalled for. I don't know why I'm so scathing whenever Mendel is involved. Or maybe it's a by-product of my recent fights with Jay and Al. If I can't even get along with them, I don't know how I could ever make a friendship with Mendel work.

"Yeah, you're probably right," he finally says. He looks up at the ceiling with blank eyes. "You know, I thought I couldn't stand you because you're so damn secretive. Always manipulating and fooling everyone, like it's all some game to you. But then I realized it was because you remind me too much of myself. And I thought, if that's the way it is for me, it's probably the same for you, too, isn't it?"

I don't answer.

"We're not very good people, are we?" He laughs softly. "Maybe that's why we can't get along."

"Being not very good people isn't necessarily bad." I think of Jay comforting me in the cave that day, of how he must have been terrified himself but focused on calming me down. How he looked out for me when he thought I was out of practice and even after he found out I wasn't. I think of Al, always honest, always blunt, and always believing that what she did was right, that she was fighting for justice and the innocent.

And I think of my own actions these past few years. How I've been sneaking off to the Order, how I've been deceiving so many people for so long that I don't feel even a shred of guilt about it anymore. What the Order has managed to become because of my choices.

"Very good people can't always do what needs to be done," I say. "The world needs people like us to get those things done and set everything straight."

"Is that what you tell yourself to help you sleep at night?" He shakes his head. "I can't tell if you're trying to cheer me up or make yourself feel better."

"Why would I ever try to cheer you up? You're a Nyte. Suck it up."

He laughs. I think he might be as surprised by his reaction as I am. But when he shakes his head again, he's smiling. "I haven't said this yet, and don't count on me ever saying it again, but thanks. For everything. You've really helped me out a lot, Lai."

Despite myself, I smile, too. "Don't mention it, Erik."

26
LAI

I MEET UP with the core members of the Order in our usual room before the meeting with everyone else starts. I'm the last to arrive.

"You said you had an update on the Councilors' experiments?" Fiona asks as soon as I step through the door.

"Always one to skip the greetings, aren't you?" I ask.

"We're incredibly short on time, in case you'd forgotten."

"I hadn't, but thanks for the reminder." Before she can reply, I say, "This morning, I passed by some . . . interesting soldiers. They were delivering something for the Councilors, but didn't know why. I don't think they even knew what it was they were delivering. I couldn't get any details from them, but I *did* recognize the buildings I saw in their thoughts."

I make my way to one of the maps on the table and point to an area in the west of the sector. Fiona, Trist, Peter, Paul, and Syon all lean in to get a better look.

"Here," I say. "This is where those soldiers were headed. It's a grouping of old factories. I thought they were only used to make bycs and other transportation vehicles, but that might just be a ruse." I bite my lip. "It might not be related to the Council's experiments. Everything was pretty vague. But . . ."

Fiona and Trist share a glance. "We will send a team to investigate," Trist says, turning to me. "The sooner the better."

"Be careful," I say. "We don't know what's there, or what the Council is working on. And if they catch on that someone is prying, who knows what they might do."

Everyone nods.

"The meeting with everyone is starting soon," Paul says. "We'd better go."

The meeting tonight is a smaller managerial one, with only Fiona, Trist, the eight captains, the various Helpers, Jay, and a select handful of others. Walker is glaringly absent. A fact no one misses.

"Shouldn't our leader be here at a time like this?" someone asks.

"You know she'd be here if she could," someone else whispers.

"What is it she's always disappearing to take care of anyway? Is it really more important than being here when the rebels made such a big move?"

I listen to these mutterings and plenty of others while Fiona and Trist call our meeting to a start. My fingers tap against my arms. This close to war, Walker might have to start making more regular appearances.

We're in one of the larger conference rooms, but despite the abundance of chairs, no one sits. The tension is so heavy it's a wonder anyone can breathe. Jay, Peter, Paul, and I hang at the back of the room.

Jay glances at me. His thoughts are touched with nervousness, and he feels out of place among all these high-ranked members. He still wonders if he's betrayed the military by joining the Order. He worries that he'll ultimately end up failing us in some way.

But when he takes my hand in his, I can feel his fingers trembling. Not with fear, but excitement. After the last few days of simply waiting to be sent into a trap, he finally feels like he's able to do something here. Not just as a weapon of the military, but as a person.

Fiona's voice rings out over the assembly. She appears, as ever, cool and unconcerned. "As most of you already know from our emergency meeting a few days ago, the rebels have invited the military to a negotiations meeting. The military's envoy is departing tomorrow morning to meet them, two of our members among them."

A few glances back at Jay and me. Jay grips his elbow self-consciously, but everyone's attention soon returns to Fiona as she goes on. "In light of this, it seems necessary for us to make preparations for either war or peace."

"It is unlikely that the meeting is not a trap," Trist says, taking over. "So we will prepare first for war."

An outbreak of mutterings makes it difficult for him to go on. The captains, however, all stand in silence or else reprimand those near them for interrupting.

"Captains Peter and Paul, and the information division, will work with Lai tonight," Fiona says once the room has quieted down again. "Captain Jair, you'll be with me and Syon as we work with the defense team."

She goes on listing groups, but I send a thought to Jay. *The whole Order will need to be prepared to act if the rebels declare war. Any suggestions on the matter?*

Me? Jay thinks back. He looks surprised to hear my voice in his head, but I guess this is the first time I've talked with him this way. **Wait, I'm still not certain I understand. Why does the Order have to be prepared for war? This is a peace coalition, isn't it?**

Well, yes, but if there's war, we need to be prepared to defend ourselves and the people around us. For that, we have to take certain measures. You're a good strategist. What do you think takes top priority?

He considers. **There appear to be a lot of members who live in Regail Hall, so securing defense here is the most important thing. But this place is secret, isn't it? So that shouldn't be too much of a problem. How *do* you keep all this a secret, anyway?**

With great care, multiple entrances to not draw so much attention, and Nytes who can cover our tracks.

He doesn't ask for details about the Nytes. **Okay. So defense here shouldn't prove too difficult. I suppose next would be stocking up on supplies? Food, water, anything that might be needed in the event of a lockdown.**

Which sounds easy enough until you consider the fact that most of our members have no money and we're already low on food as it is.

Then why not make your own?

What?

I mean, this place is kind of like the underground farms, right? There must be an area in all these tunnels that would be suitable for growing crops. It would cost a bit to start out, but you wouldn't have to worry as much after that.

I stare at him. And stare. And stare.

As the information division gathers around us, I can't stop myself from hugging him.

"Ow, ow, hey, what happened?" Jay asks, bewildered, but happy, but embarrassed by all the people around us watching.

"Jay, you're brilliant! I need you to go talk to Trist and tell him your idea, and whatever specifics it'll require. You know all about underground farms, so you know how to get one started up and how to maintain it, right?"

"I mean, it's been some time, but I suppose?"

"Perfect." I finally release him, and whatever expression he sees on my face must make him happy, because he's suddenly beaming. "Go talk to Trist. Tell him I already approve of the plan and think we should get it going as soon as possible. You'll have to write up notes and everything, but—"

"Leave it to me," Jay says. He hugs me back, quickly, tightly, before separating from our small group to go find Trist.

Which leaves me standing amid a group of people awkwardly watching me. Peter gives me a grin and thumbs-up while Paul just shakes his head with a smile on his face.

I clear my throat and try to keep any sign of embarrassment off my face. "Right, then. On to business."

The walk back to the bookstore with its secret route into Central is heavy. The excitement of the idea of the Order having its own underground farm buzzed through the meeting room like an electric current, everyone jumping on board, several people being pulled from other groups to help Jay as he listed all the supplies we'd need to begin, the conditions to look for in a good place to grow crops, the basics of how to start it up and take care of it. People took notes, ran to get other members, asked a barrage of questions. Everything had to be written down with the unspoken understanding that Jay might not be able to return to explain or answer questions after this meeting with the rebels.

Currently, both Jay and I are preoccupied with thoughts of tomorrow, now only hours away. As we make our way through the still, mostly empty streets, I look at all the precarious buildings and connecting walkways and really take them in. Will this be the last time I ever see them?

"The Order was really excited about your farm idea," I say eventually. "It was great."

"It wasn't that much," Jay says, but inwardly, he's still elated. **I was finally able to do something good and helpful that didn't involve fighting anyone.**

"Figuring out a permanent way to supply the Order with more food?" I say. "Yeah, that's not much at all."

He laughs softly before we fall back into silence.

Jay is the first to break it this time. "Hey, Lai. You think we'll make it out of this meeting with the rebels? Be honest."

"I'm always honest."

He elbows me good-humoredly.

I laugh and then stare out at the road stretching out before us, all the shops and homes, some familiar, some less so, but nevertheless an unchanging part of this path I always take. "I don't know."

"I suppose not. How could anyone, really?"

"You know, Paul's gift is to see random instances of someone's future. We could try asking him to use it on us and see if we even have a future."

Jay shudders involuntarily. "No thanks. Something like that is . . ."

He doesn't need to explain. It's a terrifying gift to have used on you. If there's nothing, you know you're going to die, but not how or when. And even if you do see a glimpse of your future, it might be just as disturbing.

Besides, Paul has been adamant about refusing to use his gift on others for years. I doubt he'd suddenly change his mind at a time like this, even if the request did come from me.

That weight from before settles back over us like too-heavy armor.

"I told Al about my gift yesterday," I say to break the silence, and because I feel like Jay should know. Given that we barely spoke to each other all day, even at the team's last joint training session this afternoon, it could be an issue during the mission. "Al . . . well, we fought about it."

I thought they were acting weird earlier. "I'm really sorry to hear that."

"It was bound to happen." I try to keep how much it upsets me not to be friends with Al right now out of my voice. "I broke the trust between us. In a lot of ways."

"I'm sure it's a difficult matter for both sides," Jay says softly. His fingers slip through mine and tighten around them. "Just give it a little time. I'm sure he'll come around. You're close, after all."

"Time is something we don't have," I say as I squeeze his hand back. I look skyward without actually seeing anything.

We continue walking for some time, hand in hand, a wall between us or above us or enclosing us.

"Hey, did you know?" Jay says. "My name used to be Jiro Kitahara."

Not the smoothest of topic changes, but I do appreciate him trying to lighten the mood. "I know."

He frowns. "Sometimes, your being a mind reader isn't very fun."

I laugh and nudge him in the side. "I didn't know because of my gift—I've read your files. But I could've guessed Jay wasn't your original name anyway. Lots of Nytes change their first names when they pick up and move somewhere else." Changing your last name is almost impossible, though. The sectors like to keep track of Nytes' movements through them. "Fiona used to be called ShinHye."

"Really?"

"Yup. She changed it when she moved to this sector."

"What about you? You're originally from Sector Four, aren't you? Did you change your name?"

"Yeah, but not by much. My name used to be Laurel."

"What's with that?" he asks with a laugh. "Since you prefer to go by Lai anyway, why didn't you make that your name?"

My laughter dies in my throat. "I couldn't completely get rid of the name my mom gave me."

"Oh."

"Isn't it the same with you?" I ask, trying for a light tone. "You just shortened your name to the first letter, after all."

He rubs the back of his neck with a soft laugh. "I never thought of it that way. When I chose this name, it was merely because I liked the sound of it."

Just when I think he's back to normal, his eyes lose their humor. "Public concern about the rebels is visibly lacking. A lot of people aren't worried about them at all. You never hear civilians talking about a war that could potentially make them extinct."

I'd noticed that as well. Their lack of concern is worrying. If they don't care about an approaching war that could wipe them out, how are we supposed to make them care about the Order? "They think the idea of it is ridiculous," I say. "Etioles outnumber Nytes by an outrageous amount. I don't think they realize it only takes a single crack in the dome to kill them all in one go. They forget their dependence on it." Luckily the military didn't.

We turn down another street. "I've been wondering about that," Jay says. "If the rebels' goal truly is to kill all the Etioles, why haven't they attacked the dome? Why pick off our scouts and supply troops like this? They're only bringing down their own numbers by confronting us head-on."

"Ellis doesn't think like that. To attack the dome directly would be a meaningless victory for her. She might resort to it if she absolutely had to, but she wants to prove that Nytes are superior by beating Etioles definitively."

"That's . . ."

"It's who she is."

He sighs. **And I suppose Lai would know better than anyone.** "I don't much care for this topic. Let's not discuss the war for a change."

I frown, trying to push the mental image of meeting Ellis in two days out of my mind. "Agreed."

So we talk about music. The pieces we enjoy, the ones we want to play in the future. Neither of us mentions leaving for the meeting tomorrow.

Jay tells me about a more difficult piece he liked to play when he was younger but that he hasn't been able to find in Central's collection. "It was the one piece my tutor never corrected me on," he says. "I played it for my father once and even he had nothing to critique."

"Do you ever miss him?" I ask. "Your dad, I mean."

"No. Not really." **Not anymore.** "Do you ever miss your mother?"

"Every day." The admission surprises me. Not only because I'm never this honest with anyone, but also because of what I said. I try not to think of Mom. I shouldn't miss her—I haven't seen her in near on a decade. And yet, somehow, I do.

When I look at Jay, I can't read his expression. I forget he's good at hiding his emotions when he wants to. I don't lean in on his thoughts.

"If you could meet her again, would you?" he asks.

It's a hard question. I don't really remember much of my childhood spent with my mom. It's more feelings than memories. I don't know how Mom would react to me if she saw me now, either. She'd probably be disappointed to see the person I've become. But despite all that, I find that I do know the answer. "I would."

Jay's head tips back as he looks up at the glass cover of the dome far, far overhead. I can't tell if he looks thoughtful or exhausted. "I'm jealous. I can't even decide whether or not I ever want to meet my father again." He pauses. "You know, he hasn't contacted me once since I entered the military, even after I was put on this frontline team. He's likely happy to be rid of me."

"How could anyone be happy with you gone?" I realize too late how cheesy that sounds and inwardly cringe.

But luckily Jay seems to like cheesy. He smiles at me, that smile that fills his whole face and rarely makes an appearance. "Thanks, Lai."

When he leans over to kiss me, I forget to be embarrassed.

27
LAI

THE COUNCIL, PREDICTABLY, did not change its mind.

When dawn breaks, all of Team One is gathered before the front gates of Central. Erik keeps shoving his hands in his pockets, only to take them out a few seconds later, then back in, then out, then in again. Jay is double-checking his pack for possibly the fourth time. Al is unexpectedly the calmest as she watches the slow foot traffic pass by on the other side of the gate. We still have yet to make up or even really speak to each other since our fight.

Anxiety roils in my stomach like spoiled milk. I'd managed to mostly hold it back these last few days, but now everything is too real. There's no avoiding it.

When Austin walks down the path toward us, it's possibly the hardest time I've ever had to not read the general's mind. I definitely can't read his expression.

He stops before all of us and we wait for him to speak. It takes a long time. "I'm sorry I couldn't convince the Council to change its mind."

It feels weird for Austin to be apologizing for anything, let alone something out of his hands.

"It isn't your fault," Jay says. "Our team was made to prevent a war. So we're going to attempt to do just that."

Al and I both nod in agreement, though I notice Erik's attention is focused somewhere outside the gates. **When we meet these rebels, will they recognize me like Devin did? Will I find out if I was actually one of them?**

"Do everything in your power to return safely," Austin says. He looks at everyone when he says this, but when his eyes land on me, I think I see something particularly painful there.

"We'll try our best," I say, because really, that's all I can say.

Once we leave the military's tunnels, the streets are quiet. Hardly anyone is out this early, and the people who are avoid us. We pass through the Gate without a problem. It isn't until we're about to board our bycs—four this time, *finally*—that I hear thoughts that are much, much closer than they should be.

I spin around as soon as I realize what's going on. The others react to my movement, whipping out their weapons and shifting to defensive positions.

From around one of the many scattered boulders, four people step out to walk toward us. Four very familiar people.

"Fiona," I say. "Paul, Peter, Syon. What are all of you doing here?"

"Can't you tell?" Peter asks.

Seeing who it is, Jay lowers his blades. Al and Erik can tell they're not enemies—especially the latter since he recognizes Peter—but since they don't know my newly appeared friends, they don't lower their guards.

"You're not coming with us," I say.

"You need help," Fiona says. "You can't go to this meeting with just the four of you—you'll never make it out alive. And we're not going to risk losing you or any of your friends if we can help it."

She doesn't mention what a devastating blow it would be to the Order. With two strangers here, none of them would mention our organization, and from the looks of Jay's thoughts, he's not about to, either.

"Lai," Erik says slowly, making me tense. "Who are these people?"

"My friends." I gesture to each of them as I say their names. "Fiona Seung. Syon. Paul Wood. Peter Wood."

Paul gives a small nod to Erik, and to Al and Jay. "Sorry to introduce ourselves so suddenly like this. But we want to come along and help."

"It's too dangerous," I say. Just imagining how much the Order would suffer if Fiona or Syon especially were lost, not to mention two of our captains on top of that, isn't worth considering. It isn't worth the risk. They should know that, and I remind them all through thought.

"There's strength in numbers," Fiona says. **You think losing you would be better for the Order?** "There's a better chance of all of us escaping than your team alone."

It shouldn't be the four of you. The Order can't afford to lose any of you. I glare at her, willing her to understand. Fiona is one of the three core leaders of the Order. Syon powers the entirety of Regail Hall. Paul and Peter are two of our most involved captains.

And they're all my closest friends.

Is there such a thing as someone disposable? "We're strong," Fiona continues. "We won't go down easily, and we can help you take on the rebels if it comes to it."

Is there a reason you don't want them to come? Erik think-asks from behind me. **Do you not trust them?**

I'm starting to get confused with all the conversations in my head and the one going on out loud.

No, I answer Erik. *I just don't want them to get hurt.*

"I think it's a good idea," Al says when none of us have spoken aloud in some time.

Even without his gift's help, Jay can sense my unwillingness to have them come along. But he's also our leader, and he wants to raise our chances of survival as much as he can. "I hate to admit it, but we could use the help," he says with a glance to me. **I'm sorry.**

I shake my head. *I understand.*

I turn back to the others. "Fine. But you all better survive."

Peter grins his usual grin, completely inappropriate given the situation. "Well, of course." His brother seems less confident, Fiona and Syon as outwardly unreadable as ever.

I jerk my thumb over my shoulder, toward the bycs. "Get on."

Fiona jumps up behind me on my byc. Syon with Al, Paul with Jay, and Peter with Erik. We don't waste any more time before kicking off and heading west.

The air is hot and dry despite it being so early in the day. Even the wind is sweltering.

"I can't believe you did this," I hiss to Fiona. "Risking so much of the Order's leadership like this. You didn't think it would be a good idea to at least *talk* about it beforehand?"

"We did," Fiona says. "You just weren't there. We knew you'd refuse if we brought it up, so we decided to just come and tell you in the moment. It worked out quite well."

I grit my teeth. Last night was so busy between last-minute preparations, Jay's idea for our own underground farm, and trying to meet with various people to sort things out that I didn't get much of a chance to really talk with any of my friends. And I certainly didn't have any reason to think I needed to go out of my way to read their minds when I already had so much to focus on.

"For the record," Fiona says, "Trist wanted to come along as well, but we made him stay behind."

"I'm *so* glad you could spare at least *one* of our leaders from this suicide mission," I say as scathingly as I can.

She ignores me. "This is the most advantageous setup. No one is going to win against Syon, and my gift allows us a wider range of strategy well-suited to escape."

"And the Woods?" I ask quietly. "You know their gifts aren't suited for battle. We have no idea what kind of Nytes we'll be up against. You shouldn't have brought them."

"I know," Fiona says just as quietly. Her admission surprises me. She never admits she's wrong about anything. "But they refused to stay behind. They were worried about you and the others."

"And now I'm worried about them." I sigh. Hesitate. "I'm worried about all of us."

"I know."

It takes physical effort to say the words, but I choke them out anyway. "Thank you, Fiona."

This is one of those rare instances when I'm being serious, so Fiona doesn't quip back at me. "You know we have your back, Lai."

"I know."

Fiona punches me lightly on the shoulder and I swerve the byc to try to throw her off. Unfortunately, her one-handed grip on me is tight.

"Nice try," Fiona says. "But you're going to have to do better than that."

"Oh, don't you worry," I say. "The day is young."

We ride until it's too dark to safely continue. We took periodic breaks throughout the day, and switched riding partners a few times when Fiona and I had had more than enough of each other, but this is our first true break. As blistering as the air was with the sun up, the frigid cold descends quickly with the fading of the light.

A dead forest rises around us. Trees with blackened trunks and leafless branches soar so high overhead they seem to rival the dome's height. Roots tangle across the dusty rock ground. A Feral keens in the distance, but Jay confirms it isn't close enough for us to have to worry. Other than that and us, life is nonexistent.

Al uses her gift to start a smokeless fire while the rest of us set up camp in the somewhat concealed protection of the trees. Once everyone has finished, we all settle around the fire.

Erik and Paul are talking animatedly as they sit down next to each other, which I find surprising given that Erik never looks that happy talking to any living thing.

"I still can't believe you haven't tried painting," Paul is saying. "Watercolor is the best."

"I prefer more hands-on work," Erik says. "Drawing is fun, too, but I do it so I can have a blueprint for what I want to make."

Paul shakes his head. "That's a shame. I have a feeling you'd really enjoy it."

Peter, ever the jealous one, drops down beside his brother. "Found an art friend, have you?"

Paul lights up, and I can't tell if it's because he gets to talk about art or if it's because his brother is close by again. They don't usually go an entire day apart. "Yeah! Erik sketches and makes furniture and models."

I raise an eyebrow at Paul's use of Erik's first name when they've known each other for all of one day, but Erik only shrugs in response.

What, he your type? I ask in his head.

Don't be stupid, Erik thinks, but he's clearly flustered. Someone has a crush. **Besides, he's already taken.**

His brother isn't.

They're twins, not the same person.

Now I'm the one to shrug. I should've known gentle Paul the painter would be able to crack Erik's shell. He has that way with people. Just like Luke. It's probably why the two of them were best friends.

As the others fill in around the fire, Jay sits beside me. We catch each other's eyes for a long moment, but there isn't anything either of us actually wants to say. Just unease.

"Now that there are more of us, we should work out a strategy," Jay says. "Why don't we start with everyone's gifts and strengths?"

Team One starts. Then Fiona, with her sword fighting and illusions. Syon—Fiona speaking in his stead—with his bow and arrows and ability to control pure energy. Paul and Peter, each with their daggers and abilities to look into the future and past, respectively.

Paul doesn't mention the fact that he doesn't use his gift, but that's probably because he knows it isn't something anyone would suggest using for a battle strategy. He's very aware of his and Peter's positions.

Nor do any of those among us in the Order mention our neutralizing power crystals. I absently check on mine to make sure it's still there, hanging with Fiona's and Syon's crystals on a chain tucked under my shirt so they're in constant contact with me. Thinking about Gabriel's last gift makes my heart heavy, especially when we might soon be facing him as an enemy. I wonder if he left together with Sara.

I still have trouble wrapping my mind around the idea that Gabriel turned on us, that he would have actually gone to join the rebels. I've tried my best to ignore it and shove the thought down the same way I do every emotion that gets in the way, but now it's unavoidable. What will we do if we see him at that meeting tomorrow? Will we have to fight each other? My stomach drops.

I carry his crystal with me always in case of an emergency, but this is the first time I fully intend to use it on a mission. It draws too much attention normally, but this is do or die. I'm going to use everything I have to ensure we get out of this alive. Besides, I have to be careful with how I use the crystal. Gabriel's gift might be limitless, but that doesn't mean his crystals are. I can activate it for a short period, but then it needs time to recharge.

But telling the others about all of that now will only draw unnecessary suspicion to ourselves.

"We need a plan that doesn't rely too heavily on assumed details, since we know next to nothing about what their numbers might be or what their abilities are," I say.

"What if when we arrive, we use Seung's illusions to make it look like there are more of us?" Erik asks. "We can throw them off."

Fiona shakes her head. "My gift only affects vision. I can't fake sounds, and they would notice the difference in footsteps and the number of people right away. Besides, they seem to have a Nyte or power crystals that neutralize others' gifts. I doubt they'd even see it."

"We won't have time to scope out the landscape beforehand," Jay murmurs. "And there's a good chance I won't be able to sense where any rebels are lying in wait. Or how many there are. They'll have the advantage in terrain and surprise in numbers."

"What if we split up?" Peter asks, putting his fingers together and pulling them apart. "Half of us meet the rebels, the other half sneaks around to attack the enemy from behind."

"I don't like the idea of splitting up," I say. "If they separate and corner us, we're done for. We need to stick together unless we have no other choice."

We continue to talk strategy for a while, but when no one comes up with anything substantial, everyone drifts off into their own thoughts. The very probable presence of Gabriel or his power crystals limits us greatly.

"I'll take first watch," Jay says when the silence has become too thick. "The rest of you get some sleep. We're heading out first thing in the morning."

I wait with him as the others drift off to their sleeping bags, Al and Erik likewise remaining. Fiona glances back at me, but doesn't linger. When I listen in on her thoughts, there's nothing in particular she wants to say, so I don't call out to her.

When it's just our team, I say, "What are you all thinking?"

"Can't you tell?" Erik asks, but for once, not meanly.

"Using my gift and asking you are different."

Jay smiles slightly. It doesn't reach the rest of his face. "I'm not sure what there is to say that isn't already obvious. I'm anxious. And more terrified than I've ever been in my life."

"Because you might die?" Erik asks.

"Because I might lose the people I've come to think of as family." Silence greets Jay's words, but he doesn't hesitate before going on. "I was so worried when this team was first thrown together. I thought it would never work. I never considered that I might come to think of you all as more than fellow soldiers." His eyes fall and his voice lowers. "But it's not like that now. We might fight and bicker a lot, but we're always all still together in the end. Knowing that you three are here with me is more comforting than I would've ever imagined possible."

Quiet fills the space his words left behind.

Across the fire, Al's eyes find mine.

I'm sorry I didn't tell you everything sooner, I say telepathically. Surprise registers on her face at the sound of my voice in her head, but I go on. *And that I used your secret against you. And didn't respect your privacy. And, well, everything else.*

I'm still mad.

My eyes fall.

But I also don't want to go into this without having made up.

When my eyes rise to meet hers, both her thoughts and expression are sincere.

You're still my best friend, and yeah, I'm pissed you blackmailed me and mad you didn't trust me sooner, but I can kind of get it, too. I don't like fighting with you. So let's stop.

Sounds good to me.

We both smile, and while I know there's still hurt and unease in Al's thoughts, I also know she'd rather be friends than let those emotions win out.

"Me too," I say aloud in response to Jay's confession. "I never thought I'd end up sharing so much with you guys, let alone *wanting* to share so much with you. I . . . don't trust people easily. For me to trust all of you is . . ."

I don't know how to finish what I was saying, or even what I was trying to say to begin with. But they seem to understand even though I don't. Something feels stuck in the back of my throat when I look at all of them, faces lit by Al's unnaturally bright fire. When did this odd collection of outcasts become so important to me?

"I don't trust people at all," Erik says. He tries to say it lightly, but even he falters. "I definitely never thought I'd end up trusting any of you. When this team first started out, I thought you were all just annoying. Secretive. Controlling. Not that I don't still think that," Erik adds, trying to get things back under control, "but I don't think it as much anymore."

That's as good as a confession of friendship as anyone is ever going to get out of Erik. And the funny thing is, we're all familiar enough with one another now to recognize that. And it's fine. It's great to even get that much, to know he does care. To know we all care.

"Yeah, well, I know I can be difficult sometimes," Al says.

"And proud," Erik says.

"Blunt," I add.

"Stubborn," Jay says.

Al half glares, half smirks at all of us as she waves our words away. "But you all still stuck around and even became friends with me. I trust you guys to watch my back—and that's not something I ever even thought I needed someone to do."

"It's something everyone needs," Jay says quietly. "And now we all have it."

We sit there in silence for a while, each of us knowing it might be the last time we'll all be together. And when I gaze up through the never-ending trees, I like to think, impossibly, that I can see the stars on the other side.

28
LAI

WE COME WITHIN sight of the meeting place around noon the next day. Even from a distance, the outline of turrets and lopsided skyscrapers is all too clear, the jagged, glittering rim encircling it all hard to miss. A shattered dome, destroyed in some war between sectors over resources. Even though I can't make out any details across the dry desert plain stretching before us, I shudder at the sight. An abandoned sector is not a place I would ever willingly choose to visit.

We slow our bycs and pass in silence through a giant gap in the fragmented glass dome, so much of which is gone that it now looks like a child stuck shards of glass around the buildings in a poor reconstruction of a picket fence. The buildings' exteriors have all faded to gray, most with long fissures running the length of them. Almost all the windows are shattered. Everything is dead.

The road beneath us is spider-webbed with cracks, heaving upward in some places and leaving huge gaps in others. Blackened roots twist through the cement, as thick around as my entire body, even though there are no trees or plants in sight. Dozens of collapsed buildings litter the street. Scattered bones and claw marks hint that Ferals have taken a liking to the place.

Empty husks of once-grand buildings watch our silent procession. The granite sky, an unusually subdued color, makes them appear eerily beautiful. Far ahead of us, I can see a tall spire rising from the center of the sector. The place where we agreed to meet the rebels. Even from here, I can see the hollowed-out crevices where parts of the spire have fallen away.

Once we reach the area, those gaping holes become even more apparent, marking the spire like knife wounds. We're in what might have once been some sort of town square. Dusty mosaics spread out around us, and off to the side sits a crippled fountain with so many splintering cracks it's a wonder the thing is still standing.

Four people are atop the short set of stairs leading up to the spire, two girls and two boys. One of them I recognize as Devin, the violence-crazed rebel who attacked me on our last mission, currently pacing across the top step. Another is Ice Eyes from our first mission, leaning against the rusted handrail. The boy sitting on one of the upper steps, I've never seen before. He has a small, lean build, bronze-toned skin, and messy black hair. His gaze instantly locks on to Erik with such intensity that he must know the corporal. The odds of Erik *not* having been associated with the rebels are quickly decreasing.

And then there's Ellis. Her long, tumbling blond hair shines in the dull sunlight. Her tall frame leans deceptively languidly against the railing behind her as she reads a small journal. When she straightens, she moves like a cat. Slowly. Deliberately. Her pale jade eyes flick over each of us as we dismount from our bycs before they finally come to rest on me.

The sight of Ellis makes my heart sick, and much as I try to ignore the unwanted emotions flooding into me, this time, I can't. Not with her.

"Good afternoon, Lai." She says it quietly, but her words carry through the dead space. "It's been a while. You never answer my messengers."

"I don't take to consorting with the enemy," I say when all eyes fall on me.

Almost all of them. Paul steps out from his place beside Fiona, mouth working without making a sound. He finally manages to say, "Joan?"

Ice Eyes looks up from her feet and blinks. Blinks again, like she's trying to see something else. "Paul?" she whispers. "What are you doing here?"

"What are you doing over there?" Paul's voice is strained. He takes a half step forward, but Peter catches his arm to prevent him going any farther. "Please tell me you're not actually with the rebels."

She stands up. Something flashes in her eyes, some kind of conflicting hurt I can't read. It doesn't help that I can't hear her or any of the other rebels' thoughts. "So what if I am? Is it so wrong to want a world where Nytes can live without fear? Without having to always look over their shoulder to make sure an Etiole isn't about to stab them in the back?"

Paul looks at her like he doesn't know who she is. "You would kill tens of thousands of innocents for that?"

She doesn't answer. She won't meet his eyes, either. I have no idea what must be going through Paul's head right now, nor any desire to pry and find out, but based on how he always talked about Joan at our meetings and the look on his face now, I can't begin to imagine his hurt.

But Paul isn't the only one whose focus is locked on Joan. Erik is staring at her with an intense look of resigned confirmation. **She's that girl from the one memory I have. The one who said the night is approaching.**

My stomach turns, but even though Erik recognizes Ice Eyes, he doesn't seem to have any desire to even speak with her. He'd been holding on to that memory for so long, and now, for him to find out the girl in it is a rebel—that it almost certainly confirms *he* was a rebel—is a heavy blow.

Before he can fully process that, though, Ellis turns her attention to him. "Erik, we're finally able to meet again!" She gives a happy little clap of her hands.

Erik slowly lifts his head to face her. "What are you talking about?" But by now, he knows that what he's suspected for weeks is true. He just has to hear it.

Ellis smiles warmly, like she's greeting an old friend rather than an enemy. It's a look I know well. It sends a knife through my rib cage. "I almost forgot. You lost your memories, didn't you? It took Cal forever to find you, and for us to figure out what happened." The messy-haired boy still sitting on the stairs looks up and meets Erik's eyes. He gives a weak sort of smile, like he's unsure of how it will be received, but Erik just stares at him blankly. "You can imagine our distress when you didn't come back. No one knew what happened to you. You just disappeared."

Erik winces as everyone turns to stare at him. Many of the gazes on him are ones of suspicion. Al's incredulity burns so strongly I feel it secondhand.

"I think you're going to have to be a little clearer there," Erik says. Amazingly, he manages to keep his usual carefree tone. But his thoughts are a jumbled mess of misery. I wish I could reach out to him telepathically for support, but he probably needs all the headspace he has for himself.

Ellis considers him with something close to sympathy. "Erik, you're my right-hand man. About five months ago, you went missing after a raid on Sector Eight."

Static ripples through the air.

Erik, Ellis's second-in-command? I had considered the possibility he'd been a rebel likely, but that he was ranked *that* high up?

Now everyone is watching him warily, which probably isn't helping his newfound anxiety. Fiona and Syon, who hadn't known about his missing memories, are openly staring at him. Al is no better than a statue. Jay and Paul are the only ones who keep their focus trained on the rebels ahead of us, while Peter looks back and forth, uncertain of who he needs to concentrate on more.

"You expect me to just believe that?" Erik asks Ellis. He gives every appearance of ignoring the change in our group. "How do I know you didn't just find out about my memory loss and decide to play that to your advantage? An easy way to try and get someone over to your side."

"Oh, Erik," Ellis says fondly. "I'm glad to see you're as distrustful as ever. But I'm not lying. Some months ago, you were leading a raid against Sector Eight. But the military was expecting you. They ambushed you and your team was forced to retreat. Only, you didn't return. We thought you were dead." Her eyes flick to the ground and then back up once more. "Then some of our people found you in the military. They said they approached you and tried to talk to you, but you didn't recognize them. After that, they dug around until they found out you'd forgotten everything."

"That doesn't make sense," Erik says. "If I really was ambushed by the military, then they would've known I was a rebel. Why would they take me in?"

"To use you." The way in which she says it, without any hesitation, sends a chill down my spine. "The military is more dangerous than you realize, Erik. Do not think for even a second that they're on your side. They're only waiting until your usefulness is up to stab you in the back."

"That's still not proof I was ever on your side," Erik says after the barest pause. But Ellis's words got to him—got to even Al and Jay, whose thoughts churn uneasily. Al is still struggling to process what's happening with Erik. Jay is trying to figure out if he should interrupt to attempt negotiations or let them continue. But he knows Erik has been searching for anything to do with his past. He can sense Erik's intensity right now.

Fiona and the others make no move to intervene, silently choosing to follow whatever my lead is.

Maybe if I hadn't spent so much time in Erik's head, and maybe if we hadn't talked at such length about his past and the few hints we had about it, I'd be more suspicious of Erik right now. But I'm not. His thoughts are distressed. He's trying so hard to reject the truth. He doesn't want to be a part of them—he doesn't even want to have ever been associated with them.

But Ellis only smiles. She tosses him the journal she was reading when we all arrived and Erik catches it reflexively. He warily looks between it and her, and she waves for him to examine it.

He flicks between the pages, skeptically at first, but then with slowly dawning recognition. And from where I stand, now I can see that it's not a journal but a sketchbook. Filled to the brim with sketches and messy scrawls.

"You always were into drawing and building," Ellis says. "Since long before we met. I'm glad that, at least, hasn't changed. That was your last sketchbook. There are more back at our base, along with your models. You were there, Erik. You were our friend. My friend."

Erik can't seem to tear his eyes from the sketchbook in his hands. **This is the first time my past has actually felt *real*. I want to know more. Do they know about my family? What was I doing before I joined the rebels?**

The strength with which he thinks these questions is alarming. He wouldn't join the rebels now as a way to learn more about his past, would he?

I finally force my way into his thoughts. *What do you want to do?*

Erik's eyes jerk around to meet mine, and he knows I'm suspicious. It snaps him out of his obsessive fervor.

He turns back to Ellis. "That was then. I'm not one of you anymore, and no matter what you say, I'm not going back."

Relief floods through me—and through Jay's thoughts. He could sense Erik's intense fascination as well.

But by the way Ellis contemplates Erik, I can't help but feel she noticed it, too. "No," she says, unperturbed. "There will come a day when you can't stand not knowing anymore and you will come searching for me. You're nearly there already. I'll wait for you, Erik. When you're ready, just look close to home for how to contact me."

Erik doesn't say anything.

In the pause, Jay steps forward. "Ms. Ellis. We have come on behalf of the military of Sector Eight in order to—"

"My offer still stands for you, too, you know," Ellis says. When I pry my eyes away from Erik, it's to find Ellis staring as intently at me now as she did that day she walked away from everything. "I do so hate the thought of us having to be enemies."

"You should have thought of that before you left." I try to keep my voice cool. Unconcerned. I don't know if it works.

Ellis considers me. Sighs. "I did. But I always thought you'd see the truth on your own one day and come find me. Sadly, I see that has yet to happen."

"Lai, do you know this person?" Al asks tightly. Her hands are clenched into fists at her sides, already dangerously close to her limit after everything with Erik.

It's hard to get the words out. "Before she left the military to found the rebels, we were officers together."

That's why she knew so much about Ellis's gift. I should've guessed they knew each other.

Ellis gives a bow with a little twirl of her hand, still maintaining eye contact with me. "It's been a while since anyone spoke of my time in the military. Do you miss me?"

I open my mouth, and for a split second, I worry the words that come out will be, "Every day." Instead, I say, "Only the old you."

"I see," Ellis says. When her eyes leave me, both relief and disappointment fill me. "Well, well, if it isn't Fiona. And you even brought Syon and the twins. How *have* you been? Still a control freak?" Despite her sarcasm, I think I hear sadness laced through her words.

"What are your conditions for a truce?" Fiona asks, ignoring her.

Ellis seems surprised by the question. "Truce? You didn't actually believe that, did you? I thought you, at least, would've known better, Lai."

"I did," I say through gritted teeth. "We all did."

"And the almighty High Council sent you anyway, didn't they?" Ellis says. "Didn't I tell you? Why can't you *see* it? They're just using you—using all of you. They sent all of you out here even though they knew it was a trap because they hoped you'd at least be able to make a dent in our forces. Pitiful."

I catch Jay's eye. Even for Ellis, she seems awfully indifferent about saying to our faces this was all a setup. We can't use our gifts on these four, either, which means there could be more rebels hidden nearby. They really do have Gabriel's power crystals. He really did betray us. But I have more pressing matters to worry about now.

"And what kind of trap might this be?" Jay asks. He discreetly hits the red alert on his MMA.

"Oh, it's quite simple, really," Ellis says. She skips back to the other rebels and spreads her arms wide. "Either you join us, or we'll kill you."

29
LAI

MY STOMACH DROPS. Even though I knew this was going to happen, even though we've been planning for an ambush, the reality of it hadn't set in until just now. There must be dozens of rebels hiding in this run-down place. We don't have a chance of winning, especially if all of the rebels are protected the same way these four are.

No. To hide that many people over such a wide range, the Nyte with the neutralization gift himself must be present. Gabriel is here somewhere.

"As I'm sure you've noticed, your gifts won't work on us, and we have more of our number hidden within this place," Ellis goes on, confirming my suspicions. "You won't be able to make it out of here alive if you refuse us." She pauses to bring her hands together. "Though I rather hope you'll join because you want to, and not under force of threat. Especially you, Erik. You have no reason to fight for the military, and every reason to come home. Please."

You're sure about your decision, Erik?

I'm not with them.

You could easily get out of this alive by going over to them. They wouldn't even be suspicious.

I watch him carefully as a muscle in his jaw works. The thought had occurred to him as well. But despite all the questions he has, despite this being his long-awaited chance to finally be able to find out about his past, despite the fact that this could be his only chance to save his life and get out of here unscathed, he genuinely thinks, **No. I'm not a part of them anymore.**

Good. I reach out to the others' thoughts so they can hear me, too. Forcing my way into seven minds at once is harder than I would've thought, but simpler than if I had more than one message for all of them. *We're going to split up and run. Me and Paul, Al and Peter to the right. Erik and Jay right and back. Fiona and Syon, front and right.*

I should be able to extend my neutralization crystal's power to Al to protect her from any direct attacks, and Peter and Paul each have their own. Fiona and Syon are a strong pair; I don't need to worry about them. And so long as Erik is with someone who trusts him, they'll both be fine.

The idea of splitting up is a terrible one, and something I wanted to avoid, but it feels like our best option. We'll hopefully be able to move faster this way, and divert the rebels' power.

Ellis's gift is shadow manipulation. If you step on a shadow that can connect to hers, she'll be able to track you. Don't let your guard down. Try to avoid fighting if you can. Just keep running. Our top priority is returning alive. Run as soon as one of them speaks.

Grim confirmation resounds through everyone's thoughts. Ellis has been watching us closely, and when I meet her familiar gaze, I almost look away again. I still remember too clearly the look in her eyes when she left. I received the messages she sent me in the form of shadow butterflies. But until I actually saw her, some part of me had rejected the idea that the joyful, sister-like Sara I knew could lead an army against her old home. Against me. I've missed her for so long that even though I know this isn't my Sara, I can still imagine it being her. I want to run over and hug her. I want to punch some sense into her. Everything I feel is a contradiction.

She opens her mouth and I tense. "I—"

My feet kick off the broken mosaic so hard I hear the skittering of pieces skipping across the ground. I swing onto my byc with Paul right behind me and we take off. I listen to everyone's thoughts as they disperse, and Al's and Peter's as they follow close behind. The fact that I can't hear Ellis's or the other rebels' thoughts still unsettles me, but that's nothing compared to the knowledge that there are groups hidden around this ghost sector whose presence I won't be aware of until they're right on top of us.

The power crystal resting under my shirt warms against my skin as I activate it. I telepathically ask Peter to extend his crystal's power to Al since he's closer to her. At the same time, I tell Paul not to activate his, that I'll cover him with my own, so that I can talk to him telepathically if need be. If anyone tries to directly attack us with their gift, it won't work. But anything indirect will still have its full effect, which leaves a lot of dangerous possibilities. Including Ellis's shadows.

"Paul, take the controls," I say, and we switch places.

I pull my compressed spear from its sheath and hold it tightly in one hand as it expands and forms into my familiar weapon. My ears and eyes strain to catch the slightest hint of anyone waiting to ambush us as we speed past on our bycs, hurtling over half-fallen buildings and debris as we go.

It isn't until after we've passed by one of the destroyed buildings that a group of rebels springs out behind us on stolen bycs of their own. I shout, "Heads up!" to warn Al and Peter, as well as Paul so he can be prepared to maneuver us out of the way of any incoming attacks.

I whirl my spear up to block a rebel's sword. I slide my shaft along the edge of his weapon until there's less of my spear underneath his blade than over—then spin the tip of my spear into the gap between him and his sword, into his chest.

Our eyes meet. I wish they hadn't.

His partner driving the byc calls back to ask if he's okay as I rip my spear out of his chest. I thrust my weapon into their byc's back engine. When I pull it out, the byc instantly drops back and collides with the pair of rebels behind them.

It's not much of a deterrent, as two new bycs appear to take their places. Behind them, more rebels zoom around collapsed buildings blocking the street. I can see Peter and Al holding their own, Al swinging her halberd, Peter maneuvering their byc to avoid the wreckage of the destroyed sector. At least the rebels can't use their numbers against us with the bycs and ruins in the way.

"Duck!" Paul yells.

I drop without question, just in time to miss the top of a decrepit archway.

The rebels behind us are not so lucky. They slam into the weakened stone structure full force, bringing it down on top of them with a thunderous crash.

For a panicked second, I think Al and Peter went down with them. Then I see their byc pull out of the dust cloud thrown up by the collapse. I allow myself a single sigh of relief before I whip my spear up and around to block the blade of another rebel coming at us from our right side. He was aiming for Paul—but *no one* touches my friends.

"Take us up a bit, Paul," I yell over the revving engines and shouts around us. He complies and we rise over the rebel who attacked us. His weapon is a polearm, good for long distances. That's going to be a pain. Worse is that a similarly equipped rebel has just appeared on our other side, too. Not good odds.

Paul, I'm going to give you directions telepathically. I need you to follow them exactly.

Got it.

Be calm. Read my opponents' movements. Catch them off balance—which shouldn't be too hard given our current modes of transportation. So long as I can throw them over the edge of their byc, it's my win.

The rebel on our right thrusts his polearm toward us. I flip my spear up to send the blade glancing harmlessly off the shaft.

Down.

The byc drops as Lefty swings her own polearm in the space we once occupied.

Up.

Before she can pull her weapon back into a proper fighting stance, I'm right beside her again. I swing my spear around the shaft of her polearm and twist up, ripping the weapon from her grip. It goes flying.

Before I can send the rebel herself flying, Righty swings his pole-arm in a wide arc, once again aiming for Paul.

I twist my spear around to block his blade. The hit sends shocks through my arms with the strength of it.

Lefty pulls a dagger out of her sheath and lunges for my side. I overpower Righty and his polearm to lift the other end of my spear up to block Lefty's blade.

Up.

Lefty is quick to slip under my shaft, but Paul steers the byc up before she can connect a hit. She lunges too far. If not for her driver grabbing the back of her jacket and righting her balance, she would've fallen off. So close.

Righty rises to our level, but before he can attack first again, I thrust my spear at his stomach. He blocks with the shaft of his pole-arm, and then Lefty is up on our other side as well.

Stop for two seconds and then go full-speed toward the byc on our right. Put them between us and the rebels on our left.

You're going to have to hold on.

Don't really have a free hand for that right now.

Just as Lefty is about to aim for another hit, Paul's arm wraps around my stomach from behind and our byc abruptly lurches to a stop. I nearly go flying. As it is, my stomach jerks up into my throat.

The rebels continue full-speed ahead with surprised looks on their faces, and after the briefest of pauses, we whip back after them.

We pull up on the other side of Righty, which cuts Lefty off from helping and makes it easier for me to concentrate on the one fight. But Righty is fast to recover. When I swing my spear at him, he knocks it back and thrusts his own weapon into the opening.

I duck, and in the moment when his polearm is extended, before he can pull it back in to defend himself, I stab my spear into his chest from below.

He sputters.

I rip my spear free with a downward motion to set the byc off balance as the dying rebel, his feet still strapped to the floor of the byc, tumbles over the edge and brings the vehicle and his partner shouting down with it.

Lefty watches in horror as her friends fall, then looks back at me with pure hate. "Why can't you bastards just die already?"

I don't say anything in response. There's no point.

Pull up beside their byc.

I don't think she poses much of a threat with a short-range weapon. Let's just run.

What if she follows us?

Then you can beat her. You're the one who said our goal is getting out of here alive, aren't you?

I hesitate, but not for long before I turn and wrap my arms around Paul. As soon as he feels my grip tighten, the byc plummets. And my stomach along with it. We can't free-fall for more than four seconds before he revs the engine and we kick forward once again, this time in a more zigzag pattern. The ground below us is fast-moving, close. All the motion is a wreck on my stomach, but I force myself to ignore it. Lefty doesn't follow us. I can still hear Al's and Peter's shouts to each other close behind. Everything is still okay.

Then the byc lurches underneath me. Paul grabs my arm before I can register what's happening, and we jump. We hit the ground rolling and spring straight back up as the byc we were riding bursts into flame. Some kind of starlight arrow with a mechanism attached to it is sticking out of the back engine.

Another explosion sounds, and I can guess that Al and Peter have found themselves similarly grounded.

I barely have time to readjust before I have to turn to defend against a rebel on the ground, this one armed with claws. When I block her first attack, her other hand comes swinging underneath my spear. I skip back just out of reach, freeing her first hand as her second shoots toward me.

I'm so far away I know she can't reach me, but I realize too late that's not what she was aiming for. Vines shoot out of the ground and wrap around my arms. *Shitshitshit*.

She rushes me, and before I manage to fully cut myself free from her vines, she slashes her claws across my arm. I'm lucky I broke free fast enough to escape any worse wounds, but my arm stings and burns and hisses and I know the cuts run deep. *Don't focus on it. Concentrate*.

Wound notwithstanding, I hold my spear at the ready, more cautious this time. I have to watch out for her vines.

But before either of us can move, someone falls into the rebel from behind and knocks her off balance.

I use the chance to send her sprawling with the heel of my foot against her jaw, but another rebel comes up behind me, sword raised overhead. Someone who's not used to fighting.

I swing my spear into his neck before he has time to bring his sword down. A sickening *crunch* reverberates all the way up my arm.

Before he even hits the ground, two more rebels are on either side of me. I twist and turn to deflect each of their attacks, raising and lowering my spear as necessary, alternately swinging and thrusting as I

spin in a defensive circle until I find the openings I'm looking for—
and then they, too, are on the ground.

There's seemingly no end to the rebels as three more step forward, this time more cautiously.

I feel a back against mine as Paul manages to break his way through to my side, his thoughts cool, daggers raised.

"Don't be reckless," he says softly.

"Same to you," I murmur back. "Don't leave my side."

Through the crowd, I can see Al from where she's wreaking havoc amid a grouping of rebels a little ways away. A one-woman army even without being able to directly use her flames. Peter fights nearby, daggers gleaming as he maintains a careful distance so as not to get in Al's way nor get too far from her.

"We need to regroup with the others," I say to Paul. "Follow me."

I don't wait for his confirmation before charging headfirst into the rebels.

It takes time to make our way to Al and Peter, but once they catch sight of us, and with Al's strength, it becomes easier.

As soon as we're all together, I say, "We have to cut a path and escape. Al, your fire?"

"It doesn't burn them." She swings her halberd round to keep the rebels at bay as she speaks. They're holding their distance now that the four of us are together, but I'm sure that won't last long.

"But you can still summon it?"

"Yeah."

I lower my voice so only my friends can hear. "We'll use it as a surprise attack. Pretend it still works, attack with confidence, and the sight of all that fire should be enough to scatter them, however briefly. As soon as they're out of our way, we'll run for the edge of the city."

"Got it," Al says.

"I'm always down for running from a fight I can't win," Peter says with a nervous laugh. Paul murmurs his agreement.

"Then get ready." I raise my voice so the rebels can hear me loud and clear. "Al, burn 'em down!"

"With pleasure," Al says. She wears a wicked grin as flames swirl around her. Looking at her, I'd believe that fire would kill me, neutralization gift or not. A few rebels fall back with shouts. When her flames turn into a towering wave of fire, about to crash down, our opponents completely break formation and run for it.

The flames follow, but Al is careful to control their speed so the rebels won't realize the fire can't actually touch them. It'd be a problem if they double back too soon.

Our way is clear. The path that leads to the outer edge of the city is open, and all we need to do is run for it. My knees are already bent to run when Al says, "Brother?" And again, a shout this time, "Brother!"

I turn to look at her, but she's already running in the opposite direction of the path she just opened, back toward the ruined buildings and a collection of rebels heading straight for us.

"Al, *what are you doing*?" I scream after her. "We need to go, *now*!"

But she ignores me and keeps running.

"What do we do?" Peter asks in a panic, looking between me and Al's quickly receding back.

"Of all the *fucking*—" Stop. Think. With every second we waste, the rebels we scattered are realizing the flames can't hurt them. Our path will be closed soon. I have to go after Al. Do I send Peter and Paul ahead to safety? They can still make it. They're not as suited to battle, they're not soldiers who've been in hundreds of fights, and the sooner I get them out of here, the better. But I don't like all of us getting separated even further. And if any rebels are waiting on the edge of the city for us, it'll be like sending them straight to their deaths if I have them go alone.

I close my eyes. Open them. "We're going after Al. Follow me. Do *not* leave my sight."

"Got it," Peter and Paul chime.

Cursing her all the while, I run after Al.

It seems ridiculous that she could've gotten so far ahead of us in such a short amount of time. But she's already fighting some of the rebels who had been headed our way. Whether any of them are her brother, I have no idea.

Nor do I get the chance to find out. A rebel brings her axe down on my spear shaft before we reach Al. I stand my ground and push back, but she's strong. Paul sweeps in from below to attack while Peter moves a little farther ahead to block another incoming attacker.

But something's wrong. I don't know why, but I'm suddenly terrified. "Peter, fall back!"

Paul darts toward his brother in the same instant the rebel swings her axe back my way. I shuffle back and forth with her, our weapons clanging against each other, until I'm finally able to slip around and stab her through her side. I don't watch as she falls.

"Paul!"

My head snaps up. Peter is on his hands and knees not far in front of me. Before him, that rebel Devin has Paul pinned to the ground with a knee on his back and a dagger to his throat. A steel ball lodges itself in my lungs.

Devin's grin widens sharply when he sees I'm watching. Paul winces as the rebel's dagger presses harder against his skin.

"You know, Sara reeeally wants you to join us," Devin says. "I'd bet she'd be super happy with me if I got you to come over. So what do you say? You join us and I'll let your friend go. Easy, right?"

"Lai, don't," Paul says. Devin shoves his face into the ground.

"Stop!" Peter looks at me desperately, panic swimming in his eyes. **Lai we have to save him what do we do.**

I wish I could give him an answer. My thoughts are whirring too quickly to latch on to any substantial idea. They're too far from us. I won't be able to attack without Devin killing Paul first. Our gifts are useless. But I can't join the rebels. There's no way. What if I pretended to agree to get him to let go of Paul? No, I won't be able to—

"Five," Devin says.

Panic spikes through my blood. What do I do?

"Four."

Peter gets to his feet and we share a look.

"Three."

I open my mouth—to agree, to lie, to do literally anything—but Paul catches my eye. He shakes his head.

"Two."

"Wait, *please!*" Peter begs.

"One. Time's up." Devin thrusts his dagger into Paul's back.

Paul screams and Peter and I run toward them, weapons drawn, but Devin stabs Paul again before ripping his dagger free of him to face us.

There's a wild light in his eyes. "I gave you a chance, you know."

I thrust my spear toward him with more anger than I've ever felt, but he sidesteps with a laugh. "Peter, get Paul," I say. "We're going."

He hardly needed an order from me to go to his brother. He kneels by Paul's side, half crying as he whispers, "No, no, no, it's going to be okay, Paul, we're going to make it out of here just fine."

I barely hear Paul's soft, strained confirmation.

I twist my spear around to try to land a hit from the side, but Devin deflects it easily. I keep attacking, pushing him farther away from Paul and Peter.

He slips under one of my swings and is suddenly right in front of me, dagger raised. His eyes shine with glee as he raises his arm to attack. Then his eyes flick to the side and he ducks out of the way as a halberd swings through the space he'd just been standing in.

Al stands there, new cuts covering her arms and sides, her breaths coming hard.

I fight the urge to yell at her. Instead I say, "We're going. And you better fucking follow this time."

She doesn't reply as I race back to where Peter has finished applying the fastest bandaging job possible to Paul to slow the bleeding. But seeing all the blood on the ground, and all the blood dripping from his back as Peter gently lifts him up, my stomach wrenches. There's no way. He's not going to make it.

We no longer have any kind of path ahead of us. A wall of rebels stands in our way, and Devin laughs at us from behind. "And just where do you think you're going? Your little fire trick won't work a second time."

Between having already used what little strengths we had earlier and my distracting anxiety over Paul, I'm coming up with a blank. How can we escape? How can we get Paul out of here?

Gabriel's power crystal burns against my skin.

Power crystals. Of course. I pull my necklace with its three crystals out from underneath my shirt and hold Syon's far overhead. As soon as Peter sees it, he braces himself and closes his eyes. Energy crackles through the air as blinding light fills the area. The rebels flinch back, and Al, but I grab her by the wrist and we all run for it.

I don't have a free hand to attack anyone we pass by, but Al does. She swings at anybody in our way, and anyone within her reach, and their cries of pain and confusion ring out around us.

The uneven road makes running hard. Holes and roots keep catching my feet, making me stumble, but we keep going without pause. Even after it seems like we've somehow managed to lose the rebels, none of us slow down.

As we run past sorry excuses for buildings, through the remnants of the glass dome that once shielded the sector, across the dry, empty plain to the relative safety of the forest, all I can think about is that moment Devin's dagger came down on Paul.

We stop soon after entering the forest. It isn't safe by any means, but we need to break for Paul. The unavoidable truth that he's not going to make it until we get back to Sector Eight pulses like a poison through my heart. A truth Peter has yet to accept.

He sets his brother on the ground, so, so gently, and starts to undo the hastily wrapped bandage from earlier. It's soaked with blood. "It'll be all right, Paul, I'm just going to clean your wounds and get you bandaged right back up," Peter says. His words spill from his mouth like a protective charm. "Everything's going to be just fine."

But Paul reaches up to grab Peter's hand before he can do any of the things he said. His fingers are trembling. Already, his skin is incredibly pale, every one of his freckles standing out. He smiles at Peter, and I think that's what breaks him.

"You shouldn't have pushed me out of the way of that attack," Peter says. Tears are already streaming down his face. "That should've been me, not you."

"Don't be stupid," Paul murmurs. "I wasn't going to let you get hurt."

"You can't go," Peter whispers. His broken words fall like shattered glass into my lungs as he wraps both his hands over Paul's. "We made a promise, remember? Together forever."

"Sorry, Peter." Paul smiles again, weaker this time. Peter's entire expression collapses in on itself. He presses his forehead to Paul's.

Without me having realized it, tears are streaming down my cheeks. I kneel beside Peter and take Paul's other hand. "I'm so sorry, Paul. I never should've gotten either of you dragged into this."

"Don't," Paul says quietly. "It was our choice. Don't blame yourself."

But how can I not? I had the chance to save them. I never should've even let them come to begin with.

Paul's hand tightens infinitesimally around mine. "Don't be like that. It'll be okay."

"You're not supposed to be the one comforting me," I say around a choked sob. My chest tightens as I watch the focus in Paul's eyes dimming. Fading.

But he smiles again, one last time, before he says to Peter, "Take care of yourself, brother. I love you." And then he says no more. His hand is still warm in mine. His blood is still wet on my fingers. But he's gone.

30
JAY

MENDEL AND I are the last to rejoin everyone. Our bycs were destroyed on our flight out of the city, so we had to go on foot. I could sense everyone's overwhelming grief a mile away. Along with one less presence than there should've been.

As I expected, when we enter the small space the others are gathered in, it's to find Lai, Peter Wood, Seung, and Syon huddled around Paul Wood. His presence doesn't appear on my grid, but the others' do, white-hot and burning in their deep, navy-black pain.

Johann stands some way back, appearing to keep watch over everyone. For some reason, his presence swirls with an uneasy, violent mix of sadness, guilt, anger, and disappointment. He lifts a hand in greeting but says nothing.

I don't think Lai even sees us. Though she's not crying now, it's clear from her red eyes that she was earlier. Her head is bowed. And beneath the river of her grief is an undercurrent of guilt that makes me worried. However, I leave her with her friends from the Order—her friends who actually knew Paul Wood—so that they might ease one another's pain.

"What happened?" I ask Johann quietly.

He shakes his head. "Later."

"Is there a reason not to talk about it now?" Mendel asks with a single raised eyebrow.

Johann shoots him a murderous look, and betrayal shoots through his presence. "Is there a reason you didn't tell me about your missing memories? Because no one else seemed surprised about that."

"That wasn't—"

"Let's not have this discussion right now," I say. I can't hold the exhaustion back from my voice. "We have enough going on as it is without starting an argument as soon as we're all together again."

They both fall quiet and look away from each other.

"Did you both hit your red alerts?" I glance at my own MMA even as I ask, but the red light in the corner of the screen is still blinking. Johann and Mendel both nod. And yet there's been no word from the military. No help sent, despite everything.

It shouldn't be taking this long. What's going on?

I refuse to acknowledge the possibility that the military isn't coming for us. That they would just abandon soldiers that they themselves forced into a trap. We've all served the sector faithfully. Even Mendel refused to join the rebels, despite his newfound knowledge that he was once a part of them. The military will help us. They have to.

However, as we eventually pick up and begin the long journey back to Sector Eight on foot, and as the days pass with no word from or sign of the military, I'm forced to accept the fact that we've been discarded.

* * *

It takes four days of traveling at a quickened pace to reach Sector Eight. Of all the bycs, only Seung and Syon's survived, and everyone was in agreement that Peter Wood should take it and get back to the sector with his brother. I wonder how he'll manage to get past the Gatesmen carrying a dead body and on a military-issue byc, but Lai doesn't seem unduly concerned over it. She's been silent the whole trip.

The military never came for us. I'd wanted to believe it was just taking time, that they had to prepare. However, by the second day, there was no point in continuing that belief.

It was just like Ellis said. They used us while they could, and then they threw us away. Why didn't I see it? No, why didn't I *do* anything about it? I always had the suspicion that the military tolerated us merely because we were useful. I just never stopped to consider the possibility that they would betray us so ultimately.

Why have I been blindly, faithfully following them all this time? Because I saw some good in them along with all the other terrible things they do? Did I learn nothing from my father?

Betrayal courses under my skin, but stronger than that is my anger. How could they? How *dare* they?

Lai stops walking. The sector is finally within sight, but she's looking at it strangely. Searching.

The rest of us stop as well. "What's wrong, Lai?" I ask.

"Something's off."

Unease ripples through everyone. If Lai says something isn't right, especially when it's the first thing she's chosen to say in the last four days, then something is very, very wrong.

"What is it?" Mendel asks.

However, Lai slowly shakes her head. "I don't know." She looks to Seung and Syon. "You guys should hang back before you go through the other Gate." Then she faces our team. "If anyone asks, it was just the four of us who went to meet the rebels. All four bycs were destroyed in the fight."

No one questions her.

She goes to hug Seung and Syon, and I worry she won't be able to bring herself to separate from them. However, she pulls back and we continue on our way. Just the four of us. I'd become so used to the others being present that now our numbers feel too small.

We all pause when we finally reach the towering starlight Gate. Despite the fact we've pushed ourselves hard the last four days to get here, now we all hesitate. Lai was right. Something feels off. The fact that I don't know what it is makes me deeply uneasy.

Johann is the one who finally steps up to the Gate and knocks. The sound reverberates through the dead air. "Team One reporting back from our mission. Permission to reenter Sector Eight."

For some reason, it feels as though both a miracle and a disaster is occurring when the starlight Gate slowly opens just wide enough to admit us. We pass through, but there are no Gatesmen on the other side. We all freeze. No part of the Gate is ever left unmanned.

"What's going on?" Mendel asks.

"I don't know," I say. "But I think we're about to find out."

We proceed to the other half of the Gate, and this time when Johann knocks, it slides open before he even has the chance to say anything. We all trade a look. And then we go in.

At first I think the area is deserted. Then, as the Gate closes with a ring of finality behind us, I realize how very wrong I was.

Guards surround us. Their weapons are all drawn and pointed at us. "Hands in the air!" one of them yells.

I slowly raise my hands. I have no idea what's happening, but there's no point inviting any unnecessary conflict. Lai and Mendel mimic me, and after a lot of hesitation and with anger coursing through his presence, Johann eventually does the same.

"We're from the military, just returned from a mission given to us by the High Council. Why are you treating us like this?" I ask.

"Because," the woman who spoke before says, "the High Council has ordered your arrests."

31
LAI

AUSTIN IS THE one who finally comes to meet us. My team stands in a completely empty cell made of starlight metal. After we were arrested, they brought us to the nearest prison that had an anti-Nyte cell and shoved us all inside without saying anything more. But I had already gotten what I needed from them.

I run my thumb over the edge of the card in my jacket pocket as a door in the hallway opens. A few seconds later, the general stands before the bars of our cell.

Erik immediately shoots up from where he was sitting on the ground, and Al finally stops her senseless pacing. But Jay stays seated in his corner of the cell. Only his eyes rise to meet the general. The betrayal and fury in his thoughts—at the military and at himself—have been too strong for me to try talking to him.

"What the hell is this, Austin?" Al demands. "Why are we in this cell?"

Austin gives each of us a look-over before he sighs. "I'm glad you're all safe."

"What the fuck is going on?"

"There was an attack by the rebels," Austin says. "Around the same time you were meeting with Ellis, a group of rebels infiltrated the sector and struck some of the factories in the west. We still haven't ascertained their goal in the attack. But the Council feared it meant you had gone over to them."

"Why would we have come back here if we'd joined the rebels?" Erik asks.

"As spies. Double agents."

"This is bullshit!" Al explodes. "It took us days to get back here on foot from a trap we were forced into, we're all injured, and the first thing the Council does is throw us in jail?"

"I'm sorry. There was nothing I could do. You will all have a fair trial in a matter of days."

"Fair trial?" Jay asks. I've never heard him be scathing before. It hurts. "We're Nytes. No one's going to believe us. Everyone's going to treat us as guilty until proven innocent, and we have no evidence of our innocence. What's even the point?"

Silence greets his words.

Austin looks at his feet, then at me. I can tell from his expression that he's struggling. "I'll do everything in my power to prove your innocence. Your records of loyalty, the red alerts you sent—even the injuries you've sustained. It's all evidence. Just wait for me."

"Not like we've got anything else to do," I say flatly.

Austin flinches—something I've never seen before—and I know I should feel bad. It's not his fault we're in this mess. He's trying to help. But I don't have it in me to hold back right now. Paul's death still scrapes against the backs of my eyelids, still gnaws at my chest. Why are we the ones suffering over and over again because of the Council's whims and designs? I'm through with it. I'm through with them, and anything to do with them. Including the military.

"I'll come again," Austin says. "I wanted to inform you of the situation as soon as I could. Just know that I'm working on your defense."

If he's expecting thanks, he's going to be waiting for an eternity. We all know how any trial with a Nyte will go. Especially a trial involving potential rebel spies.

When no one says anything, he reluctantly takes his leave.

At least his visit confirmed what I heard from the earlier guards' thoughts. Those factories the rebels attacked. They were the same ones the Order was going to investigate. The ones we suspect the Council is doing their experiments in.

From the sounds of it, the rebels destroyed most of the factories, but the guards earlier thought something had been stolen, too. That *that* was why the Council was panicking and why they went so far as to have us arrested.

My fist tightens until my fingernails dig into my palms. I can't believe I didn't see that Ellis's meeting was not only a trap but a diversion as well. Stupid, stupid, stupid. Of course she'd have another trick up her sleeve. That's how she is.

The real question now is what she stole. Was it the experiment for somehow controlling Nytes? That would be sure to make the Councilors desperate. And put the rest of us in danger. If Ellis has a weapon like that and decides to use it against all the gifted still in the military and the sector in general . . .

"Well, since we've all finally got some personal time together,"

Al says, "do you all want to tell me why I was the only one who didn't know about Mendel and his apparent memory loss?" With nothing to do with her anger at the Council, it's now giving way to her anger at us. And beneath it all, the years-old anger at her brother, who in great part brought us to this point.

"It wasn't any of your business," Erik says flatly. He's already sat back down on the floor.

"But it was Lai's and Kitahara's?"

"They found out. It just happened."

"Right," Al says, her sarcasm fuming. "Of course they did. And I guess the fact that you were a rebel wasn't *anyone's* business?"

"Like I knew!" Erik says. He jabs a finger at Al. "And even if I had, what would you have wanted me to say? 'Hey, so I don't remember my past at all, but I'm pretty sure I was a rebel. Oh, but don't worry, I'm not anymore, so we're all good!'"

"A little warning would have been nice, instead of finding out from the enemy in the middle of an ambush!"

This feels like the point Jay would normally step in. But he remains silent in his corner, too tired, too done with everything to try to play neutralizer for the millionth time since this dysfunctional team was formed.

"I thought we were a team," Al says. "I trusted all of you. Then I find out everyone's been keeping secrets this whole time, and I'm just supposed to ignore that?"

"You're sure one to talk," I say with a snort.

She whirls around to face me, expression furious. "I've never lied about who I am as a person—and you're the last person I want to hear talking right now. You think I can't tell you're hiding things from me?

You think I never noticed those nights you disappeared from our room? I never asked you about it because I trusted you. But now I think that was just a mistake." She laughs once, short, humorlessly. "This entire team was a mistake. I don't care what secrets you all have. You can keep them to yourselves and deal with them yourselves. I don't want anything more to do with any of you."

I grab the front of Al's shirt and shove her into the wall with my arm against her collarbone. "Are you fucking kidding me?" My voice comes out low and with all the anger I've been holding back these last four days. "You don't want anything more to do with us? You say that after you *ran back* when we had the perfect chance to escape and Paul got killed because we went back for you? It's your fault he's dead. If you hadn't destroyed the plan because of your own selfish, reckless—"

"I never asked you to come back for me. That was your choice."

"You seriously think I would've considered leaving you for even a second?"

She hesitates.

I let go of her. "Was it even worth it? Did you kill him?"

". . . No. He ran away."

I laugh. "Of course." But as much anger as I feel toward Al, the bulk of it isn't really directed at her. Not truly. I'm the one who gave the order for Peter and Paul to follow me. The way was clear and I could've sent them to safety. But I didn't. They didn't know Al. Going after her wasn't something that involved them. But I dragged them into it. Paul's death was my fault.

"So you're going to snap at us about keeping secrets and then not even reveal your own?" Erik asks drily. He laughs, a harsh, sarcastic sound that seems more suited to the Mendel we all first met rather than the Erik we've come to be friends with. "Wow, what a just, upstanding teammate you are, Johann."

Al's eyes flick to him furiously. "Fine. You wanna know? I'm a girl, and I'm looking for my brother to get revenge against him for killing our parents. I saw him with the rebels at that meeting and tried to kill him, but he got away." At Erik's blank look of shock, she asks disparagingly, "Happy now? So glad we finally have everything all out in the open."

"What do you mean you're a girl? And you're trying to kill your own brother? You think those aren't secrets worth—"

"Can we just stop already?" Jay asks. He doesn't speak with authority, but maybe because it's one of the only times he's spoken, all of us look at him. His eyes are downcast but not defeated. Just tired. And resentful. "This isn't helping anything. The ones we *should* be angry at are the Council, not each other. Being divided like this doesn't do anything to help us."

Al, Erik, and I share a glance.

"Then what do you propose we do?" Erik asks slowly.

Jay closes his eyes for a long moment. When he opens them again, he finally stands up. "We fight back. We all know how this stupid trial is going to go. So before they can screw us over any further, I say we break out of here."

"Break out?" Al asks incredulously. "That's your plan? We're surrounded by starlight metal, in case you forgot—no gifts, remember? How exactly are we supposed to get out of here?"

"You rely on your gift way too much, Al," I say when Jay hesitates. I flick the card I'd been playing with out of my pocket. The one

I swiped from a guard on our way over here. "Some Etioles are so wary of Nytes' gifts they forget to watch out for the normal things like sleight of hand."

They all stare at me.

"What?" I ask. "I lived on the streets before I joined the military. You think I didn't pick up a few useful tricks? Besides, I do believe I'm our resident expert on prison breaks. I know what needs doing and what needs to be stolen." I raise an eyebrow. "That is, if you're all feeling up for it?"

We all share a long look. There's still a lot of anger and distrust. But more than being upset with one another, we despise the Council. None of us wants to remain here to be pushed around by them any longer.

Jay puts his hand forward. I place mine over his. Al's over mine, and Erik's over hers.

"Let's get out of this dump."

ACKNOWLEDGMENTS

THERE HAVE BEEN so many people who have helped me with this book in so many ways over the years that it feels impossible to be able to sufficiently express my thanks to everyone here. But I'm sure going to try.

First of all, I have nothing but gratitude for the team that made my book into what it is today. My truly amazing editors Holly West and Anna Poon, who have shown an endless amount of patience and understanding toward me, even when I was being difficult or asked way too many questions or was just generally panicking. You guys are the best. To Jean and Lauren, who believed in my story and gave it the chance to go out into the world. To Katie K., who created a truly badass cover for my book (it's so epic and I love it so much. Thank you!). And to all the many people on the Swoon Reads team who worked on this book whom I don't know by name: thank you, my behind-the-scenes saviors!

Of course I have to thank my mom for raising me as a reader, and both her and my stepdad for their constant encouragement of me pursuing my dreams—even when that led to me getting an English degree and moving halfway around the planet. And my fullest thanks to Kristin Dodson, who first made me seriously think that I could become a real writer. I'd always written as a hobby, but because of your passion for writing and your belief in mine, I felt like my dream could become more than that.

Perhaps the true MVPs here are Paris Powers, Sydney Catlin, and Natalia Bravo, who read the very first draft of my book back in high school when it was, well, terrible. But none of you ever showed anything but enthusiasm for it and supported me so much—and continue to do so even now. You all mean the world to me. And my thanks to Ricardo Angulo, Georgia Jackson, and Shane Hall for reading my next-but-still-truly-awful draft in college, and especially to Ricardo for also reading the next version I wrote from scratch. You read a lot of my crap, and wow, do I appreciate that immensely. And thanks still to Karen Brown, for guiding me through a much later and hopefully less horrible draft. You've been an amazing mentor and supporter to me over the years.

To Megen Nelsen, without whose constant encouragement and amazing advice, I might have quit pursuing the publication of this story long ago. You are such an inspiration and wise as well, and I wish you ALL the success. To Maria Dones, whose writing makes me want to become a better writer myself, and who helped me out in many a time of panicked anxiety. To Hannah Azok, and our many, many hours spent writing and editing together in various Gustos and Saizeriyras across Tokyo. You made this process, which could be so overwhelming at times, so enjoyable. Thank you.

My endless thanks to Elena Nielsen, who has done so much to keep me sane through pretty much the entire publishing process when I was far from home, family, longtime friends, and basically every support system I've ever had. You helped me through a lot of hard and stressful times, and I don't have words for how much your ceaseless support has meant to me.

And of course, my thanks to all the readers who helped get my book published in the first place! Swoon Reads is such an amazing community, and I am so thrilled and thankful to be able to be a part of it. Everyone's enthusiasm and encouragement has been so amazing. It is such an honor to be an author chosen by such passionate readers, and I hope I was able to do well by everyone.

So much effort and passion has gone into this book from a huge amount of people, and I am beyond happy to have been able to share this journey with everyone. It's truly been a humbling experience, and I wouldn't change a thing. To everyone, thank you so, so much.

Check out more books chosen for publication by readers like you.